Praise for Cookie Encounter:

... one of the most accurate depictions of a never-churched non-Christian that I've read in Christian fiction...and I'm looking forward to future books in the series.

Carrie Schmidt, Reading is My SuperPower

A very awesome book cover, great font & writing style. A delightful very well written romance book. It was very easy for me to read/follow from start/finish & never a dull moment. There were no grammar/typo errors, nor any repetitive or out of line sequence sentences. Lots of exciting scenarios, with several twists/turns & a great set of unique characters to keep track of. This could also make another great romantic movie, or mini TV series. Not something I normally read but I really enjoyed it.

Tony Parsons, GoodReads reader

Cookie Encounter has been a hit since we added it to our collection. We have two copies that have checked out a total of eight times in just three months! That is a tremendous turnover rate for any book. We are glad to see it doing so well. It's a testament to great word-of-mouth buzz.

Ryan Johnson, O'Fallon Public Library

Published by Paddle Creek Publishing

Heir Force: A Military Inspirational Romance
Copyright © 2018 by Michelle Connell
www.michelleconnellwrites.net

Heir Force is a work of fiction; all characters are a figment of the author's imagination. Any resemblance to actual people, living or dead, or to businesses, companies, or institutions is used in a fictitious manner.

Cover design © Lucy Burton
Layout design © 2016 BookDesignTemplates.com

ISBN: 978-0-9968570-2-4 (pbk); ISBN: 978-0-9968570-3-1 (ebk)

Paddle Creek Publishing
O'Fallon Illinois

Publisher's Cataloging-In-Publication Data
(Prepared by The Donohue Group, Inc.)

Names: Connell, Michelle.
Title: Heir force : a military inspirational romance / Michelle Connell.
Description: O'Fallon, Illinois : Paddle Creek Publishing, [2017]
Identifiers: ISBN 9780996857024 | ISBN 9780996857031 (ebook)
Subjects: LCSH: Families of military personnel--United States--Fiction. | Soldiers--United States--Fiction. | United States. Air Force--Fiction. | Man-woman relationships--Fiction. | Orphans--Fiction. | LCGFT: Romance fiction.
Classification: LCC PS3603.O5451 H45 2017 (print) | LCC PS3603.O5451 (ebook) | DDC 813/.6--dc23

To the men and women of our armed services who serve across our country and around the globe. And to the veterans who served in the past, including many of my family members and my husband. God bless you.

Heir Force
A Military Inspirational Romance

~~Michelle Connell~~

Paddle Creek Publishing

O'Fallon Illinois

Chapter 1

May 2000

"Just put one foot in front of the other, Kate. You'll be fine." John turned toward Kate, his blue eyes pleading.

"Ugh. You know how Ruth is. She'll make my life miserable." Ruth Vandervort was Kate's enemy in the office and almost everyone else's also. She was rude, abrupt and sometimes down- right cruel. It didn't help matters that she previously dated John, however brief it was.

Kate Langston talked with her boyfriend, John Kern, apprehension on her face. Both wore the United States Air Force uniform: black T-shirts, camouflage pants, black boots. They sat side by side on a lumpy castaway sofa, in the lounge of Building 755, the Security Forces building. They were currently stationed at Scott Air Force Base, Illinois, about twenty miles east of St. Louis, Missouri.

Kate didn't like the situation, feeling helpless with everything out of her control. She didn't like it one bit. She should be used to it, having lived the Air Force life for the past ten years. Her time, her wishes, and her desires were not her own.

"Kate, just carry on. Don't worry about her." John started to say more, but changed his mind.

Kate leaned her head on John's shoulder, not caring about PDA. "I don't want you to go." She tried to swallow the lump in her throat. His upcoming TDY was coming too soon and she didn't feel prepared.

"Me either," he whispered.

What worried her so much this time? It wasn't as if they hadn't gone TDY before. Sometimes they were both gone simultaneously to different parts of the world. It never bothered her. Until now.

A whiff of John's woodsy aftershave trailed under her nose and she breathed in deeply.

An airman walked in and cleared his throat. Kate reluctantly got up and moved to a window, her back to John. Her throat swelled and her eyes misted.

The intruding airman left a minute later after making a racket at the soda machine in the corner, jarring her nerves even further. John walked over to Kate and squeezed her shoulder before leaving the room. She turned to watch his retreating back, feeling uneasy. She walked back to her cube to grab her hat before she could go to lunch off base.

A few minutes later she spotted Spencer Coleman in the hallway outside the bank of cubicles in the main part of the building. He was a friend to both her and John, but he and John were friends for years before she met either of them. Spencer headed her way.

"Going to lunch?" he asked.

Kate tuned out the beeping computers, clacking keyboards, ringing phones, a myriad of conversations going on at once, and the squawking scanner at the help desk. It always took a moment to get used to the noise at work.

She nodded, looking up at him as she passed. He was several inches taller than her five-foot, ten-inch frame.

"Me, too. See you later," he said. He was probably headed for the food court, attached to the Base Exchange, the military department store.

Kate glanced back at Spencer, watching him twirl his keys. He did that all the time. She shook her head before pulling the building door open, a wave of fresh air hitting her, reaffirming her decision to leave the canned air conditioning behind. She headed across the parking lot to her car. She wanted to eat lunch in peace. Not that she felt like eating much.

John worked a different shift this week, so their lunch breaks didn't coincide. Which was just as well, considering her mood. She unlocked her car door and slid into the driver seat of her Toyota. Kate put the key in the ignition but didn't start the engine. Instead she rolled the windows down and removed her hat, tossing it to the passenger seat along with her small leather cross body bag. She wasn't the purse-carrying type. The breeze blew her brunette hair around her face. She kept her hair short, first for easier management, and secondly because of Air Force regulations.

Leaning back on the car seat, Kate watched a pair of sparrows sparring on the curb, while considering her feelings. If she were to name the feeling, it would be fear. The realization made her shudder. *But why? Fear of what? That John would meet someone else? That he would get hurt? That they would grow apart?*

Every day in the life of an airman, whether in their field of Security Forces or not, there was always a chance of danger. One certainly couldn't control the lunatics in the world who hated Americans and what they stood for.

Kate had met John and Spencer at Peterson AFB in Colorado several years ago where they were doing tactical training. Spencer and John had been friends for years, stationed at two prior bases together. With Kate, they made a trio. Kate had fallen for John, but liked Spencer too.

Then the three got split up, sent to three different bases, and now were all together again at Scott Air Force Base. Kate and John had stayed in touch with letters, emails and calls. Occasionally she had emailed Spencer, too. Then John and Kate both arrived at Scott within a month of each other and renewed their friendship, which over the last year had blossomed into some sort of love relationship, though John hadn't actually used the 'L' word. Yet. Kate still held hope.

Kate wasn't hungry for a full lunch, but she could at least get a taco and an iced tea, southern sweet, just the way she liked it. The food court on base had a Taco Bell, but she needed to leave the military world, even if only for an hour. Her brain needed it, her mental psyche needed it, and her spirit needed it.

She drove through the Georgian Housing area and stopped for the light at Scott Drive. She turned left, passing by the commissary on her right, and drove through the Belleville gate. She picked up speed as she turned east onto Carlyle Avenue, the main drag nearby that would take her past the local YMCA, the Wal-Mart plaza with a smattering of fast food places to the north and Belleville Area College to the south. A mile or two further she turned left into the fast food joint and parked facing the street.

Since the weather was as perfect as it could be for the area, she bought her lunch and ate it while sitting in the car. The constant traffic noise going by was her only entertainment. She let her mind wander, staring mindlessly out the window as she ate mechanically. She drove back to work, putting her emotions aside.

That afternoon, Ruth struck again. "You think you're so smart, Langston. I bet you cheated. Somehow, I bet you did." Kate ignored her sneering lie and focused on her reports. She opened the one she'd started before lunch so she could finish it—if her nemesis would leave her alone. She continued with her report of a drug incident in base housing from the previous night.

Somebody else heard Ruth and hollered, "Hey, Langston, you gonna help me study for my test next month? I could use your brains."

Kate just ignored him, knowing he said it to get Ruth off her back. Everybody in the office knew Ruth ridiculed her and why. Kate tried to bide her time until Ruth's next leave in a few weeks.

"Hey, Vandervort," another airman that Kate didn't know hollered, "maybe you should trade in your camouflage cap for a dunce cap."

Snickers echoed around the room but Kate ignored them. She had enough to do without Ruth's troublemaking. Apparently others in the office were bothered by Ruth's rude comments as much as she was. Kate tuned it out as best she could.

Kate felt more than saw Ruth's menacing stare and tried not to react. She could feel her black beady eyes lasering through her back, but she kept typing without stopping.

She feared she might lose it. She busied herself in her cubicle, minding her own business.

"Go lay an egg, Carter," Ruth shot back.

Kate hit the print button, walked toward the printer stationed on a desk across the room and removed her report. She just removed it off the tray when she heard loud footsteps coming down the hall.

"What's going on around here?" Lieutenant Thompson bellowed. He stood in the corridor with his hands on his hips.

Everyone in the area stopped what they were doing and quickly stood to attention.

"Oh, just a little banter between the troops, Sir," an airman Kate didn't know bravely answered.

Kate kept her eyes on their supervisor and it was a good thing or she might have busted out laughing if she saw the serious look the young airman was trying to put on his face. She curled her toes in her boots, trying to remain calm and collected.

Lieutenant Thompson looked at Kate directly. "Is this true, Langston?"

Her toes on her right foot uncurled so fast, she thought she broke a nail. Kate swallowed before answering. "Absolutely, Sir. Just a little camaraderie among comrades." She kept her eyes just a smidgeon to the left of his head, so she couldn't see into his piercing eyes.

He didn't say anything for a moment as he glanced around the room. "At ease then and carry on. Vandervort, I need to see you in my office. Now."

Kate didn't dare look Ruth's way and turned to her document on the printer tray. She took a deep breath and hoped Ruth wasn't in trouble on her account. Kate had no control over the exam results, or Ruth's attitude, which she ignored as much as possible.

She had to wait to deliver her report to Lieutenant Thompson, since he was busy with Ruth. She gathered the papers on her desk and started filing them. She decided an iced tea sounded good, so she left her cubicle for the break room.

When she got home, the sight of Buttons running for her always cheered her up. Buttons was her mixed mutt she had fallen in love with at the local rescue kennel. His coloring reminded her of a butterscotch and vanilla candy. He always had a way of helping her forget the stress of her day.

"Ready for your walk?"

Buttons started jumping on her legs. "Hold on, let me get out of this uniform first." She plopped on the bed in her room and unlaced her black boots, tossing them to a corner. She pulled out some sweats and a T-shirt with the St. Louis Cardinals across the front. She wasn't a big fan, but watched the games when they were playing well and made it to the playoffs. She seemed to become a fan of whatever team was most popular at each base. In truth she was a chameleon fan, in favor of whatever the local team or teams were where she was stationed. So it was the St. Louis Cardinals baseball team and the St. Louis Blues hockey team.

"Ok, Buttons, let's head out."

Kate enjoyed the breeze and the warm spring sunshine on her shoulders as they briskly circled the track near her apartment complex. She watched a couple playing tennis, a sport she never understood. She preferred racquet ball or bowling, not that she was any good at either one. Walking was more her style. And pace.

After a treat for Buttons, and a shower for her, she put a quick salad together and made a fruit smoothie in the blender. Buttons always took off when he heard the blender. Salad and smoothie in hand, she picked up her library book and read until bedtime.

The next afternoon when she got home from work Kate made her double fudge brownies with a caramel center and set them aside to cool before John picked her up. She didn't indulge in sweets much, but the brownies were requested for their dinner at Spencer's place. There would be a foursome, with Andrew, a friend of Spencer's.

She opened the door when John arrived. "Tough day?" he asked. Kate let him in before answering. She led him to the living room after he put his dish on the kitchen counter. They sat on her sofa, leaning against a blanket in a southwestern turquoise pattern.

"Just long. I'm waiting for Ruth to go on leave, and then it won't be as bad."

"I see." He rubbed her shoulders after sitting beside her. He wore khaki cargo shorts and a red polo. "Is your outfit new?"

She turned toward him, surprised. "Actually, it is."

"It looks nice on you." His eyes appraised her choice of the blue floral print top and slacks that hugged her curves perfectly.

"Thanks. I bought it last week." One of her favorite stores at the mall was Christopher & Banks, because they sold pants in 'tall' which she needed for her height.

John stopped his massage and patted her on the shoulder. "I guess we should go. Don't want to be late for dinner."

Kate hid her disappointment and said, "I guess so. I'll get my dessert."

It was a short drive to Spencer's bachelor pad. Kate was amused at his lack of decorating skills, but never let on. Spencer was taller than John by several inches. His blond hair was cut short, but a little longer in the front so that it sometimes flopped to one side or the other. He was actually quite handsome, but Kate had already been interested in John when they all met years ago. Spencer was always the southern gentleman and a great host. He hosted several cookouts throughout the year for whoever was available.

Andrew arrived a few minutes after them. He stood a few inches shorter than Spencer and had brown hair. He always jumped in to help like he was your best friend, even if he didn't know you.

Kate didn't really want to do the group thing with John leaving so soon, but they'd made these plans weeks ago around their various schedules. And John didn't want to cancel or change it to just the two of them, which was what Kate secretly preferred. *Oh, well.*

Spencer lived in a comfortable two-bedroom condo owned by a widow who lived next door. Martha Pettigrew (Mrs. P they called her) and her husband bought both sides years ago, and rented out the other side to a military family or person for as long as they needed it. They never had any problems, according to what Spencer had told her and John once.

Spencer grilled steaks and Andrew brought a veggie tray, John brought garlic bread and a salad to round out their meal.

"Great steaks, Coleman," John said.

"Yes, thank you." Kate agreed. "Thanks for cooking for us."

"My pleasure."

"Veggies aren't bad, either," John teased Andrew.

"Funny. Didn't know you were a sit-down comedian," Andrew responded.

Conversation centered on the price of gas (too high at nearly $4 a gallon), their low pay (always, no matter the rank), and who would make it to the playoffs (Kate could care less). She had offered to rinse the dishes and load the dishwasher, which the guys were quick to let her do. No surprise.

Kate finished the dishes and Spencer pulled out his Trivial Pursuit game and she prepared to lose like usual. She didn't care though, it was still fun and they laughed at some of their guesses.

Later that night as Kate readied for bed, she thought over the evening. It seemed to her that Spencer was eyeing John about something. But every time she looked at either of them, they pretended nothing was going on. She wondered what those two were cooking up now. She wondered what it might be before falling asleep.

Chapter 2

On Monday morning, Kate had an email in her inbox requesting she see Lieutenant Thompson. She didn't know what it might be about but walked down to his office. No sense in delaying it if he had bad news. Kate knocked on his door frame and waited for Lieutenant Thompson to acknowledge her. He was on the phone, but he waved her in, gesturing to the chair in front of his desk.

She ignored his conversation as best she could, which was difficult from her perch. The sunlight coming through the windows in the office dimmed as clouds gathered across the sun's path.

Kate tried to keep her legs still, but they jiggled up and down. She clasped and unclasped her hands as she glanced around the office. Framed awards and photos adorned the walls and the office was decorated in typical military fashion, which was practical but not very warm. Most offices had the same pale walls, blue plastic molding, and industrial carpet in dark blue tones and inexpensive dark-wood furniture made to look expensive.

Lieutenant Thompson finally hung up the phone and folded his hands on his desk. "Thanks for coming right away. Wasn't counting on that," he pointed to the phone.

"Sure. What did you want to see me about, Sir?" Kate didn't know what to expect, so she sat forward in the chair, her boots flat on the floor like a pair of tight bookends.

"I'm hearing rumors of a personality conflict in your area. Anything you want to tell me about?" Her boss leaned back in his chair, putting his hands behind his head.

"Sir, I..." Kate faltered and looked at the ground. How was she supposed to phrase her answer?

Lieutenant Thompson spoke, which made her look up again. "Kate, just tell me what's going on. I think we've known each other long enough that you can just play it straight with me. Agreed?"

Kate studied his bushy eyebrows a moment before speaking. She slumped against her chair. "Truthfully, Sir, ever since John and I started dating and especially after I got my last stripe, Ruth has been awful. I try not to engage, but it's getting bad enough that everyone in the office is defending me or trying to deflect her from me. It's embarrassing." Finished, Kate looked out the window.

"Thanks for being frank with me; I appreciate it. I think I've heard enough to get Ruth transferred. Nobody will be the wiser. It doesn't do to have problems in the ranks if they can be dealt with. Things are hard enough with troops spread thin and all these conflicts all over the globe."

He paused to straighten a stack of papers on his desk. "If this problem affected troops on the battlefield, that's another story altogether. I'll take care of it." He leaned toward his desk again, signaling the end of their conversation.

Kate stood up. She wasn't sure she agreed nobody would know why Ruth got transferred, but it was out of her hands. "Thank you for listening to my side. I've tried to be as truthful as possible." Kate finished speaking and saluted. Lieutenant Thompson nodded and said, "You're dismissed."

She decided to go to the break room for a tea before heading to her desk, so hopefully nobody would know where she had come from. She walked down the hall, lost in thought and nearly ran into Spencer.

"Whoa, you're not on earth, Kate." Spencer put his hand on Kate's shoulder to steady her after their near collision.

"Sorry, just lost in thought."

"More like space. Everything okay?"

"Yeah, fine. Just something I can't talk about right now."

"Alright then. See you later."

Kate nodded, resuming her way towards the break room.

****

John picked Kate up promptly at seven and they left for the restaurant shortly after. His navy slacks paired with a gray and red polo along with his tanned skin made him appear like a magazine model. Her heart skipped a beat when he kissed her before opening the car door for her.

Kate and John ordered their meals at Cheddar's, a casual restaurant not far from the base that specialized in pasta and chicken. Kate didn't like cooking chicken, so ordered it often in one form or another when eating out. She just didn't like the texture when handling raw chicken. Her nickname was Chicken, though she was seldom called that.

John was leaving in three days and this would be their last time together before he deployed. Kate could barely eat anything, and John's silence wasn't helping. He seemed to be in his own world.

Their meal was eaten mostly in silence, and Kate was worried. "John, what are you thinking about?"

He swallowed his mashed potatoes before answering. When he looked her in the eye, his face was serious and reflective. "Everything. Why I'm doing this, why I have to leave again, how much I hate the desert. Leaving you and my friends. Worrying my parents."

Kate reached for John's left hand and nodded. She thought the same things before deploying too. And it was possible she could get sent somewhere anytime, as she'd been stateside for five months.

"I'm ready to get out. To do something else and stay put."

John's announcement startled her. This was new. "Really?" Maybe this is what he'd been trying to say for the last few months. And maybe what was holding him back from proclaiming his true feelings.

"It's time." John looked away from Kate.

"You only have sixteen months left of your tour, right?"

He nodded, picking up his iced tea. "Yep, and it can't go fast enough."

Their server brought their ticket and John removed his wallet, leaving a generous tip with the bill.

Later that evening, Kate realized she didn't feel any less fear about John getting out and wondered if he was going to break up with her. He didn't really go into what he would do after getting out or where he would settle. Or more importantly, who with.

The next few days flew by and before she knew it, Kate hugged John goodbye the night before he left. She wiped away tears as she drove home, wondering what caused the dread she couldn't shake.

Two weeks later, Kate received an email from John:

Arrived safely. Sand still stinks.
Later, John.

Kate took a deep breath. But the cloud over her didn't disappear. She drove to the park near the apartment complex where she lived to eat lunch alone. She sat in the car, with all the windows down, nibbling on her sandwich while staring at walkers and joggers going around the track and children playing on the jungle gym. Oh, to be young again with no worries about your coworkers or best friends being in harm's way 24/7.

The day was mild for an Illinois spring. Cardinals and robins flitted nearby, the robins looking for worms in the fresh cut grass. The sounds of spring, including the music of insects floated through her open windows. At least she wasn't hot, sometimes spring was more like summer and it could change from winter to summer in a day.

Nearly every day Kate felt an unexplainable sadness. It wasn't only because John was half-way around the world. She thought they were in love, but he never declared it. His actions showed he was, but he never actually said, "I love you." Their relationship was like a tug-of-war—a game she never enjoyed. But the fact that she hadn't known he was considering getting out of the service and that he was ready to stay put, certainly bothered her. Shouldn't she have known sooner?

Back at the office after her quiet but unsettling lunch, Kate had stacks of reports to enter into the Air Force data base, Security Forces Information Management System or SFIM, for short. It was one of her tasks to enter any disturbances or incidents around the base into the system. At least it was mindless work to a certain degree. She could type eighty words a minute with her eyes closed.

At least her nemesis, Ruth, was gone for two weeks and Kate could breathe a sigh of relief. Ruth felt that Kate didn't deserve her promotion and let her know every chance she got. Kate didn't appreciate working with a bully constantly over her shoulder. Kate worked out regularly and had to get a massage once a week, to get the kinks worked out of her neck and shoulders from all the stress, and not just from Ruth; but from her line of work, the travel, her relationship with John. In other words, stress from every aspect of her life. Kate still tried to get the Health Net Federal Services to cover her massages, especially since it was workman's comp—in her opinion—but to no avail.

Kate took a few phone calls, checked her schedule for next week and finished her paperwork which she laid on her boss's desk. Lieutenant Thompson had already left for the day.

Her day was nearly over and nothing new appeared that needed taking care of, so Kate grabbed her bag and hat and headed for the window to sign in her M9 pistol she carried on duty.

Spencer caught her on the way out. "Heard from John lately?"

"Yeah, the sand stinks. He's okay, I guess." They walked down the hall together, their boot steps in unison on the tile floor.

Spencer nodded. "I'll email him this weekend. I need to ask him a favor." He waited for Kate to reply, but she was lost in her own world. "Kate?"

"Hmm?" She realized Spencer wasn't done speaking with her. She stopped in front of the door. "What?"

"Are you okay? Do you want to do something this weekend?" It wasn't unusual for Spencer, Andrew, John and Kate to get together or parts of their group, depending who was around.

"I'm fine. Thanks." She turned toward the door, put her hat on, and strode into the searing sunshine.

Spencer stood inside the door, thinking about what he thought Kate felt. He knew why John hadn't used the 'love' word with Kate and he also knew she wanted to hear it. But she was too proud to probe John. Spencer hoped John would step up to the plate when he returned from Iraq in three-and-a-half months as he found it difficult to keep John's secret and even harder to keep it from Kate.

A few seconds later Spencer walked out the door but headed in the opposite direction for his Acura. He tried to push his feelings for Kate aside. He knew John beat him to her and had to respect that. But he also knew Kate would be in for a shock when John returned. Because Spencer was going to convince John to tell Kate his secret. They couldn't keep their relationship in limbo forever because of it.

As he drove home, he fervently prayed for John's safety. How would Kate handle hearing the reason behind John's secrecy? Spencer sighed, letting the wind blow his blond hair every which way.

There wasn't anything he could do about it.

Not for Kate, or for a particular little girl in Iowa.

Chapter 3

Scott Air Force Base spreads across more than 3,500 acres in the western part of southern Illinois and employs about 5,500 active duty personnel, another 2,300 Air National Guard and Reserve members and close to 5,000 civilian employees. Adding over 2 billion dollars to the area's economy, it's considered one of the largest employers in the state.

Several times the base has narrowly missed the base closing and realignment list. Named after the first enlisted man who died in an air accident in 1912, Corporal Frank S. Scott, the base has since grown to include many groups under the 375th Air Mobility Wing, and under each group, several squadrons. Kate, John, Spencer, Andrew and other friends worked for the Security Forces Squadron, or SFS for short. Kate's friend Jen worked in the Supply Squadron. Kate sometimes thought it was all rather complicated and was glad she didn't have to keep it all straight. She had a hard enough time keeping her life straight.

Kate's cube was in the middle of a section, two down from Ruth Vandervoort's, which remained blessedly quiet. She liked the new security building, made of brick. The one-story building had classrooms, a break room, a locker room with nearly 600 lockers, several offices and banks of computers all housed in one location instead of in various buildings across the base.

Flags, patches, awards and other Air Force memorabilia adorned the inside walls as well as many of the cubical half-walls. In another area was the phone center, where airmen answered emergency calls and sent the appropriate help. Kate worked in one of the cubicle areas when she wasn't on patrol or at the gate. Her duty area was laid out in a square of cubicles in the center of a large room, with walled offices for superior officers around the perimeter and the law/help desk up front. Each cubical was shared with personnel who worked the different shifts.

Now John and Ruth were both gone, and she was fretful for one and relieved about the other. Each day that passed seemed to make Kate feel worse. She said a quick prayer each morning and night for John, not sure that anybody heard them.

****

Monday morning Kate had a staff meeting and barely arrived on time. She slid into a plastic chair next to Spencer, as it was the only empty seat in the conference room. His face lit up and he said, "Good morning."

"If you think so," she replied. She slapped her hat in her lap, not having time to stop by her desk first.

He frowned and looked away.

Kate only half listened to the spiel about multi-cultural diversity. Frankly, she was quite sick of the word *diversity*. She wondered if CEOs in China or Japan held these kinds of meetings and what happened to the US being known as the "melting pot". But no one ever asked her what she thought.

"We're all in this together, and we need to support each other," the speaker droned on. Kate had heard it all before, at every base and every year since she signed her life away. Air Force life wasn't as glamorous as she'd hoped, and the pay wasn't great considering the danger, but it had many benefits. She met all kinds of people, had a free gym membership, free health care, traveled to new places, and carried a gun. She saw more of the world than the average Joe and she enjoyed traveling, except to Saudi Arabia or Afghanistan.

"You all right?" Spencer whispered.

"Fine," she answered automatically. "Just bored," she added.

"Ditto." He smiled, encouraging her. "Want to go to lunch later?"

"Sure, why not?" Kate replied without thinking. What did she say yes for? She didn't want to give him the wrong idea. But before she could change her mind, Spencer spoke up.

"Great; my treat." Spencer seemed pleased, but Kate didn't know why. It hadn't been that long since they had dinner at his place.

The meeting of no purpose finally ended and Spencer followed Kate out of the room. "I'm parked in the back forty." He turned down the hall.

"Okay, I'll see you later. Wait for me by the back door?"

He turned back around and said, "Sure."

Kate thought she heard him whistle, but it could have been somebody else in the hallway. She ignored most of the banter around her and walked back to the main cube. She wasn't in the mood for it and was a little perturbed with herself that she agreed to have lunch today. She liked Spencer well enough and he had great manners and was generous almost to a fault, but her heart belonged to John and she missed him terribly. She figured John put Spencer up to "watching out" for her, and he was trying to do that by asking her to lunch.

Kate plopped into her wheeled chair, rolled up to the computer and started typing up forms and notes from incident calls she had responded to. When she looked at the clock a minute later, it was already lunch time. She had been so busy, the time flew by.

She got up from her chair and stretched. Then she put on her hat and checked her hair for any strays. Her top desk drawer held a compact mirror, extra chap stick and lotion, tissues and other assorted things she didn't like to carry around. She found the mirror quite useful, even though at the moment it showed her frowning face. Kissing her index finger and touching the framed photo of John sitting on the desk was something she liked to do before leaving her cube.

"Ready?" Spencer asked as Kate walked up. He stopped spinning his keys and leaned away from the wall where he had been waiting.

Kate nodded. She walked through the door Spencer held for her. She headed for the back parking lot. Her friend fell in step beside her. The late morning heat radiated off the parking lot and the bright sunshine reflecting off the cars was nearly blinding.

"Pasta Garden sound good?" he asked, his long legs slowing to match her shorter ones.

"We don't have to go that fancy," she replied, looking at him.

"We need someplace quiet." He stopped walking and stilled his keys.

"We do?" Her heart skipped a beat. She wondered why they needed a quiet place, but she didn't voice it aloud.

Suddenly it felt like there was a boxing match going on in her stomach. She gulped, trying to remain calm. Spencer beeped the locks to his sedan several feet away and smoothly stepped ahead to open the door for Kate.

"Spence," she started to protest. She used his shortened name, but in frustration, not friendliness this time.

"Kate." Spencer looked down on her, a serious expression on his face.

"You don't need to open my door," she finished.

"I don't mind, ladies first and all that." He swept his arm toward the car.

"You're quite the gentleman, as usual."

"I try." He waited for her to get in and shut the door.

Several minutes later they were seated across from each other in a quiet corner. Kate opened her cloth-wrapped silverware and draped the napkin across her lap. She sipped her water, trying not to appear nervous. She fidgeted with her bag's strap while she studied the menu. Her stomach growled as soon as the scent of tomato sauce and garlic bread drifted by her nose.

She ordered veggie lasagna, no extra cheese and he ordered a pasta trio.

"I'll take half home for dinner." He rubbed his hands together in anticipation.

Kate raised an eyebrow, not sure he could leave half for later. "Did you email John this weekend?" she asked.

Spencer nodded. "I haven't heard back yet."

"Me either. I sent mine Friday afternoon." She swallowed a sip of water before continuing, "He said the oddest thing."

"Yeah? What's that?"

"It wasn't in his email, but at dinner before he left. He said he's ready to get out. Did you know anything about that?"

"Really? Nooo. Did he say anything else?"

Kate looked at him with a questioning glance. "Anything else? Uh..." She thought for a minute about their dinner conversation that night. "No." She was curious. "Why, what do you know?"

Spencer almost choked before he answered. "Bite went down the wrong pipe. Nothing, nothing." He swallowed more water and changed the subject. Kate had a hard time staying focused. If Spencer didn't know John was thinking about getting out, that was weird. Very. They were pretty close. It was also strange that Spencer asked if he had said anything else. *What was going on? What else should John have said?*

Kate mentioned she needed to get her oil changed. "John did it last time. Where should I go?" she knew she could trust Spencer's judgment.

He rattled off an address.

Kate was startled for a minute until she realized what address it was. "Seriously?"

"Sure, I even have a garage. It's easy."

Kate gave a half chuckle. "How much do you charge?"

"Hmm. Now there's something to consider."

"Very funny."

Spencer saw Kate's hesitation, and said, "You know I'm just helping while John's away. He asked me to help you and watch out for you."

"Oh, he did, did he?" Kate sat back against the leather seat, a little upset. This was news to her although she suspected as much. She thought that maybe John would ask Spencer to, but she didn't know she needed 'looking after'. She was a grown woman after all, in the air force, and fiercely independent according to others she'd worked with over the years. She just considered herself a woman of the new millennium, nothing unusual to her.

"Don't act so surprised. We've been friends for years, longer than you've known him." Spencer took a bite of his salad.

She admitted to herself that he was right. Sometimes she forgot that they had a longer history than she and John did.

Spencer started to say something more but stopped.

She looked at him. "What? What aren't you telling me?" She picked up her fork and turned it over and over.

"I shouldn't be telling you this much, but if anything happens to him, he has a letter for you."

"He does?" This wasn't exactly a revelation that she liked. And she was hearing it from the wrong man. She felt something plummet in her stomach. She didn't know if she could eat.

Spencer nodded. He looked like he was going to say more, but didn't.

"What kind of letter? I'm sorry I never said I love you? What?"

"I can't say anything else. Okay? Just know that he cares for you and he wants to return to you as soon as he can. I'm sorry I can't say more." Spencer sighed and looked away.

Kate absorbed this news, not too happily. She knew John had some sort of secret, because he acted like he wanted to tell her something many times, but always changed his mind. Kate figured he would tell her when he was ready. Then his latest deployment came up. So now she knew there was something else John needed to tell her. And apparently it was in a letter that Spencer knew about.

It was her turn to change the subject. "Well, when do you want to do this oil thing?" Kate put her fork down, re-signed. She'd worry about John's letter later.

"Any afternoon this week is open except Wednesday."

"Tomorrow?"

"Sure."

"What do you need to buy? Or rather I need to buy?"

"I'll flip through your car manual, if you have it."

"No manual." She didn't know how many prior owners her beater had before she bought it shortly after she arrived at Scott.

"I'll look it up online. We can take care of it tomorrow and get a bite after if you want."

"How about if I cook?" Their circle of friends got together often, so the two of them might as well.

Spencer perked up. "Really?"

She laughed for the first time in weeks. "Sure. I owe you one for your mechanical expertise."

"You don't; but I'm sure I'll enjoy it all the same." He gave her a wide grin.

"How about meatloaf?"

"Mashed potatoes and gravy?"

Kate smiled. "You got it." She dug into her lasagna with more energy than she felt since John left.

Spencer knew what kind of car Kate had of course, but he didn't know its specs. He asked her about the model and related questions which she answered as best she could. Mechanics wasn't her thing. Spencer grabbed the check saying, "Don't even try."

Kate opened and shut her mouth, without a word.

They walked out to his car and he opened her door but she didn't protest this time. A minute or so into the drive back to the base, Kate commented, "Thanks, Spence," she said, leaning back. "I needed this."

"I thought so. And the diversity meeting was boring."

She couldn't help smiling. "Indeed."

Chapter 4

After work Kate drove across the base to the commissary for the ingredients she needed for the meatloaf. She felt a little lighter than in recent days. But being separated from John, who she thought was the 'one', didn't sit well with her. Not to mention the cloud that continually hung over her. She couldn't shake it.

When she got home, she changed out of her uniform and made a cheesecake so it would be chilled for her and Spencer's dinner the next night.

"Ok, Buttons, let's go for a walk." She laughed as he tried to run around her, while she tied her tennis shoes. She grabbed his leash and they went out into the sunshine, heading west through her apartment complex. They headed to the nearby dog park.

When they got back after a twenty-minute power walk, she fed Buttons, then vacuumed and dusted so tomorrow all she had to do was make the meatloaf while Spencer worked on her car.

****

The next morning was cloudy and Kate hoped the predicted storms would be either over by dinner time or hold off until after she got her oil changed. She knew Spencer would not appreciate working on her car during a thunderstorm. She kept her fingers crossed.

When she checked her email before going into work, she had a message from John. She almost dropped her glass of juice when she saw it. She quickly opened and read the message.

> *Dear Kate,*
>
> *I've been busy with training and now things have slowed down some. I still don't like the food here and there's not much to do, entertainment wise. I think about you constantly and wish we could see each other. Take care of yourself.*
>
> *Miss you,*
>
> *John*

She quickly wrote back that she missed him too, and told him that Spencer would change her oil later and signed off, *miss you lots*. She got up from the table and gave Buttons a huge squeeze before going to work

At noon, Jen followed Kate home so Kate could leave her car for Spencer to work on later. He would be driving her to the auto parts store to pick up the correct items. But as they drove back to the base after a quick bite to eat, they heard thunder in the distance. After getting dropped off and thanking Jen, Kate sought out Spencer.

"What do you think about our afternoon plans?"

"We can still get the oil, and hope for the best." He looked at her, letting her decide.

"Okay," she agreed. They would meet up later.

After a couple hours of driving patrol around the base without incident, she finished early and searched for Spencer. "I'm done, so I'll be in the break room."

"I'm almost done. I'll be there in twenty." Spencer typed faster on his reports.

Kate nodded. She was glad she kept a book in her desk for times like this. A few minutes later she felt a presence behind her and turned around to see Spencer watching her.

"All finished?" she asked.

He nodded.

"Why didn't you say something?" Kate closed her book after replacing her book mark.

He shrugged. "I don't know," he answered finally. Kate glanced at him, a curious look on her face. But Spencer had already turned around, his keys spinning on his finger. She put on her hat and scooped up her belongings. "Mind if I put this back in my desk?" she held up the book.

"Not at all. I'll be by the door."

She nodded, wondering why he was acting so funny. She heard thunder rolling and wasn't happy to hear a downpour right afterward. *Figures.* She put the book back in her drawer and went back the way she had come.

"I have an umbrella," Spencer offered. He already had his hat on and the umbrella ready to pop open as soon as they stepped outside.

The pair walked in a stilted fashion to his car, trying to stay in step. Spencer was at least four inches taller than Kate so it wasn't easy. The rain drove down at an angle, soaking them. They tried to walk faster, but it was awkward. "We're getting soaked," Kate groaned.

"I hope you don't melt," Spencer teased.

"I'll try not to." They reached his car and he opened the door. She slid in, trying to dry off with a tissue from her bag. She heard him open the trunk, but she couldn't see what he was doing. When he got in, he handed her a towel.

"Oh, thanks. This is much better."

She finished drying off, while he started the car and turned on the defrost. She finished drying off her uniform the best she could and started on Spencer's. She dried off his sleeve and his cheeks.

"There. That's the best I can do." She handed him the towel and their fingers touched, sending an electric shock through her arm. It was so unexpected, she gasped.

Spencer looked concerned. "You okay?" He took the towel and finished wiping down his uniform before tossing the towel to the back seat.

"Yeah; sorry."

"No problem."

While Spencer drove, Kate pondered what had just happened. What was that spark and what did it mean? Out of the corner of her eye, she watched Spencer navigate through the storm, driving slowly through the gate on base and not much faster in town due to the limited visibility. They pulled into the parking lot of the auto parts store and sat watching the rain for a minute, waiting for it to let up.

"It's not looking good," Kate said.

"Nope. How long do you want to wait?" Spencer asked, looking at her and then out the windshield.

She looked at her watch. It was half past four now, and the meatloaf needed to bake for forty minutes, but she needed fifteen minutes to prepare it.

"You need an hour or so?" she asked, not answering his question yet.

"Maybe." He looked at her, waiting.

"How late is too late?" She looked at the rain, a frown on her face. She didn't care that much about the oil getting changed, but having company for dinner was something she was looking forward to. But she didn't want Spencer to be unsafe trying to help her.

"Tonight?"

She nodded.

"Midnight."

"Are you serious?" She laughed, swatting him on the arm. "I don't want to stay up that late."

"I don't have anything better to do, do you?"

"That's not the point, and you know it."

"So?"

"Spencer, work with me here."

"I am. I'm still waiting."

Kate noticed a small grin on his face. "For?"

"How long?" He repeated his original question.

"Oh, right. I need almost an hour for the meatloaf and potatoes."

"So, it will take about the same amount of time for both of us. If we can just get out of the car." He readjusted the defrost and turned down the radio.

"I forgot to tell you that I heard from John this morning. He said he's been busy training. He's fine."

"Great! Maybe I have a message, too. I haven't checked the last few days."

Kate nodded. She looked out the window. "Looks like it let up some. Want to run for it?"

"Sure. I'll get your door," he said, but Kate was already out and running for it.

Spencer shook his head, running after her. Kate waited for him inside the door. "Well, that was fun," she said.

"Something like that. Come on." He led her to the area where they could find the oil. Spencer picked up a few bottles and some boxes. Kate just followed, letting him do his thing. This was definitely out of her realm. "Got everything I need. You need anything?"

She looked around the store. "I think I'm good." She gave him a small smile.

Spencer walked over to the checkout. Kate pulled out a debit card, but Spencer said, "Let me get it. It'll be faster."

She didn't want to protest and make a scene, so she kept silent. Spencer paid cash which surprised her. She took the bag while he got his change. "I'll pay you back in the car," she said. "I've got cash."

"Nope. I got it." He headed out the door.

"Spencer, I'm paying for my car's maintenance." She stalked off after him.

Now I've probably made her mad, Spencer thought. *Oh, well. Wouldn't be the first time; and not likely the last either.* Kate beat him to the car, and crossed her arms impatiently. Spencer walked slowly on purpose, so she had to listen to him when he got to the car. The rain had slowed to a sprinkle.

"I've paid, and that's that. I'll do what I need to do and if there's any problem, I'll have the receipt. So, are we cool?" He spoke slowly and succinctly as if to a stubborn child.

"I'm getting wet." Kate answered through clenched teeth.

"So, are we cool with that?" Spencer repeated, making sure she looked at him. He adjusted the umbrella to cover her.

"I'm not only cool, now I'm wet. Will you please open the darn door?"

"It's unlocked." Spencer grinned as he walked to the driver's side of the car after opening her door, much to her chagrin. He slid in next to a cool and stiff Kate.

"You're making it difficult for me to be independent and self-sufficient, you know."

"So glad you brought that up, actually." He started the car, turned down the country music, turned the defrost on high, and flipped the wipers back on before he turned to her. "Why are you always refusing help and trying to be so self-sufficient, anyway? What are you trying to prove?"

"What's that supposed to mean?" She reached for the towel in the backseat.

"Have you ever been a damsel in distress?"

"Of course not! And why should I be?" Kate dried off her arms and legs vigorously with the towel before tossing it to him.

"Gosh, Kate, you make it sound like it's a crime." He took the towel and dried off.

"Maybe in my book it is." Kate stared straight ahead.

Spencer didn't say anything, but pulled out of the parking lot and headed for her apartment. After a few minutes of silence, he said, "I'm sorry. I just try to do the right thing, and sometimes I forget it interferes with women's lib and all that."

"I'm not a libber. Just fiercely independent."

"You got the fiercely part right," he muttered.

Kate dropped her head against the head rest. "I'm sorry, too. I just miss John and I'm tired of Ruth's bullying and tired of the heat, and—"

"It's okay. I get it." Actually, if he told the truth, he didn't. But it wasn't worth arguing about. He figured it probably had something to do with her mother leaving her when she was a child and never getting over it. He knew Kate tried to put on a strong front, but he didn't know how deep it went and whether she ever had counseling to deal with the emotional trauma. She didn't seem to let others get too close, except for John, and he didn't seem to be as close as she wanted.

As he drove down Interstate 64 back toward her place, he thought about Kate and John. Kate always tried to act cool and tough. And John had a secret, sworn by Spencer to never mention it unless he absolutely had to. He hoped that day never came. Because he didn't know how Kate would handle it if or when she found out. For she would definitely be a damsel in distress then.

****

Kate glanced through the car window and noticed the storm had eased up and would probably be only a memory by the time they got home and changed. She figured Spencer probably had old clothes with him, to make it easier to crawl around under her car.

After they got to her place and got Buttons to settle down at the prospect of a new playmate, they changed out of their wet clothes.

Spencer asked, "Do you have a place I can hang this sopping thing?" He held up his uniform.

"I'll get you a hanger and you can put it over the shower head."

"Very practical."

"Don't start."

"Yes, ma'am." Spencer dropped his head in mock submission. Secretly he was wishing he could dry her off, but he had to reign in those thoughts. He played with Buttons for a minute waiting for the hanger. Then he asked for her keys and quickly went back outside.

Kate shook her head, going to the kitchen. She was surprised how tan Spencer looked in his navy polo and shorts after he changed in her hall bathroom. It had been a while since she'd seen him in summer clothes since they had all been in business casual at the dinner a few weeks ago before John left.

With Spencer outside, she turned the kitchen radio on to a jazz station and found the pot for the potatoes and the pan for the meatloaf. So what had happened in the short time they drove to the store? There had been an electric shock between them and then an idiotic argument. She filled her pot with water, turned on the burner and pulled five russets from the bag. While she peeled the potatoes over the left side of the sink she thought about their conversation at lunch yesterday and their silly argument today. She wished John were here for the umpteenth time. She wanted to ask him what was going on, but she didn't want to do it by email.

She chopped onions for the meatloaf, grated cheese, and opened tomato sauce, a myriad of thoughts running through her mind.

While she cooked, she could see Spencer from the kitchen window that overlooked one end of the parking lot. He was pouring oil in, she thought. The rain had completely stopped, but it was still cloudy.

Kate knew Spencer liked her and always had, but she belonged to John and Spencer respected that. She tried not to banter and joke with Spencer too much, because she didn't want to lead him on. She slid the meatloaf in the oven and set the timer.

Even though John seemed reserved at times, she was pretty sure he loved her. She was troubled by the fact he never said so in those exact words, but was afraid to ever ask, even as stubborn as she was. She was afraid there was something or someone from his past that he was afraid to bring up. And she didn't want to ruin what they had, so she kept her worries to herself. It seemed like a Catch-22 scenario and it confused and irritated her.

With the potatoes boiling along, Kate took out the salad fixings and a bowl and sliced the onion, romaine, mushrooms and tomato. She looked forward to their meal and the leftovers she could have for lunch.

She peeked back out the window, but couldn't see what Spencer was doing. A few seconds later she heard a knock and opened the door.

"All done?"

"Yep. She's already to go."

"Thanks, I appreciate it." She had forgotten to offer him something to drink earlier, so asked him, "Would you like something to drink?"

"Please. Do you have any tea?" He was washing up at the sink.

"Sure. I'll get it." She poured his tea and more water for herself. Spencer settled on a stool at the counter. She placed his tea in front of him and he thanked her.

Kate busied herself with washing a few of the prep dishes. "Dinner will be ready in just a few minutes."

"Can I help?"

"You could set the table and get out the dressing, if you like. Otherwise, there's not much to do."

"I can handle that." He knew where most things were in her kitchen, having eaten there often.

Kate put the bread in the oven and put hot pads on the table. She wiped down the counters and checked the potatoes. All she had to do was heat up the gravy.

Spencer finished setting the table and walked back to the kitchen. "Smells scrumptious. I feel like you're getting the short end of the stick."

"How so?"

"It didn't take that long to finish my task."

"That's okay; I would cook anyway."

"You cook a whole lot more than I do. Lean Cuisine and pizza for one is the extent of my cooking, unless I grill."

"Well, we're even."

"I suppose."

Kate still wondered about their conversation in the car, but didn't want to ruin the evening by bringing it up again.

Instead they talked about how things were going in Afghanistan and Iraq.

"We're every country's hero, but our own," Spencer lamented. "We can't be there forever; they've got to learn to defend themselves."

"Yeah, the United States always seems to come to everybody's rescue at the expense of young lives." Kate hoped troops would be pulled out of Iraq soon so that John and all the others could come home and stay home. She only had another year and a half of her tour and she was ready to settle down in one spot. Depending on John's plans, she hoped they could marry and finish his tour and choose a location they both agreed on.

They were each lost in their own thoughts for a minute when Kate noticed blood on Spencer's finger. "What's that?"

He turned his hand around to look at it. "A little scratch looks like." He licked the blood off his finger.

"Looks more than that," Kate said. She got up and rummaged through her medicine cabinet in the bathroom. She came back with a first aid kit. "Here let me see," she held out her hand.

"It's nothing."

"Nothing, my foot. Look how deep that is." She poured iodine on a cotton ball and wiped it clean, then dabbed on a little antibacterial cream and covered it with a bandage. "Can't have you getting an infection on my account."

"Thanks, nurse Kate. I feel so much better already."

"Very funny. Now eat your meatloaf before it gets cold."

"Yes, ma'am." He didn't mind obeying her this time.

Kate set the medical kit on the table before finishing her own dinner. After they cleared the table, Spencer offered to dry the dishes. Kate agreed and they had the kitchen cleaned up in no time. Even Buttons got a little scrap and was happy. She packed a plate for Spencer which he accepted, saying, "Thanks for the great dinner."

"Thanks for the oil change."

"You're welcome. Goodnight."

Chapter 5

The next morning after arriving at the office, Kate's boss informed her she'd be leaving in a few days for Germany. "Get your affairs in order, you know the drill." Lieutenant Thompson dismissed her. Kate groaned silently. But she had to do what she had to do. The guy she was replacing had gotten injured and had to be sent home. She drove home after work and ran through her mental TDY list:

Clean out the fridge

Empty all garbage cans

Hold the mail

Call the kennel to make reservations for Buttons

Get caught up on laundry

Water the two plants still living

She pulled out her green duffle bag and left it on the bedroom floor. She gathered uniforms and civilian clothes to wash and started a load of laundry to stay caught up. She called Spencer Kennel in O'Fallon (no relation to her coworker) and made a reservation for Buttons to ensure they would have space when she needed it.

After making her lists and setting aside clean uniforms on her bed, she grabbed Buttons' leash and they went for a jog/run through the dog park. The sun was partly hidden by clouds but it was humid. The park had recently been mowed and the scent of fresh cut grass mingled with the dust from the nearby ball diamond, making Kate sneeze as she kicked up dust and grass from the path.

Kate pushed herself as she ran, her shoes making a rhythmic pounding sound as she continued running around the oval. She ignored others around her and tried focusing on her breathing and the pressure in her lungs. She and Buttons both needed to run, to get some exercise and fresh air. Buttons easily kept pace with Kate's strides and seemed to enjoy it. After four rounds on the path, she slowed to a jog to wind down, and then did some stretches on the bleachers by the ball field.

When they got home, Kate filled Button's water bowl and gave him a treat. "Good boy," she said, patting him on the head. Buttons wagged his tail and went to his bed to enjoy his small bone.

Kate didn't want to treat herself to what she really wanted—a chocolate extreme blizzard from Dairy Queen, because it would defeat the purpose of her exercise. She had to maintain a certain body mass and weight for the uniform. Instead she had a Greek strawberry yogurt. *It's almost the same.*

Before going to bed she emailed John letting him know of her pending TDY. She told him the weather was getting hot and she missed him terribly. There wasn't much else to say.

A few days later, Kate was washing up her mug at the sink in the break room. Spencer walked in with coins in his hand. "Oh, hi, Spencer." She shook her mug and dried it with a paper towel.

"You look like you're on a mission."

"Yep, leaving for lunch with some of the girls. Kind of like a baby shower, but a lunch hour version." Her keys and gift sat on the table.

"Ah, well have fun." He bought his soda from the machine.

Kate rolled her eyes. "I'll try," she answered. Baby showers really weren't her thing, but she did want to honor Leslie with a gift. Especially since she and her family had orders to PCS (Permanent Change of Station, the military's long way of saying move) a few weeks after the baby came. She didn't mind other people becoming moms; she just didn't want to be one herself.

Kate walked out the door and put her hat on. She had picked out a couple of boy outfits, hoping they were the right size. She really had no clue with such things so included the gift receipt, just in case Leslie needed to exchange them.

At the café where the shower was, Kate found a seat with Jen and Kelly after adding her gift to the collection of others wrapped in pastel blue and white. Kelly was talking with another coworker, so Kate waved to her.

Jen asked Kate, "How you doing?"

"Fine I guess. But I keep feeling as if there's a fog around me and it's driving me crazy," she admitted aloud for the first time.

"Well, maybe you just need some girl time. I'm glad you're here." Jen lightly squeezed Kate's shoulder.

Kate smiled. "Thanks. Maybe you're right. Have you ordered yet?"

"No, let's go. I know exactly what I want; how about you?"

"The strawberry chicken salad, definitely."

Jen gave her a knowing smile. "Me, too."

When the two got back to the table, Kate said to Leslie, "Congratulations." Leslie was short with glasses that made her look a little like a professor.

"Thanks, Kate. And thanks for coming."

"You're welcome. I hope all goes well."

Leslie chuckled. "Me too."

Kate and Jen discussed their latest library books they were reading. They often exchanged each other's books before returning them. Jen was from Minnesota and held similar values to Kate's. They had met one day at the base gym and swapped phone numbers since they had both said they were new to the base. Jen worked in Supply, so had a more regular schedule than Kate's rotating schedule, but they saw each other often.

Kelly was her other closest friend and a liberal from California. Kate tried not to hold it against her. Kate liked her because she wasn't afraid to say what she thought and was a little on the wilder side.

****

Kate left for Germany two days after the baby shower. She flew in to the Frankfurt airport and took a shuttle to the base at Ramstein and checked into billeting. Her assignment was for three months and since she was single, was assigned to a small apartment in temporary living facilities or TLF.

Car insurance was much higher in Germany, so Kate would be stuck taking a shuttle back and forth to work, the gym, and the commissary.

She would become a temporary part of the 435th Security Forces Squadron, after finding her sponsor and taking a two-day orientation class. *I can hardly wait to sit in on another boring class.*

On a three-day weekend, Kate took a train to Paris. She went to see the Eiffel Tower since she was so close. The train was crowded and she didn't know very much French. But signs were also in English or in symbol form and she could get around well enough.

The area around the tower was pretty and looked like a park at home. Couples and families picnicked nearby or strolled through the grounds. Kate was happy for the opportunity to see it and snapped lots of pictures from various angles.

Paris looked very clean and she loved the architecture of many of its buildings, with their old world charm. After her visit to the tower, she looked for a bakery.

She stopped in Les Gourmandises d'Eiffel and her mouth watered at all the pastries arranged on pretty doilies in the display cases. She finally settled for a couple of chocolate croissants and a cup of coffee. The croissants were flaky and buttery and nearly melted in her mouth. She bought a loaf of bread to nibble on back at the hotel.

****

Six weeks later Kate picked up a newspaper at the Chicago airport before getting her connection to St. Louis. She hadn't kept up too much on the world news lately. She found her seat next to a middle-aged woman who played a handheld bingo game. Kate glanced through the paper, scanning headlines before she read the first section. On the front page was a story about the latest roadside bombings in Iraq. Kate felt a chill snake down her spine causing her to shiver as if she felt a breeze.

Her seatmate commented, "These planes are always chilly, aren't they?"

Kate didn't realize her seatmate had paid any attention to her. "Uh, yes they are." She readjusted in the too-tight plane seat and looked around. Nobody seemed to be alarmed or worried about anything. *It's just nerves.*

The flight was nothing to write home about and after she retrieved her bags, she hailed a taxi to get home. Spencer had emailed her an offer to pick her up, but she didn't want to trouble him. Besides, she needed some time to readjust to the time change and didn't feel like talking.

The next morning right after a late breakfast from the nearby cafe, Kate picked up Buttons.

"Hi, Buttons! I missed you." She didn't know if dogs had memories or not, but he certainly was always excited when Kate got back from a trip.

The weather had turned from summer to the early stages of fall while she was away. The days were still hot, but the evenings cooler. This summer had been pretty bad from what she'd heard from others.

Kate had a couple days to herself after her TDY, so she drove to the base library and stocked up on a couple mystery novels and some thriller and suspense movies. She loved Agatha Christie for her great settings and plots, Robert Whitlow for his legal thrillers, and Jacqueline Winspear for her Maisie Dobbs series. Armed with her free entertainment, she stopped at the shoppette and picked up some trail mix, tortilla chips, and salsa to munch on.

The following Wednesday, Kate drove to the Security Forces building for her first day back to work. She walked into the building, expecting much more noise. The closer she got to her cube, the quieter the hallways were. There was still work activity of course, but it took on an eerie atmosphere and made the hairs on her neck stand up. She didn't hear a lot of conversation or machines beeping or keyboards clacking. Several of the cubes were empty.

Something had happened. Kate slowly reached her cube which was empty. She put away her belongings in a drawer, locked it and tossed her hat on the desk, giving her hair a quick brush with her fingers. She walked down the hall to Lieutenant Thompson's office and heard muted tones as she got closer. Several of her coworkers, including Spencer and Andrew, stood around Lieutenant Thompson's desk listening.

Kate stopped at the doorway, saw the huddle around the desk and started to back away, not knowing what the meeting was about. Lieutenant Thompson noticed her movement and said, "Kate, I'm afraid you need to hear this too."

She gingerly took a few steps forward again, before she realized what he was talking about. Lieutenant Thompson was still speaking, but Kate's brain stopped listening after she heard him say, "I'm afraid that John was one of the airmen...killed while on patrol in Iraq."

Gasps filled the air and suddenly the clouds hanging over Kate let loose and the dam broke. She felt pressure on her arm and glanced to see that it was from Spencer's hand before she said, "Not possible," and ran out of the office.

Her head felt like it was in a vice and all the blood drained from her face. She could hear nothing except the roar in her head and had no idea where she was going, but she knew she had to get away from there and as fast as possible.

She heard footsteps running after her but she didn't stop. She ran out of the building through a side door, pushing the door so hard it hit the building. She ran across the parking lot and half way across an empty field before she fell to her knees sobbing. With her hands she pulled at her hair, nearly pulling it out of her scalp. *This can't be. He can't be dead.* She felt a hand on her back and then a body plop next to her. She didn't bother to look, not caring who it was. Whispered conversation went on around her and then she heard somebody say, "Leave them be."

No! No! No! This can't be! John cannot be dead. She just spoke to him by email a few days ago. He had wished her a safe flight home. *It had to be a mistake.* She wiped her face and looked around her. It was then that she realized Spencer was the one beside her.

Kate had never seen his face red or streaked with tears, but she couldn't help anyone else right now. She didn't want anyone near her and shook off Spencer's attempt at comfort.

Shock and immense sadness overwhelmed her mind and body. John couldn't be dead. It wasn't possible. She wouldn't believe it. Tears streamed down her cheeks and she didn't bother to wipe them away. She curled into a ball, ignoring anyone who tried to touch or speak to her.

Several minutes later, she sniffed and slowly sat up. She pulled her knees up to her chest and stared at nothing. *How could this happen? Why him? Why now? What was his se-cret? How can I go on now?*

Spencer couldn't believe the news either. He had a hard time comprehending John would never return. He would miss his buddy, the one he saw movies with and played practical jokes on. They encouraged each other whenever the going was tough and enjoyed weekly get togethers whenever possible. *Why was it always the good guys?*

How would Kate react to the shock that was coming? Spencer would do his best to help her, but he didn't know if she would want help after finding out what neither he nor John could tell her. He set his emotions aside the best he could.

Though she rebuffed him earlier, he knew it was only because of her grief. He moved closer to her and rubbed her back. "Are you a damsel in distress?" he asked quietly.

Kate wasn't aware of anyone else and thought everyone returned to work. To her left, she saw some green fatigues in her blurred vision. At first she didn't comprehend the words. They sounded foreign and she wasn't sure she heard them right. After a few silent seconds, the words registered and she understood. She slowly raised her head and made the mistake of looking at his crushed features and just as she started to answer, "I don't know," Spencer pulled her into his arms.

"I'm so sorry, Kate," he sobbed.

She broke down again, grateful for his arms around her. She couldn't keep herself together. Not this time. She gave in, letting the tears flow, not caring whether they soaked his uniform. *To heck with protocol.* This was war, and she didn't give a flip about regulations. Maybe she never did, and it was all a façade, a front to keep her strong in appearance only. She was only human after all.

Maybe Spencer had been right when he said Kate didn't have to keep it all together. Life was rough on a good day most of the time. The constant coming and going, training, moving, and making and losing friends could all get a person down after a while. Nothing was in her control. Not life, death or anything in between.

She continued to cry, not caring who saw or heard her. She had a right to break down. She cried harder when she realized she didn't get to say goodbye to John. The last time she and John talked, they talked about mundane things and nothing important. *How would she go on without him?*

They cried together, holding on tight to each other as if they were afraid to let go. She had never seen or felt so much emotion coming from him and it broke her even more.

Chapter 6

Spencer was in trouble. Big time. He swiped tears from his cheeks and thought about John never coming home, never sharing another meal or a blockbuster movie. They would never share jokes or listen to each other's complaints about the military life they lived or discuss their dreams and hopes. He and John would never tease each other again, never provoke each other on the running field or spend a holiday together.

Spencer sighed as he thought about what would happen now. It felt like a pile of cinder blocks anchored his insides, leaving him with a heavy sickening feeling. He tried to comfort Kate, hugging and crying with her. Coworkers from the building were coming out in pairs now that the news spread about John. He felt pats on his back and shoulders. But they weren't going to help.

Spencer prayed for the days and months ahead and for the reaction from Kate when she got John's letter. Spencer regretted not pushing John harder to tell Kate his secret. But he didn't want to ruin their friendship over it, either. It hadn't been Spencer's decision.

Too late now.

He let go of Kate and wiped his face with the back of his hands. The news of John's death seemed so foreign and unreal. *How can he be dead? How will I deal with Kate once she's read John's letter? How will she react?*

Oh, God, help us. She is so going to need it.

Kelly came outside and rubbed Kate's shoulders, "I'm so sorry, Kate, honey." Kate stood up to hug her friend. "I can't believe it; I can't believe it. I didn't get to say good-bye," she wailed on Kelly's shoulder.

Kelly just held her, knowing there weren't any words that would help. Others trickled out of the building to offer their condolences. Spencer grieved for himself but much more for Kate. She didn't know what else was coming which made Spencer sick to his stomach.

Andrew squeezed Spencer's shoulder. "I'm so sorry, man. I know you two were close."

Spencer gave him a weak smile and a pat on the back. "Thanks. Appreciate it."

After a few minutes, Spencer and Kate were alone again. He followed Kate as she slowly ambled back toward the building. He watched her slump down to sit on a bench outside the door, and plopped next to her. A pair of uniform pants and boots appeared in their vision and he scooted over a bit. Their commanding officer, Major Connors, must have asked Lieutenant Thompson where they were. He and Kate slowly stood up and half-heartedly saluted.

Connors was a cool guy, not a hard-nosed jerk like some officers they knew and had worked under. Spencer knew he had a sense of humor, though he didn't see him often. He also knew he was fair.

Though the Major's tall frame towered over them, he never used his height to lord over anyone. His blue eyes often twinkled and he loved to share a good joke. At this moment, his eyes held only sympathy.

Major Connors gestured with his hands, the 'at ease' signal and remained silent for a moment. When he finally spoke, it wasn't a reprimand. "I'm sorry, Kate, Spencer. These things are difficult to take, but they happen."

"Yes, Sir," they both answered in weak tones.

He held his hand up. "But don't go just yet. Now, as a human being as well as an officer, I'll be the first to offer my condolences. John was an excellent airman. One of our finest. He'll be missed around here for sure.

"Funeral services are being worked out through the Air Force Mortuary Affairs Operations." He turned to Spencer, "Spencer, are you willing to be the Funeral Liaison Officer between the family and the unit? It seems Mrs. Kern knows you?"

Spencer swallowed down a lump before answering him. "Of course; I'd be honored. Let Mrs. Kern know I'll help in any way." He wiped his face and stood straighter. As the FLO, he would be in touch with John's parents in Minnesota through the AFMAO to let the unit know of the official funeral service information. And he would be responsible for relaying the family's wishes to the affairs office, in addition to informing the family of the funeral procedures.

"We'd be grateful. I'll let the Affairs office know and give them your contact info."

Then the Major Connors turned to Kate. "I'm assuming you'd like to attend the funeral."

Kate nodded, not able to speak.

"Fill out the normal leave forms and I'll have Lieutenant Thompson sign them. The service will most likely be mid-week next week," he turned to Spencer, "just keep us informed. Spencer, as the FLO, you'll be going under TDY orders and I'll be attending along with the First Sergeant, etc."

"Thank you, Sir." Spencer replied. The officer turned to Kate. "I'm sorry Kate. If there's anything we can do, let us know."

She nodded, already turning to go. He whispered to Spencer, "Watch her now."

"I will."

Then Spencer walked along beside her. He cleared his throat before asking, "Want me to take you home or somewhere?" She barely saw his red face and swollen eyes. But he seemed to be in control for the moment.

She seemed to hesitate at first but answered, "I guess." She took a few steps before she stopped. "I have to get my things."

"I'll wait here." Spencer ambled back to the bench and plopped down, raking his hands through his hair, before putting his hat askew on his head.

A minute later, Kate returned with her cap shoved on her head, her eyes red. Spencer said quietly, "My car's this way." As much as he wanted to, he wanted to hold Kate's hand, but protocol wouldn't allow it unless they were out of uniform. He stuffed his left hand in his pocket, the other holding his keys which he didn't spin on his finger. He would miss his friend and the jokes and memories they shared. But he knew things would change after he finally told Kate what John could not.

And he dreaded that conversation worse than a root canal.

****

The car was silent. Not even the radio was on. Spencer couldn't remember when or why he had turned it off. He didn't bother turning it back on. He still had weepy eyes and wasn't in the mood for music. Somehow silence seemed fitting.

Instead of driving straight to her apartment, Spencer drove to the park nearby where he sometimes jogged on Saturday mornings. He wasn't sure he could trust himself to be alone with Kate in their grief. Though he had always had feelings for Kate, he saw early on that Kate had eyes for John.

He backed off, and tried to think of other things, but he saw her almost every day, which made life difficult. Now with John gone, he felt guilty. He just couldn't win. He turned the engine off and powered the windows half-way down. Kate, with tears still falling, hadn't noticed Spencer had parked. He let her be, lost in his own thoughts.

John had been one of his best friends since they'd both been through basic training in San Antonio. They had stayed in touch through emails and phone calls and then found each other stationed together at Castle AFB in California nearly eight years ago.

After being at Castle together, they had gotten orders that sent them in different directions, John to Eglin AFB in Florida, and Spencer to Wright-Pat AFB in Ohio. Though they stayed in touch, they were then reunited again at Pope AFB in North Carolina. They tried to be roommates when they were on the same station, since they had the same morals and values. Well, most of the time.

Spencer had been sent to Afghanistan and Saudi Arabia a few times, but never to Iraq. It still didn't seem real that John would never come back.

He let himself shed the tears that he could no longer hold at bay. He leaned over the steering wheel, his head resting on his crossed hands. He let himself cry until he couldn't anymore. At some point he felt Kate's hand on his shoulder, which he ignored.

If Spencer had been in a jogging suit, he would run hard for an hour at least. He felt a pressure on his heart and emotions that he needed to drive out. The tension in the car along with Kate's sniffing started to get to him.

He opened the door and said, "I'll be back." He put on his hat and took off down the trail. He couldn't go as fast as he felt like, wearing his stupid boots, and his hat flying off, but he ran anyway.

Kate asked, "Where are you going?" But he couldn't answer. Not yet.

Now things would really get complicated. As he picked up speed on the track, he thought about what he had to do now. *I have to find John's letter in the file safe and give it to Kate, which I'm not looking forward to. My signature as a witness on the form enclosed with the letter wasn't going to help. Kate's going to get quite the shock. I hope she doesn't faint. She's so stubborn and self-sufficient; he wasn't sure what she would do.*

He let the wind and the rush of his half-jog, half-run ease some of the weight on his shoulders, wiping the tears from his face, the wind stinging his wet eyes. He continued along the path until he had to slow his pace. The sun had been shining when he started, but now clouds were rolling in, reminding him of the last storm that came through. He had tried to reign himself in that day at Kate's, trying not to have feelings for her. Her stubbornness was partly what attracted her to him. He never did find out why she was so gung-ho on being independent, but he was sure he would find out soon enough.

Especially when she found out she was going to be a mother.

Chapter 7

For several days, Kate found herself wandering her apartment, looking at photos of her and John on dates at the zoo, or at the St. Louis Arch, or with other air force friends. She cried until she had no more tears.

Jen came over one afternoon after her shift with a small bouquet of carnations and daisies and a card. "I'm so sorry, Kate."

She stayed for a while and sat with Kate, but they didn't say much. In the silence they stared at the walls or watched Buttons playing with his rope. Kelly called and brought over some German chocolate cake, which Kate appreciated but couldn't eat. She put it in the freezer for another day.

Spencer called to give her the funeral information. He offered to come over so they could arrange the same flight, but she didn't want company. As soon as she hung up, she called for a flight to St. Paul/Minneapolis. John's family lived in a suburb of the Twin Cities.

She made sure her blues uniform was in regulation form and packed it in her garment bag along with her black pumps wrapped in a towel to keep them from getting scuffed.

Two days later, the day of the funeral, was bright and sunny, the complete opposite of Kate's mood. She didn't pay any attention to the scenery during her cab drive from the airport to her hotel. Somehow she blocked out the traffic and noise along the freeways. She knew the Mall of America was around somewhere, but she certainly wasn't interested in anything like that. That morning she dressed in her dress blues uniform and fixed her hair and makeup in a robotic state. Spencer booked into a different hotel but was coming by to pick her up from the lobby of her hotel.

Now she would meet John's family for the first and last time. The thought upset her and she grabbed a tissue from her bag.

****

Spencer straightened the ribbons on his blues jacket, swallowing his sadness. He had seen John's family several times over the years when they had visited John at Castle and Pope. They were proud of their son and tried to visit him at each base he was assigned. The last time Spencer had seen them was two years ago, when he had been a guest in their Minnesota home.

He knew this day would be tough for all of them, especially Kate. He prayed for strength and wisdom for the weeks and months ahead.

Spencer considered the letter written by John, now sitting on Spencer's desk at home. He would have to give it to Kate and soon. He'd rather stand still through a tornado.

Spencer recalled previous exchanges he'd heard between Kate and John when Kate would say something like, "I'm never going to be a mother and there's no changing my mind." Or, "Motherhood, it's not for me!" Spencer didn't take her too seriously, and hoped she had been joking. If she was really against it, he'd find out soon enough.

He focused on the task at hand, which was the funeral. He ran down the stairs to the lobby and out to the cab, feeling like a twenty pound pumpkin weighed down his stomach.

****

Kate sat in the pew behind John's parents, Spencer beside her. Various other family members and the group from Scott Air Force Base, including Major Connors, sat in rows behind and to the right of them. She tried not to cry whenever she heard someone else sniff. *Be strong.* She stared at the bouquets of carnations and roses, several arrangements in the red, white and blue colors of their beloved country. Several peace lilies, with their huge white blooms in stark contrast to their dark green leaves, adorned the stage along with other house plants that she couldn't identify.

The pastor talked of peace and a reunion of some kind in heaven when those who also knew Jesus would one day be together again. Kate had heard John talk a little about religion, but she had never thought much about what she believed. And right now she didn't want to think about it. She was so angry that John was gone and left her behind. She had so many questions and would never get the answers. It felt like she was left hanging with nowhere to turn.

As far as funerals went, John's service seemed to be more uplifting than others she'd attended. That gave her food for thought as she followed the line winding into the fellowship hall.

After the service, Spencer and Kate and a few others had lunch with John's family. His mother, Mrs. Kern, had said she heard so much about her, and Kate wondered how much John had said. She wore a maroon dress with small white flowers all over a material that looked like it would never wrinkle.

"Kate, I know the next few weeks will be difficult for you, but please feel free to call me if you like." Mrs. Kern handed Kate a lavender envelope with a scent that reminded her of a spring garden. "You can open this later." Mrs. Kern squeezed Kate's hand and said she'd be praying for her.

Kate said thanks, wondering why his mom would be praying for her. Shouldn't it be the other way around?

After eating what little she could get down, Kate said goodbye to John's parents and left. She was anxious to get out of her blues and to have a good cry by herself. Spencer called after her, but she kept her pace, ignoring him. Confused and hurt, she made a quick exit to be alone.

****

Spencer jogged outside the church trying to catch Kate before she left, wanting to set up a time to get together. But he let her go for now guessing she'd get a cab back to her hotel. He felt the same way, wanting to be alone with his thoughts and memories of John. He returned to the fellowship hall and visited with John's parents. Spencer ate a few bites of ham, mashed potatoes and some Jell-o salad with pineapple and coconut in it. Comfort food. *But today it wasn't very comforting.*

Mrs. Kern leaned over and whispered, "She'll be alright."

Spencer nodded. "Still, it's hard."

She continued. "It is, but there's always the Comforter to help in times like this." She pushed her plate away. "And we were very proud of him; still are." She wiped her eyes and gave Spencer a wobbly smile.

He nodded, not wanting to say anything.

Mrs. Kern sipped her coffee before asking, "Now, will you be taking care of Kate?" She gave him a knowing smile.

Spencer turned in the direction that Kate took off. He turned back to Mrs. Kern and sighed. "If she'll let me. She's very stubborn."

"That's what John said. But he liked that in her, though sometimes it was a problem. I think she'll need you, Spencer. I know the three of you have been friends for a while, and that you liked her from the beginning, but that she chose John. You're a gentleman, and can be available to her now. Don't let her push you away."

Spencer thought about what he had to tell Kate. "I won't, even if she tries." He sighed, crumpling his napkin.

"Good. You take special care of her and you'll all be fine."

"All?" He was startled at her statement.

Mrs. Kern smiled. "Yes, *all*. We know. John finally told us recently by email and that he was afraid Kate wouldn't accept her. But I think time will heal all of you." She squeezed his hand. "May we stay in touch?"

"Of course, Mrs. Kern. That would be great, actually."

"She's our granddaughter, you know."

"I didn't—"

She didn't let him finish. She waved her hand as if to swat away his words. "It's not your fault, Spencer, and we understand. John made his peace and told us the mother has been very sick and that Sarah would go to an orphanage until you can pick her up. With our age, it would have been too hard for us, but we know you two will take care of her like your own."

"Absolutely. I won't be able to marry Kate right away."

"Take your time and let her heal first. She'll come around." They sat in silence for a minute, listening to the chatter and laughter around the room. Posters with messages of God's love, power and hope adorned the walls. *Did Kate believe in God's love?*

"Give Kate our regards, and we'll talk soon." She got up and Spencer followed suit. Mr. Kern was involved in a conversation with family members and seemed oblivious to their conversation. Mrs. Kern gave Spencer a hug and he felt some closure.

"I have to tell Kate soon; I want to get it over with."

"I understand. Just be her rock. She'll bash against you but absorb her anger as best you can and she'll get it all out eventually. I think John mentioned Kate's resistance to motherhood. But, you'll all adjust in due time. She'll be shocked for a while, and understandably so. Becoming a mother the normal way is enough of a change," she stopped and gave Spencer a smile, "but this will be quite the challenge, indeed. If I'd known about Sarah sooner, I would have encouraged John to share the news with Kate."

Mrs. Kern adjusted her handbag on her arm. "I'm sorry you have to do his dirty work, Spencer. Go easy on Kate, I'm sure she's capable and will come around."

"Thank you, Mrs. Kern. I needed this. It helps a lot."

"I hope so, but I also want to thank you. For being such a great friend to John and keeping him on the straight and narrow as best you could. We know he wasn't perfect." They hugged and then she said, "And thank you again so much for your help with the funeral and being the go-between. That was a big help."

"You're very welcome. Glad I could do it." He couldn't say anything else. He said goodbye to Mr. and Mrs. Kern and left the church, feeling a whole lot freer than before. Now all he had to do was tell Kate and be ready for her assault.

One thing at a time.

****

Several days passed and Spencer hadn't heard from Kate. He saw her at work, but she ignored him and many others around her. She refused to join in any kind of banter and she no longer smiled. She focused on her work and left as soon as it was done. Kate seemed like a cardboard cut-out of herself, very stiff and wooden.

Finally on a Friday, Spencer drove to her apartment and rang the bell. He held the envelope in his hand, geared up to face the oncoming hurricane. He felt he better inform Kate personally before some government agency or an attorney did.

But there was no answer. He didn't hear Buttons barking either, so maybe they were on a walk. He leaned on the door frame. A neighbor noticed Spencer and said, "She ain't home, man. She left yesterday with a bag." The neighbor held an empty laundry basket.

"Oh. Thanks. I'll come back later." Spencer wondered where Kate took off to. He didn't know she had any leave coming, not that he knew every detail of Kate's life. *So much for getting this over with.* He'd have to wait for her return.

For the next several days, Spencer went to work on auto pilot. He did what needed to be done and left early most days. He waited to hear from Kate, but she never called. Jen and Kelly didn't even know where she took off to. Finally, two weeks later he heard through the grapevine that she was back.

Chapter 8

Two Fridays after his first attempt, Spencer drove to Kate's after work. This time when he knocked, she opened the door and backed up. She looked awful. Her hair was a mess and her eyes were red. Something smelled in the apartment and Spencer wrinkled his nose. "Kate, you've got to—"

"Don't preach to me, Spencer. You're the one who came over uninvited."

Whoa. He paused at her hardness. He said a quick prayer for strength. For both of them.

"Kate, may I come in? I need to talk to you." He nervously fingered the letter in his hand. He had a sinking feeling this wasn't going to go well.

She left the door open and left him standing there. He gingerly stepped into the malodorous atmosphere and shut the door. He took a deep breath—through his mouth.

He found her sitting on the sofa with her arms crossed as if she was done already with whatever he came to say.

"Kate, do you mind if I open a window?" His stomach had been doing summersaults before he arrived; now he felt like heaving from whatever was rotting in her trash.

"Once again, you're here uninvited." She gestured toward the patio door. Spencer felt worse by the minute. He quickly opened the patio door and breathed in a lungful of fresh air. Not only did he need it physically, but also emotionally. He said another quick prayer for strength and to keep his cool.

Leaving the door open, he pulled the screen closed. He took another deep breath and slowly stepped to the sofa. He watched her stare out the door, noting her tank top and shorts, thinking she was still in her bedclothes. *How long has she been like this and where did she go during her leave?* He knew she didn't have any family except for her mom who Kate didn't even know for sure was alive.

"Kate, can I get you something to eat? Or drink?"

"No."

"Did I do something wrong?"

"No."

At least not for the moment. He took a quick breath before asking Kate, "Do you remember our conversation at The Pasta House?"

"How could I forget?" she snarled.

Another deep breath. He held the envelope toward her. "This is John's letter." He spoke in practically a whisper, hoping to hold back her coolness.

She gulped and stared at the envelope he held out.

"What now?" She snatched the letter from his hand and plopped back on the sofa. Spencer lowered himself slowly in his seat, but on the edge in case he had to defend himself against whatever reaction she responded with.

Kate flipped the envelope over a time or two before she finally ripped it open. She pulled out several sheets of paper, including one in John's handwriting. Just seeing his script jolted her.

Spencer eyed her warily and saw her stiffen as she read. He braced himself.

She scanned the letter at first and then read it word for word.

> *Dear Kate,*
>
> *If you're reading this, you know I'm no longer living. I have always loved you, but I couldn't say so. Because I had a secret. One that I was afraid you wouldn't accept. I remember you saying more than once, you didn't ever want to be a mother because yours left when you were young.*
>
> *Kate, I have a daughter, Sarah, who's living with her mother in Iowa. But Sarah's mother is dying of cancer and she will become my responsibility unless something happens to me. Sarah will be your legal daughter if both her mother and I die. Enclosed you will find the necessary documents you need to find her. Only Spencer, the lawyer, and Beth, Sarah's mother, know. We were young and stupid, but Sarah is not a mistake. I know you will love her with every fiber of your being once you absorb the shock. Please allow Spencer to help you in getting her settled in and don't blame him for keeping my secret as I've asked. Because Sarah will legally become a ward of the state before you adopt her, you will get a monthly stipend from the Iowa government to provide*

for her. There shouldn't be any snags with the paperwork, but the attorney's contact info is enclosed if you need any help or have any questions I haven't answered in the paperwork or this letter. The legal office on base can assist you as well.

Kate, this was the hardest letter I've ever written. Please know that I love you, and I trust you with Sarah. Please love her as your own and tell her her daddy loved her.

I love you, Kate, and please forgive me.

Love always,

John

Kate dropped the letter and the other papers on the floor, her vision blurry. She couldn't read anymore. This couldn't possibly be happening. There was no way she was going to be a mother. And especially to a stranger who was also John's flesh and blood. *What on earth had he been thinking? How could he have kept this from me? How could he possibly do this to me?*

She was now going to become a mother, her worst nightmare. *And now I have to tell this daughter that John loved her? How can I possibly do that? He never had the nerve to use those words with me.* The audacity of it all made her want to scream.

Why didn't he tell her anyway, so she could wring his neck instead of Spencer's?

"Kate? Are you okay?" Spencer watched Kate, concerned. He gingerly moved next to her, waiting for the screaming, or something. It was now four weeks after the funeral. He didn't think he could wait any longer, given the circumstances and knowing Sarah's fate was in her hands.

Kate jumped up, startling him. "Am I okay!? Are you kidding? No! Absolutely not! I'm now a mother of a little girl I know *nothing* about. A little girl I didn't know existed until a few weeks after her father died. A little girl who I'm supposed to tell her father loves her, when he could never say that to me? *Do you think I'm okay?*" She snatched up a cup of pens from the end table and threw it against the wall. Then she stormed off to her bedroom and slammed the door.

Spencer heard her yell through the door, "You can leave anytime!" And then something thrown at the door. He picked up the papers and folded them neatly back into the envelope and laid it on the table. *Thanks, John. It's going to be a long night.* He took off his shoes and put them by the door, then opened the patio door wider to air out the place. He couldn't quite place the stench, but it was bad.

Since he apparently had time on his hands, he picked up the pens Kate threw and went to find the source of the bad smell to take care of it.

"Wow, Buttons, you look awful." He whimpered and jumped up when he saw Spencer. "Come here boy. You poor thing. Are you hungry?"

He found the dog food container and poured some into his dish. Then he changed his paper and pad in the kitchen floor after mopping up the mess from several day's worth of waste. He spied a load of dirty dishes in the sink and loaded the dishwasher. He tossed a loaf of moldy bread from the counter, wiped down all the counters and cupboards and took her stinky trash outside to the apartment Dumpster.

Spencer returned to Kate's apartment, washed his hands and grabbed the leash hanging on a peg by the door. "Come on Buttons, let's go for a walk." He used his copy of Kate's key to lock the door, since he had one. He, John, and Kate watched over each other's places when they left for their TDYs. "I bet you haven't had a good walk all week. And when we get back, you're getting a much needed bath."

When Spencer and Buttons returned, Kate's apartment was still quiet. He had left a lamp on in the living room. Spencer hoped Kate had fallen asleep and would be in a better mood later. Fat chance of that. He ran the bathwater for Buttons, and gave him a good lathering with some dog shampoo he found on the shower shelf.

"Okay, let's get you dried off." He pulled down the bath towel and wrapped Buttons in it, then carried him to the living room where he gave him a good rub down. At least Buttons and the apartment smelled better.

It was now evening and the stars were starting to come out. He stepped out on the patio, thinking. *Well, I've done it now.* The bomb had been dropped and he had to figure out how to clean up the aftermath. The scent of roses drifted through the air from a neighbor's potted bush. He certainly didn't feel rosy at the moment. His stomach was still tight and his shoulders tense. Mrs. Kern had been right. He's going to have to be a rock for Kate to thrash against for a while. He better get used to it.

Once again, he found himself praying. *Lord, I need your help. I can't do this alone. Kate's livid and I have to help her come around. Show me how.*

He went back inside, found the television remote and settled in, with Buttons beside him. "She'll eventually come around. I hope." Buttons crawled up on his lap, curling up as if he understood what Spencer had said.

An hour later, his stomach growled and still no sound came from the bedroom. He checked the kitchen for anything edible. He didn't find anything but sour milk and rubbery carrots. "Has she been eating, boy?" Buttons was sticking close to him, so he put him back on the leash and drove to the store. Since the commissary was closed, he drove to the grocery store nearby.

Buttons barked when he left him in the car, but Spencer told him, "I'll be right back, I promise." He spun a cart toward the produce section and bought apples, bananas, carrots, mushrooms, green leaf lettuce, fresh cilantro and some red potatoes. He added soup, soy milk, eggs, and a few other items. He walked back to the car, stowing the bags in the back seat while Buttons barked furiously.

"See, I said I'd be right back." He slid in the front seat and Buttons tried sitting on his lap. "Sorry, Bud, but not while I'm driving." He scooted him over on to the passenger seat. "Stay." Buttons whined, but he settled down.

Back at Kate's, it took Spencer two trips to bring in the bags and then he unloaded everything, hoping he put most things where Kate liked them.

"Now, how about an omelet for a late dinner?" Buttons seemed to know what Spencer was saying and didn't let the human out of his sight.

As Spencer chopped mushrooms, tomatoes and peppers, he wondered if he should try and wake up Kate, but figured she might need the sleep, so let her be. He and Buttons shared the omelet and then Spencer washed up the few dishes and unloaded the dishwasher since it had finished its cycle.

Then he attacked her living room. He did everything except vacuum. He piled up her mail in one neat stack, leaving it on the kitchen counter. He dusted, watered her plants, and gathered more dishes to wash.

Afterwards, the two of them settled in for a movie and a long night. He rubbed Buttons' belly, played ball and pulled tug-of-war with his rope toy until Buttons wore himself out and fell asleep.

Spencer pulled a blanket off the sofa back and stretched out, with the television remote in his hand. He wasn't leaving until they had it out. All of it. He had been sworn to secrecy by his best friend, who was now dead and whose girlfriend now hated him for it.

About midnight, he heard some noise from Kate's bedroom and the door opening. He braced himself for more abuse. He switched off the television and waited.

"Why are you still here?" Kate's voice sounded hoarse and she looked awful. Her hair was even messier and her eyes were red and swollen.

Spencer rubbed his eyes with one hand and stood up moving his hands to his back pockets to keep them still. He took a deep breath. He said in a whisper, "Because we're not done."

Kate's jaw dropped and her eyes bulged. "Not done?! What do you mean not done? You have more bombs to drop in my lap? What more damage are you going to do to me, Spencer?" She dropped to the floor, and Spencer walked over to hold her while she cried. After a minute, she whispered, "Why did he have to die?"

"I don't know, Kate. I wish I knew." He let her cry on his shoulder for as long as she needed. When she fell asleep, he covered her with the blanket he had used earlier and made her as comfortable as he could. He leaned against the living room wall in the semi-darkness pondering her unanswerable question until he finally fell asleep beside her.

Chapter 9

Bright sunshine peeking through the slats in the blinds hit Spencer in the face and woke him up. He felt a chill. He didn't know where he was at first or why he felt so stiff. When he rolled over, he felt a bruise on his leg. It had been a long time since he'd slept on a hard surface. He moaned and remembered why he was on the floor. And realized he'd forgotten to shut and lock the patio door after Kate's collapse. He remembered the fiasco from the previous night and groaned inwardly. Maybe he could fall back asleep and wake again to a better scenario. And maybe the Cubs would win the National Championship.

Kate was still asleep with Buttons curled up at their feet.

When Spencer glanced at them, he felt compassion and vowed to do what he could to make this a better day. He got up and walked around quietly, trying to get the kinks out. He bent his knees one at a time and waved his arms up and down over his head to get his joints to pop. Then he closed the door most of the way, but left the blinds partially open, turned the lamp off, and headed to the kitchen to see if Kate had any coffee. Normally he didn't indulge, but he knew it would be a long day. Thank goodness it was Saturday.

Spencer found some coffee grounds in a canister and started a pot in her small machine. He took out the eggs and turkey bacon and the pan he used last night. Before he started cooking, he opened her apartment door to check for the *St. Louis Post-Dispatch* which was delivered right to her door. The headline read, "Troops Pulling Out of Iraq". He refolded it and tossed it in her recycle bin under the sink. He knew troops were pulling out, bit by bit. But it was too late for John, and thus too late for Kate. She didn't need the reminder.

He cracked the eggs and cooked the bacon, waiting for Kate to wake up. When he was done he took out two plates and served it up, putting it on her dining table. He went to search for Kate, since she was no longer on the living room floor. He walked down the hall to let her know breakfast was ready.

Strange sounds came from the direction of the bathroom, and they didn't sound good. Spencer knocked on the door. "Kate, are you all right?"

"Leave me alone," she croaked before making retching sounds. That's what he'd heard. Was she sick? He was pretty sure she was just upset last night, not sick to her stomach.

Spencer tried the door, found it unlocked and cautiously opened it.

"Can I help?" The odor of fresh vomit assaulted his nose. He averted his eyes, but as he moved them away, he spied an orange pill bottle on the counter. Now confusion overrode the stench. He looked from her to the bottle and back again. *Surely she didn't. No....*

When the realization of what she was doing sunk in, he felt like he was going to be sick himself. He snatched up the small bottle, scanning the label to see they were a type of sleeping pill.

"What do you think you're doing!?" He looked from the pills to her and back again. He fell against the door jamb, livid.

"None of your business," she yelled before another episode wracked her body. Spencer, still holding the bottle with the remaining pills, stalked down the hall and dumped them down the kitchen sink before she dare stop him.

She stomped right behind him, trying to grab his arm. "Hey! Those are mine and you can't take them! What do you think you're doing?"

Spencer spun around and threw the empty bottle toward the trash can where it bounced off the rim and rolled under the cupboards. "You have a lot of nerve! What do you think *I'm* doing?! Saving a friend's life, that's what. What are you trying to pull here, Kate Langston? How could you?" He had used a few choice words, surprised at how easily they slipped off his tongue.

"None of your business! I don't have to answer to you!" She kicked at the empty bottle and ran for the hall bathroom again.

He stormed after her, yelling, "Yes it is. You're my business now. And you know better. That's not the answer, Kate."

Kate slammed the bathroom door and then he heard the lock turn. Spencer stomped back the way he came, jarring pictures on the walls. He sucked in air, shaken. He raked his hands through his hair, yanking on it before letting go. Back in the kitchen, he kicked the stupid medicine bottle before picking it up. What was he supposed to do now? He pounded the counter with a fist, making the dishes rattle.

He leaned on the sink, gulping for air and swiping away angry tears. Great sobs wracked his body. He had no idea Kate would react like this. *I didn't sign up for this. I didn't ask for my best friend to die or to keep a secret from his girlfriend. And I certainly didn't ask for Kate to put herself out of her misery. What am I supposed to do?* He stood there, trying to deal with his own crushed emotions, waiting for his heart rate to return to normal. Several minutes later he splashed cold water on his face at the sink before finding his shoes.

He ran out the door, slamming it behind him and headed for the path around the apartment complex. He ran as fast as his legs could go, his feet pounding the pavement as hard as his heart pounded inside his chest. Around and around he went until he could hardly move anymore. He slowed to a walk, reducing his heart rate and breathing to cool down level. The next few months ahead were going to be rockier than he thought. He slowly walked back to Kate's door, bracing himself for the next round.

****

Plopping into a chair in Kate's dining room, Spencer considered what he should do. He heated up his breakfast and picked at it while he thought. Ordinarily he knew he was supposed to report Kate's suicide attempt to their First Sergeant, but he didn't know if it was necessary. He didn't see Kate as suicidal, just lost. And highly vulnerable. He'd have to keep an eye on her. He slumped down at the dining room table, his head resting on his arms, clenching and un-clenching his fists.

Buttons came in, whimpering. Spencer sat up and wiped the corners of his eyes on his shirt sleeve. Buttons eyed Spencer with a nervous look. Spencer slowly lowered his hand and reached down for him.

"Sorry, boy. Come here." Buttons jumped on his lap and shuddered. "Sorry, life's a little rough right now." Spencer rubbed the puppy's back, asking God what he was sup-posed to do now. If he was going to be any help to Kate, he had to keep himself together. He absently rubbed Buttons' back lost in thought. He didn't hear Kate enter.

"What do you mean; I'm your business now? That sounds like I'm a problem, or a burden. What the heck does that mean?"

Spencer turned to face her. Kate had cleaned up, but her eyes were red and puffy. She stood in a ready-to-fight stance, legs apart with her hands on her hips. Spencer looked down at Buttons. He answered in a half whisper. "I didn't mean it that way. I just meant that John wanted me to look after you and make sure you would be all right if anything ever happened to him." *And help you be a mother to his child.*

"How the curses am I supposed to be 'all right'?" She leaned on the dining room wall with her arms crossed. An-gry tears coursed down her face.

Spencer got up from the table, still holding Buttons. "I guess we'll have to figure that out together, okay? I'm not exactly in a bed of roses myself, you know. You're ticked off at me, my best friend is dead, and I have to help you become a mother against your will. Piece of cake, huh?"

He kept rubbing Button's belly, not risking a glance at Kate.

****

Kate never gave Spencer's situation a thought. She had only thought of herself. She swallowed her guilt and it was a minute before she could respond.

"I'm sorry. I didn't think about how hard it was for you too." She wiped away fresh tears with her hand. She gestured back to the bathroom. "That's not like me," she whispered and started crying harder. She slid down the wall, plopping to the floor.

Spencer put Buttons down gently and sat next to Kate, wrapping his arm around her. Buttons tried licking her tears. Poor guy was as bewildered as they were.

"I didn't think so," Spencer said, tears running down his own face. "But I better not ever catch you doing anything that stupid ever again," he said, his voice hoarse.

"I won't; I promise. I'm so sorry."

"I don't know what I'd do without both of you..." his voice trailed off. Spencer had imagined this moment many times, his arm around Kate, but under much happier circumstances.

Kate sat up abruptly and said, "I need you to go. I can't deal with this right now." She rubbed Buttons' back, almost in a trance.

"But what about Sarah?" Spencer was a little worried from Kate's lack of concern for the orphan.

"I don't care about Sarah right now! She isn't my problem. She's fine where she is." Kate got up and strode to the door. "Now go. I'm done with this mess."

Spencer's heart dropped to the floor. *This can't be happening.* "But Sarah is left all alone..."

"I don't care. I didn't make this mess and I don't have to clean it up. My so-called boyfriend has turned out to be a jerk and I'm so mad at him that if he weren't dead already, I'd kill him. And I'm just as mad at you for not telling me!" She yanked open the door and waited.

Spencer let out his breath and slowly walked through the door, worried for the little girl in Iowa without parents. Spencer had no choice but to leave. He would have to convince Kate somehow over the next few weeks to understand her responsibilities and to help her the best way he could.

Paying off the national debt would be easier.

****

Spencer drove home with thoughts of how he could convince Kate to do the right thing by Sarah. He understood Kate's shock and knew she still grieved John's death and understandably so. It hadn't been that long ago that John was here and then suddenly gone.

The Indian summer temperatures were still hot by day, but the days were already getting shorter with the sun setting earlier. Spencer found himself pulling into his driveway, wondering how he got there. Apparently on autopilot. He spotted his neighbor lady walking over to his driveway and stopped to chat with her.

"How are you, Spencer?" Mrs. Pettigrew was in her late sixties and had hip replacement a couple weeks ago. She leaned on her walker while waiting for Spencer's answer. Her husband died a year ago after having a stroke. Spencer had helped them with projects like clearing out leaves from their rain gutters and trimming their bushes under the front window. The couple called him for help on occasion since their children lived out of state.

Spencer debated how to answer. "Doing all right, I guess. How are you?"

"Hanging in there. Just got off the phone with the grandkids in Ohio. They're already giving me their Christmas lists." She laughed. "Always something they want, those two."

Spencer grinned. He remembered being excited about Christmas months ahead, too. And flipping through toy catalogs.

"Would you be around tomorrow to give me a ride to church?" Mrs. Pettigrew wasn't allowed to drive yet. Spencer took her to church whenever he had the opportunity and wasn't working.

"Love to. I'm going to need the inspiration and encouragement myself." Spencer toed a weed growing in the sidewalk between their duplexes.

"Oh? Anything I can pray about?" Mrs. Pettigrew leaned her head to one side ready to listen.

"It's Kate. She's going to be a mom now. And she's not interested in the job. I feel partly responsible in not telling her sooner." Spencer shared the details with Mrs. Pettigrew who gestured him to come over and sit on her porch. She had gone inside for a minute and came out with some fresh-squeezed lemonade tucked into the basket of her walker.

Mrs. Pettigrew had been living here when Spencer moved in a few years ago. She had met John, Kate, Andrew, and Kelly and knew about their deployments and other activities and kept them in her prayers. Her own husband had been a Squadron Commander before he retired.

"You made a promise to John and you kept it. The responsibility was his to tell. But, it sounds like Kate is going to need a lot of support and prayer." Mrs. Pettigrew sipped her lemonade before going on. "Life is never easy when you have the love and peace of the Creator, but when you don't even have that…well, life can be darn right traumatic at times. Kate doesn't go to church, does she?"

Spencer shook his head. "No. I've invited her and John a few times, and John came sometimes, when he'd been here, but Kate always declined. Says she doesn't need the help of an unloving and mean God."

"Ouch."

Spencer nodded, remembering past conversations with Kate that left him wondering why he liked her in the first place. He wasn't supposed to be attracted to someone outside his faith. Maybe subconsciously he was hoping Kate would come to believe in God.

"I agree with you that life can be very traumatic and stressful without God, but even with his help, life is often difficult. Just because someone believes in God, doesn't mean their life will be easy."

She nodded and then said, "I'll double up the prayers on her behalf."

Spencer got up, thanked her for the lemonade and said he'd be there in the morning.

"See you in the morning, then. Enjoy your evening."

Spencer nodded, and said, "You too, Mrs. Pettigrew. Thanks."

Chapter 10

Two hours after Spencer left, Kate's phone rang, waking her up. She thought about not answering, but curiosity got the better of her.

"Hello," Kate answered.

"Hey, Kate. It's Jen, how you doing?"

"Awful." She started to cry and moan.

"Kate? I know John's gone, but—"

"I'm a mother," she wailed.

"Pregnant? With John's—"

"No!"

"Kate, you're not making any sense. I'll be right over."

Ten minutes later, Jen knocked. Kate ran fingers through her hair and opened the door for Jen.

"Wow, you look awful." Jen gingerly stepped inside, not sure she wanted to come in. She followed Kate to the living room after shutting the door. Buttons came running to see who was so brave to enter.

"I feel awful."

Jen sat down. "Now, what on earth are you trying to say? Are you pregnant?"

Kate sank into the sofa. "No." She wiped fresh tears off her cheeks. "John has a daughter."

"What!? From who? When? How? Never mind that last one," she waved her hand as if to erase that question.

Kate looked at Jen's astonished face, which had been her own look earlier.

"Have anything to drink?" Jen got up, heading for the kitchen. She opened the fridge and took out a lone wine cooler left from a previous get together. She needed a minute to absorb Kate's news. She came back after opening the bottle, took a swig and handed it to Kate who looked like she needed something more along the lines of brandy, which she knew wasn't around.

Jen sat back down in and they passed the bottle back and forth.

"John had a 'celebratory one night stand relationship' after getting his last promotion and he got a girl pregnant. It wasn't until the child was a year old that he found out he was a dad. He never told me, because as you know, my mother left and I have chosen not to have any children of my own. Now the little girl's mother is dead. John's dead. Her name is Sarah."

"But—"

"I know. John named me as her legal guardian." Kate flopped her head on the sofa back with a long sigh.

"What!? Why?"

"No. Idea." She sighed out a long breath of frustration. She added, "Figured we might get married eventually and maybe he'd take custody after he settled in one place, I don't know." Kate threw up her hands in irritation.

Silence filled the room like a heavy fog coming in off the ocean. "Wow." Jen drained the bottle, setting it on the table with a loud thunk. "Sorry."

Kate shook her head.

They sat in silence a few minutes. "Are you going to keep her? How old is she? Where is she?"

"I'm not sure I have a choice in keeping her—it's legal and all that. It's such a shock. I don't even know the first thing about being a mom. And according to the papers, she's around two or so."

"Wow." Jen leaned her elbows on her knees and looked at Kate. "That sure explains a few things."

"What do you mean?" Kate asked, not sure she wanted to know.

"Kelly told me once that John sometimes talked about a little girl he knew, but never said her name or how he knew her. And sometimes it seemed like he was kind of sad when he'd see school children or something. She wondered if he had a child somewhere, but didn't ever ask. Now we know."

"Yep. And now she's mine."

"Kate, I'm so sorry. If you need anything, please let me know. I'll be praying for you double-time."

"I think it's going to take a whole lot more than prayers to get me through this one." She sighed and added, "For the next sixteen years."

****

Jen, Kelly and Spencer met for lunch on the Friday before Spencer had to leave for a couple weeks of training in Texas. They met at the Stars and Strikes Bowling Alley on base where they ordered the daily special, a taco salad. They chatted at their table, while the line to order from the Spare Time Grille grew. The group luckily beat the lunch hour rush.

The three of them sat a square purple table in matching chairs near the center lanes. Large bowling pin designs were on the walls and a bright blue carpet in geometric designs covered the floor. A small room opposite the lanes housed additional tables and chairs for meetings and a small shop offering bags, balls, and shoes was situated behind the register.

Some of the lanes were occupied with airmen having a good time. The bowling alley was a popular place to eat and get exercise at the same time. Plus the snack bar had take-out which was a big plus.

"I don't know what we can do," Kelly said. She tossed her straw wrapper into the middle of the table. "The other day I tried talking to her and she said, 'I'm not dealing with that right now. Discussion closed.'"

"I don't think there is much we can do except pray," Jen offered. She stirred sour cream and salsa into her salad with a plastic fork.

Spencer folded his hands, elbows on the table. "There's got to be something. Sarah is an orphan in Iowa, waiting for something to happen."

Jen spoke up. "Maybe not. She's only two, right?"

Spencer nodded.

"She's probably fine. It's Kate we have to worry about. Sarah is most likely well-cared for, maybe a little bewildered, but little kids are pretty resilient. Kate is the one we have to concentrate on." Jen poured more salsa on her salad. "If Kate doesn't come around soon, then we really have a problem."

"You're right, Sarah's probably fine," Spencer agreed. "I hope Kate understands her position and takes her responsibility seriously. It would be worse if she took it on with a rotten attitude."

"That would definitely be bad," Kelly said. "So, I'm not the praying type," she grinned at Jen and Spencer respectively, "so what can I do?"

Jen and Spencer looked at each other before answering. "Encourage her, keep her spirits up," Jen said.

And Spencer added, "Remind us to pray and talk some sense into her."

"That I can do." Kelly finished up her salad. "I have to run an errand. See you guys later," Kelly pushed in her chair and took her tray to dump in the trash on her way out.

"Thanks, Kelly," Spencer said.

"Sure." Kelly put on her hat and waved goodbye.

"I've been wearing myself out praying for Kate," Jen said.

"Me too. Have been for months."

Jen looked at Spencer with a questioning look.

"Never mind. Not worth discussing."

"You sure?"

"At least not now anyway." Spencer finished his tea and set his cup down. "Finished?" He gestured towards Jen's tray.

"Yes, thanks." She gathered her trash and piled it on her tray for him to take.

Then they walked out to the parking lot to their cars. "Keep me posted, and I'll do the same," Jen said before beeping her car to unlock it.

"You have my number? I'm leaving in the morning."

"Oh, right." She pulled out her phone and waited for him to give it to her. Then she gave him hers. "Have a safe trip."

"Thanks."

****

Kate continued to work like a robot and took little notice of what was going on around her. In the back of her mind she knew there was a little girl several states away waiting for her. But she just couldn't deal with it. Every time she thought about motherhood, the idea made her insides quiver like a five-and-a-half point earthquake.

At home, after each shift, she took out pictures of her and John and wiped away tears at what could have been. She thought about all the times John looked like he had something to say or had a secret. Now she knew what it was. And it made her so sick, she couldn't think straight.

Spencer had been gone on his TDY for several days already and Kate was used to being alone. Kelly had tried talking to her one day, but she blew her off. Kate had no desire to discuss the situation.

Kate knew that this motherhood thing was nibbling at her, making her almost physically sick. She slept more and did less when she wasn't working. The idea of parenting alone plagued her as much as an infectious disease.

She needed to do some shopping at St. Clair Square in Fairview Heights, which was the nearest mall without driving across the river. She stopped near a crowd of children and their parents in the center of the mall where they waited for a short train ride. A little girl who might be close to Sarah's age caught her eye and she found herself mesmerized by her. Kate nearly froze in place when she thought about what Sarah might look like but she forced herself to move on to the store she was looking for. Before she walked away, the little girl in a jumper and boots gave Kate a huge smile.

That evening, Kate was trying to read in bed but kept re-reading the same paragraph repeatedly and still couldn't comprehend it. The image of the girl from the mall kept popping up in her mind. Kate couldn't stand it any longer. She collapsed against her headboard and wailed, "I can't do it! I can't; I can't!" She began sobbing.

I can.

Kate looked around to see who spoke. "Who's there?"

I Am.

Kate's eyes opened wide. She'd heard that phrase before...a long time ago. She'd been a child when she had gone to church with her parents. A memory, a warm and comforting one, rose up to remind her she was not alone and never had been. Events from her childhood came to mind, one after another of happy times being with her parents and grandparents. Ever since her mother left, any warm or comforting memories she had were forgotten along with God.

"Oh, God! Are you still there?" Kate wailed.

I Am.

The still small voice spoke volumes to Kate's weary spirit. "God, I need your help," Kate whispered in the lamplight. "I can't do this alone." She wiped away tears with a tissue.

I know. I am here.

Kate's anxiety lessened when she realized God would help her with the impossible. Her knowledge of God was only what she gained as a child, but she remembered God helping David with a giant, and Moses freeing the slaves from Egypt. Surely, he could help her with an adopted child.

Immediately upon that realization, Kate had another thought. Though Sarah wasn't her daughter by blood, by not accepting her, Kate was doing the very thing she vowed she would never do and that was to leave a child behind. She doubled over when she realized that's exactly what she was doing. Sarah needed her. Kate had no choice but to pick up the pieces and care for Sarah as if she were her own flesh and blood.

Kate nearly gagged as the tears continued and her throat constricted while these thoughts tormented her. She had to get Sarah and she had to get her *now*. How could she not have realized this sooner?

Buttons tried to get in Kate's lap, but she picked him up gently and put him on the bed. She wiped tears from her face and stood up. She had to find her phone.

****

Kate dialed Jen's number as soon as she found her phone in her bag. When Jen answered, Kate babbled, "I'm a failure already!"

Jen said, "Kate! Slow down. What's going on?"

Kate shared with Jen the revelations of the last few minutes. "Now I'm a horrible mother and I haven't even started yet!"

"Kate, calm down. You'll be okay. Listen, I'll pick up some hot chocolates and I'll be over in a few minutes. Will you be okay until I get there?"

"I'll try." Kate hung up and decided to take Buttons for a short walk. Her anxiety needed an outlet. Though it was obviously dark out, there were numerous lights placed around the complex which were bright enough to make her feel safe.

The night was crisp, the stars twinkling miles overhead. She tried to calm her beating heart and pace herself, but she was nearly running around the tennis courts. *This was crazy. She had so much to do. She was going to be a mother!*

Chapter 11

Before Jen left the house, she texted Spencer to let him know Kate was coming around. Jen didn't know if Spencer was back from his TDY yet or maybe sleeping. At least that's what she thought Kate was doing when she babbled earlier—coming around. Jen put her phone in her purse and left for the nearest café and ordered the hot drinks through the drive through window.

A few minutes later Jen was listening to Kate's story. Kate ended it with, "So, how can I possibly leave her there a minute longer?"

Jen told her about the conversation at the bowling alley. "Kate, don't go overboard in a panic, Sarah is fine." She blew across her cocoa to cool it down so she didn't burn her tongue. "Call the place where she's staying and let them know you're coming. Are you going by yourself? How much leave do you have?"

Kate stared at Jen. "I have no idea. Should I fly or drive? What's the easiest way to transport a toddler?" Kate turned on her computer and waited for it to fire up. She was going to get a laptop soon and probably ditch this old dinosaur.

Jen answered, "I have no idea how to travel with a toddler. Never done it. How much time will you have to get her?"

Kate groaned. "I don't know that either. Why does everything have to be so difficult?"

"It's not necessarily difficult. It's just different. You're on a whole new learning curve."

"You got that right. I have about thirty days of leave; that I do know."

Jen laughed. "One thing at a time. You'll figure it out." While they were still talking, Kate's phone beeped an incoming text. She picked it up from the coffee table where she had left it after calling Jen. The text was from Spencer and it read:

Everything ok?

Kate called him. "Hi, welcome back."

"Thanks. Jen texted me a little while ago. You okay?"

"If being a mother overnight is something 'okay'."

Spencer's heart skipped a beat, hoping this meant she was going to get Sarah soon. "Want me to come over?"

"Sure, the more, the merrier." She threw her free hand up in the air with a why not gesture, not that he could see it.

"On my way."

Kate hung up and glanced at Jen. Kate shrugged and went back to the computer in the next room where she researched time and distance from St. Louis to northwest Iowa. Then she tried to figure out if it would be cheaper to fly or drive. She didn't like math.

"Jen, I have no idea what I'm going to do." From where she sat at the computer, Kate could still see Jen in the other room.

"Kate, you know Spencer, Kelly, and I will help you. That's what friends are for. I know it's going to be strange, different, and tough. But you can do this. God's with you too, remember?"

Kate nodded slowly, absorbing what Jen said. "I guess so."

A few minutes later Spencer arrived and Jen let him in as Kate was lost in thought. "She's spaced out at the computer. But she's fine."

"Good. I've been worried." Spencer slipped off his shoes in the entryway before following Jen to the living room. Spencer could see Buttons asleep in his bed near the sofa.

"Kate? Are you okay?" Spencer stopped in the doorway to the living room, remembering the last time he'd been there. He was a little concerned at Kate's facial expression. He slowly walked into the living room and sat next to her. She had left the computer and rejoined Jen.

"Hmm?" Kate noticed Spencer's arrival. "Oh, sure. Fine. Just trying to figure out how in the world to bring a toddler home. That's all."

"Can I help?" Spencer didn't quite feel like he could relax yet, so didn't get too comfortable.

"I don't know." Kate zoned out again.

Jen and Spencer eyed each other. Jen shrugged. "I'm going to go and let you two figure things out. Let me know if there's anything you need me to do, okay?"

Kate snapped out of it and got up. "Sure, Jen. Thanks for coming over and for the cocoa."

"You're welcome. Call me tomorrow?"

Kate nodded, following Jen to the door.

When she walked back to the living room she didn't sit back down. She cleared her throat and looked at Spencer.

"I owe you an apology. I'm sorry for kicking you out last time. Since then, I've had time to think about things and realized I'm not doing the right thing by Sarah."

Spencer stood up and walked over to her and put his hand on her shoulder, squeezing it. "Apology accepted. I'm here to help anyway you need, okay?"

Kate nodded. "I'm still a little mad at you, you know."

"I figured as much. I was between a rock and a hard place, as they say."

She nodded. "Can I get a hug?" Kate felt a little emotional thinking about the next chapter in her life and all it would involve. Tears threatened for the hundredth time that month.

"Of course," Spencer whispered. He stepped closer to Kate, wrapping his arms around her. He wished once again, the circumstances were different. Maybe someday they would be able to hug each other with love rather than grief. He held her there for several minutes, one hand on her head, the other across her shoulders. He could smell her flowery shampoo.

Kate squeezed him back, needing the reassurance and strength he gave her. Her cheek rested against his soft polo shirt. *His hand on the back of her head felt tender ...and ...like it belonged. Why was she thinking that? She'd have to give it more thought later.*

"I'm glad you're rethinking things about Sarah," Spencer spoke into Kate's ear, breaking through her thoughts.

After a brief moment, which Kate thought could go on longer, she moved back and said, "Thanks. I needed that."

"You're welcome."

"How was your trip?" Kate moved back to the sofa. Spencer sat in Jen's vacated place in the chair opposite her. They talked about his trip and the training he did and then Kate offered him something to drink which he declined.

Kate cleared her throat again. "Spencer, before we go any further, just how long did you know about Sarah?" Kate leaned back in the sofa, her arms crossed.

"Kate, this isn't—"

Kate put up her hand and pointed a finger at him. "Don't even. Don't give excuses for John and don't sugar coat it or I'll get up and leave. Tell me what I want to know." She meant business. She was almost back to her normal self.

Spencer sighed and gathered his thoughts. "Kate, after John made his previous rank three years ago, a bunch of us went out, and I was the designated driver. You know I don't drink much. He met a girl, and somehow ended up with her somewhere. Apparently he and she...you know..." His hands rolled around, in a you-know-I-mean gesture.

Kate nodded in silence, waiting for him to finish.

Spencer cleared his throat. "Anyway, he didn't know anything about the baby until she was a year old. The Red Cross had to locate him, because by then he was at a different base, and he and the girl didn't exactly exchange phone numbers."

Spencer took another deep breath and glanced at Kate before continuing. "Honest to God, Kate, he didn't even tell me until last year that the mother was dying and that he may get custody later. He had to fly home and get a paternity test before he signed papers for child support. I had no idea though that he might die and actually leave Sarah with you until a few months ago when he updated his will before his latest…last TDY." He had to swallow before he could finish. "So, I've only known a few months about the will and you being named Sarah's legal guardian."

"So you didn't know anything about Sarah until she was a year old?"

"No. I didn't know he had…you know…" He cleared his throat before adding, "It wasn't any of my business. And he didn't have custody."

Kate absorbed this information, not speaking. After a few minutes with the soft snoring from Buttons the only noise in the room, she finally said, "I can't believe he never told me! What did he think I'd do?"

"He thought you'd run away, because he knew you never wanted to be a mother."

"But this is different!"

"How so?" Now Spencer was confused.

"Because she isn't *mine*. She doesn't have my lifeblood in her and I won't abandon her. I could never do that." Kate leaned her head on her hands while resting her elbows on her knees.

"John didn't know that, Kate. You were always so adamant about not being a mother, and he didn't know how you'd react if he told you." Spencer spoke in quiet tones, his voice full of regret. Regret for John, for Sarah, for Kate and himself. *What a mess.*

"Did he really think that I would take care of her, and raise her, knowing I didn't want to be a mother?"

"He knew you would try, out of love for him. And only if he died, which he didn't plan on doing, of course."

Spencer smiled at the irony. He knew Kate, in all her stubbornness would be a fine mom. He had no doubts. She'd always put her mind to whatever task that was before her. Maybe it wouldn't be so bad after all. And if he could help her, all the better. He'd always wanted a little girl.

Kate got up to find the envelope from John. It had gotten buried under mail and magazines on her end table.

Spencer asked, "Did you read all the papers in there?"

"No, not yet." Kate pulled them out and unfolded them. "Oh..."

"Why? What now?"

Spencer didn't answer. "I'll just wait for you to read them. I think I'll get that drink now." He got up and left the room, giving Kate time to digest the other papers in the envelope.

Kate started scanning the other papers. "What?! Are you kidding me?" Her raised voice woke up Buttons, who growled. She shushed him and he settled back down.

Kate however did not. "Spencer!"

Spencer almost choked on his water in the kitchen. *Uh oh. He was in for it now.* He set his glass on the counter and turned around, ready for Kate's next onslaught.

"Yes, Kate?" Spencer tried to play it innocent.

"Do you know exactly what these papers say?" Kate huffed.

He zeroed in on "exactly". "Not *exactly*, no." And that was the honest to God truth.

"Let me enlighten you. The papers say that John, my dearly departed boyfriend, would *prefer* that I bring up Sarah in the church and homeschool her. The church I got no problem with—" Kate noticed Spencer's left eyebrow go up. "But the homeschool part, I have an issue with. How do you homeschool a child and work full time, in the air force, no less?" Kate's voice rose with each syllable.

Spencer suppressed a smile. "Since when do you not have a problem with church?" He wondered what exactly happened during his TDY. He took a swig of his water while she answered.

Kate sighed. "I realized that I was doing to Sarah what my mother did to me and that God has been there all this time but I forgot about him. He didn't move away—I did."

He looked at her with awe. "I see. Just making sure you didn't get any visits from aliens or charlatans while I was away." Spencer's hope soared at this new revelation in Kate's life. "I'm glad you and God are on speaking terms again. It won't make things easier necessarily, but you'll have more peace."

Neither spoke for a moment until Spencer asked, "So is that all then?"

"What do you mean, is that all? That's certainly way more than I bargained for." Kate tossed the papers onto the counter. "Good gravy, he wasn't exactly a saint, you know."

"Hey, John did go to church when he could, you just didn't want to go with him, remember?" Spencer cleared his throat before adding, "And, he didn't swear, didn't drink too often; yeah, that one time; he tried to do the right thing and knew God loved him in spite of himself. It's true every church is filled with hypocrites, you know, because they're full of humans who aren't perfect. Like John. Like me." *And hopefully like you.* "And if we were perfect, we wouldn't need God at all."

Kate leaned on the counter, silent. If she were to think about it, and had been going to church all this time like she should have been, she'd be another hypocrite herself. She had been harboring anger for years at her mother for leaving her. *Who was she to be judge and jury? Was anybody ever better than anybody else? Not really.*

"One thing at a time, Kate. I'm here to help you. I think John would want me to, now that he's gone." He set his glass on the counter.

Kate nodded, tears slipping down her cheeks. "You're right. Again."

Chapter 12

A few days later, Kate looked for Spencer when she got to work. "Hey, Spencer."

"Hi, how are you doing?" Spencer spun his key ring on his fingers and had his hat on.

"Fine I guess. Are you free after work?"

"Sure." Curious, Spencer dropped his keys into the front pocket of his uniform pants.

"Can you come over?"

Spencer thought about giving Kate a hard time, but reconsidered, thinking she'd been through enough lately. He simply asked, "What time?"

"Five?"

"I'll be there."

"I'll have something for dinner."

Spencer gave her a small smile. "I won't be late."

Kate nodded and headed for her cube. Spencer headed out the door, needing to run an errand across the base. He adjusted his hat and walked to his car. *I hope Kate wants to discuss how to bring Sarah home and that she lets me help. I'm more than willing to help her as much as she'll let me.* He tried to keep his heart from thundering in his chest. He knew she had a long way to go before she could think about falling in love with him. He hoped it worked out that way.

Because his heart was already gone.

****

Spencer stopped by his place right after work to change out of his uniform, and picked up some iced teas before going over to Kate's. He had no idea if she had anything besides coffee.

After eating a simple but delicious dinner of Mexican rice bowls and salad, they cleared the table and Kate loaded the dishwasher, putting away leftovers. During dinner they had skirted the elephant in the room, chatting about work mostly. Buttons waited patiently for little tidbits to come his way, but was sadly disappointed when he didn't get any. The humans seemed to be too focused on themselves to pay him any attention.

Once dinner was over, Spencer and Kate sat back down at the table and Kate got serious. "Spencer, I need your help." Tears slid down her cheeks and she wiped them away with a napkin. "This is too big for me."

"I understand, Kate." Spencer swallowed a lump in his throat. "I'll help however I can, you know I will."

"Good. How much leave do you have right now?" She toyed with her napkin, putting holes in it.

Spencer put down his tea. "Plenty. When do we go?"

"As soon as possible. Sarah's lost both parents after all." Kate wiped her eyes with the napkin before leaving the room for a minute. She came back a minute later, with a map in her hand. She studied it for a few minutes and said, "It looks like it'll take about twelve or thirteen hours as the crow flies to get there." She tossed the map onto the table and sighed. "We have to pack, get leave approved and buy clothes for a two-year-old."

Spencer sat in silence.

"So young not to remember either parent--how sad." Kate tapped the map with a finger. "I need diapers, clothes, toddler food, a car seat, stroller, bibs—"

"Kate," Spencer interrupted. "They have most of that where she's staying."

"Oh. Then I need a crib, educational toys, safety gates..." She looked around her apartment and groaned.

"Kate, I think we need to call our First Sergeant first."

"That too." She got up and came back to the table with a notepad and pen. He sat in silence while watching her write furiously. Suddenly she dropped her pen and announced, "I have to move."

"Move? Why?" Spencer was having a hard time keeping up with her abrupt turns in their conversation.

"I only have a one-bedroom apartment. I can't sleep with a toddler in my room." She picked the pen up again and rapidly tapped the tablet with it. "Could my life be any more upside down?"

"Only if you have to deploy."

Kate glared at him. "Are you for real?"

"Well, you asked." Spencer was trying to lighten the mood but was obviously failing.

"It was rhetorical."

"I know." He grinned at her, which only made her frown.

"What would I do, if I *did* have to deploy? Who would watch Sarah?"

"Kate, I didn't mean to—"

"I know you were joking, but what if I did have to go? There's a likely possibility." Kate put her head on the table, lightly bouncing it up and down while groaning.

"I would keep her."

Kate looked at him, surprise on her face. "You? Why? How?"

"Why not?"

"Because she's not your responsibility... you're not a parent...you're not—"

"Qualified?"

"I didn't say that." Kate looked down at the floor. She knew she wasn't the least bit qualified, but now motherhood had suddenly been thrust on her and by George, she was going to give it her best.

"In every other way, you did. But yes, I would do it. With pleasure. I have a few nieces, but no, I'm not a daddy." *Not yet.*

"Spencer, are you serious?" Kate looked at him like he just landed from Mars.

"Of course! John was my friend too, you know."

Kate sighed. "I know. Sometimes I forget. Sorry." She rubbed her temples, thinking about how her life had changed so drastically in such a short time. "Well, that's a relief. I only have a few million things to do." She sat for several minutes, her pen flicking the notepad again. She knew she needed help with this one. *How on earth will I cope? John is gone and I'm going to be his daughter's stepmother.* She knew she had to swallow her pride. She would definitely need Spencer's help. And probably a lot of other people's.

Kate turned to Spencer and searched his face while he stared out the window lost in his own thoughts. Kate saw compassion, confusion and something else ... love? For her? *If it is, she couldn't deal with that right now.* She had enough to deal with already without exploring those feelings. She took a deep breath.

"Spencer, will you help me? Please?"

Spencer turned from the window and looked at Kate. After a few seconds of silence, he answered, "Of course, I was planning on it. But I have a few conditions." He cleared his throat and swallowed.

"Like?" Kate wasn't sure she wanted to hear them.

Spencer reached to put his hand on her arm. "Remember that day?" He gestured with his other hand toward the hall bathroom. "Promise me you'll never do anything that stupid again." She glanced at his hand, knowing what he referred to and nodded. "Promise you won't edge me out." He wasn't sure if she'd agree to that one. He waited for a few seconds in agonizing silence. She nodded again, still not looking at his face. "Promise you'll be the best mom, under the circumstances and to get help if you need it." She nodded again without hesitation. "That's it."

Kate slowly brought her head up and looked at him in the face. "Spencer, you know I'll do my best. And I won't do that," she pointed toward the bathroom with her arm, "ever again. But, I'm still a little overwhelmed and certainly not qualified—"

"Hold on, Kate." Spencer scooted his chair over so he could reach her hand. He squeezed it and didn't let go. "Think about any other parent. Granted, they may have nine months to prepare or a little less if they're adopting, but parenting is learned by on-the-job- training. Nobody is "qualified" for parenting. Things will be bumpy for a while, sure, but that's to be expected. All you can do is love Sarah with all your heart and do your best." He squeezed her hand again, wishing he could kiss her.

"Thanks, Spence." She squeezed his hand with her own. They sat in silence for a few minutes absorbing the last several hours. Not wanting to let go of Spencer's hand, she picked up the papers that were with John's letter with her free hand. She read through the legalese and decided to call the attorney's office listed on the letterhead to ask some questions.

Kate knew she had enough leave saved for a trip, but how much time did she have to get settled with a newly-acquired child? Kate tapped her pen on the tablet, lost in thought.

"When do you want to leave? We can talk to the First Sergeant in the morning and explain the situation. I'm sure this is a little odd, even for the air force."

Kate looked over at Spencer, "No kidding."

"Add oil change and tire pressure for my car." Spencer pointed to her notes.

"Huh? Oh." Kate jotted that down and then made more coffee. Spencer refilled her cup when the pot stopped brewing and sat back down.

"Here's the list so far," she pushed her notes toward him.

"Looks good. I'll go get the oil changed in the car and check the tires and gas up before we go."

"I'll call this attorney after talking to the First Sergeant to get some details before I pack."

"Good, I'll see you tomorrow."

"Thanks, Spencer."

He nodded before slipping on his shoes and made a mental note to recharge his phone as soon as he got home. He didn't have a landline. He heard Kate sigh behind him and turned to her. "You'll be a good mom, don't worry." He squeezed her arm to reassure her.

"I'm not so sure about that. But I'll give it my best. For her...for John...for me."

"That's all we can ask." Spencer finally let go of her arm and left. *Oh, boy. What a month we've had!* He ran to the car and mentally made a list of what he needed to do before they had to leave. If he got to go. There was a chance he wouldn't be given permission. He'd soon find out once Kate called Sergeant Nelson.

****

After driving home from Kate's, the first thing Spencer did when he got home was throw a load of clothes in the washer, and then found the phone charger in a kitchen drawer. He went to bed, knowing what he had to do in the morning.

After a quick breakfast, he changed into old sweats to change the oil. His duplex had a garage and he already had six quarts of oil on hand. When that was done, he went through the refrigerator, dumping out old leftovers and milk. He added the dishes to the dishwasher and ran it. Then he bagged what little perishables he had left and walked over to Mrs. Pettigrew's.

"Leaving again?" Mrs. Pettigrew asked when she saw him with the plastic sack.

"Yep. My own mission this time. Going to pick up Sarah, Kate's new daughter."

"That's great news." Mrs. Pettigrew reached for the bag and said, "Come in. I have some Snickerdoodles fresh out of the oven." She was without her walker, fully recovered from her earlier hip surgery.

"Don't have to tell me twice." Spencer wiped his feet on the rug before stepping in.

"You can tell me how God answered our prayers for Kate." Mrs. Pettigrew seemed quite pleased at Spencer's reason for leaving.

Over cookies and iced tea, he updated Mrs. Pettigrew on how Kate came around. "I'll help her any way I can, but boy she can be stubborn."

Mrs. Pettigrew refilled his tea. He nodded his thanks. "Stubbornness goes both ways. Good and bad," she commented.

"True. But I hope she uses it to be a good mother to Sarah. I think she will." They chatted a few minutes more and when Spencer left, he held a package of cookies and had assurance that Mrs. Pettigrew would watch over his place. Again.

Back home, he took a shower. While under the hot water, he thought about the last few days. He was relieved that Kate was pulling herself back together. He hoped she really was. He worried about her.

After getting in bed, he made a mental note of food items to buy and reminded himself to get out the cooler and rinse it out.

The next morning he drove to work, knowing he and Kate would meet with Sergeant Nelson at some point. First

Sergeants, often called First Shirts; were like counselors, pastors, and liaisons all rolled into one and often acted as go-between for the troops and higher ups. It took a special person to fit the role, and Nelson fit as well as any Spencer had known so far in his career. The special duty was usually a three-year term with some additional pay for being on-call 24/7. Nelson was known to be fair, but didn't let himself be taken advantage of.

Spencer hoped their trip would be stress free and that he and Kate could come to some understanding and forgiveness. It hadn't been his idea not to tell Kate about John's troubling secret. He had tried to get John to fess up early on, so John and Kate's relationship could move forward. But he had stood by his friend and now he was paying the price.

Spencer showed the guard his ID at the gate and drove on to the office building where he and Kate could sign their emergency leave papers. *What a mess.* But at least they were dealing with it. He had no idea how the trip home would be coming back with a bundle of two-year-old in his car, but they'd find out.

He pulled into a parking spot and ran into the building, looking for Kate or Sergeant Nelson. Airmen rushed from office to office, holding papers or conversations in the hallways. Phones rang, printers printed and normal other office noise filled the air. Spencer found Kate in the hallway, outside Sergeant Nelson's doorway.

"Hey. Is he here?" Spencer leaned on the wall next to Kate.

"I'm not sure. His office was empty, but the light was on. Maybe he's making coffee or something."

"You're probably right. He drinks a gallon a day, I think."

Kate smiled and nodded. "Probably."

"All packed?"

Kate shook her head. "Doing laundry and finishing the cleaning."

"Me too. Laundry's done though." He turned to his right as he heard footsteps approaching.

"All right you two, step into my office." Sergeant Nelson held a large mug in his hand, steam rising from the top. Spencer grinned over at Kate before they sat in the chairs in front of the First Shirt's desk. Sergeant Nelson could be mistaken for a football player since he was tall and broad through the chest and shoulders. Spencer always tried to keep on his good side, just in case he found himself playing football on the opposing team. One never knew what activity you might find yourself doing on those required "team building" days.

"So, explain this to me again. Something about Kate adopting and you need to go along." Nelson took a sip of his java and set the mug down, then leaned back in his chair.

Kate deferred to Spencer. Spencer explained John's situation, the will and that he was a witness and proof of Kate's identity.

"You're mostly moral support."

"I guess so, Sir."

Sergeant Nelson nodded and turned to Kate, "Are you prepared with childcare and all that's necessary to take care of this child?" He waited for her answer.

Kate gulped before answering. "No, I'm not. I just found out I was adopting, more like inheriting this child, a few weeks ago."

"This child's not yours?" Kate saw a quick look of surprise on the sergeant's face before it disappeared.

"No."

He leaned toward the desk again and picked up his mug. "Well, this makes things interesting."

Spencer and Kate looked at each other, not sure what he was thinking.

"So, let me get this straight." He gestured toward Kate. "You're the adoptive mother, the legal guardian of a daughter who isn't yours, but who's been 'willed' to you. Did you know about her before?"

Kate shook her head, afraid she would start crying or screaming. Most likely screaming. *This is so not my month.*

Nelson rubbed his forehead. "And you," he turned to Spencer, "did you know about her?"

Spencer hesitated before answering. "Yes, but she wasn't mine either and I was sworn to secrecy."

"Why?" After a few seconds, he said, "Never mind. Irrelevant. And not my business." He leaned back in his chair, his hands folded behind his head. He sighed before saying, "I don't know that this has ever happened before. But I do know that emergency leave is granted to airmen adopting overseas or even stateside for that matter. But for both of you to go for the same reason, from the same squadron, to the same destination, and not married; I don't know."

Spencer knew the difficulty of their situation. The air force had to know at all times where an airman was located when not at work in case of emergency. It was unusual for two unmarried airmen to go to the same location unless it was for training.

He asked, "Sir, could you just grant me regular leave, but let us go to the same destination? Nobody had any idea Sarah's parents would die within months of each other. It's not like we planned this."

Nelson leaned forward and steepled his hands, resting his elbows on his desk and sat quiet for a few minutes. "That works. And for Kate, emergency family leave." He picked out some forms from a folder in a metal stand resting on his desk and handed them over. "Just fill out the usual boxes and I'll sign them. Kate, you can have three weeks, Spencer one."

"Thank you, Sir." Spencer took the form and pen Nelson handed over and began filling in the blanks. Kate took hers and did the same.

When they were finished with the paperwork, they had to finish their shifts but made plans to pack the car after dinner and leave early in the morning. "I'll Google the route later, and print out directions. What time do you want me to stop by tonight?" Spencer asked before going his way.

"Eight o'clock okay?"

"Works for me."

As Kate drove back to the Security Forces building, she contemplated what had happened in her life during the last few months. *Where had my nice, quiet independent come-and-go life gone? How on earth am I going to adapt to the life of motherhood with no preparation or parenting classes? And a single mother at that.*

All her life she took classes to prepare for the future-- school and college for life skills, air force classes and training for her job, driver's education for her license. She hadn't signed up for this, and had no training whatsoever. She was blessed though to have so many friends willing to help her and she would definitely count on it.

Kate was relieved to get some time off, even though it was for picking up a daughter she didn't know existed a month ago. She had a few days to absorb this adventure, and an adventure she was sure it would be. In her wallet there was a long list of things to buy before the drive back home.

She couldn't believe that Sarah was the reason John hadn't told her he loved her. *Have I been that adamant about not being a mother because my own abandoned me?* She thought about that for a few minutes and realized she had. In the presence of her coworkers, she swore several times she would never be a mother. *What would they think now?*

On the other hand, how could I abandon Sarah? It wasn't her fault both her parents died and left her behind. It was all so tragic. Being left behind by one parent on purpose was one thing, but by death of both parents was a whole other issue.

After work, Kate stopped for some tacos since she wouldn't be cooking. In the refrigerator was a yogurt and banana for her breakfast, otherwise it was all cleaned out except for the cheese and milk Spencer had bought the other day. All she had to do was fold her clothes and pack the diaper bag with what she thought were essentials. The big stuff like high chair and crib, she would have Spencer help her with after their return.

She left the diaper bag and her bag of parenting magazines purchased the other day by the door and then folded her clothes into her suitcase. In the bathroom, she packed her makeup and extra toothbrush. Buttons moped around, watching her pack. But what he didn't know was that Jen was going to stay here with him. Jen lived with two roommates, so she was looking forward to staying alone for a week.

Kate took Buttons for his evening walk and breathed in the clean night air. The days were getting shorter as fall slowly took over the long summer days. Leaves blew around their feet as they trekked around the walking trail. A hint of smoke from a nearby chimney floated through the air. Kate always liked the aroma signaling the change of seasons.

After their walk, Kate gave Buttons a treat which he took to his bed to enjoy. While she did last minute tasks like watering her two houseplants, she felt grateful Spencer was going with her for support. She realized that it must have been hard for him not to tell her John's secret.

Spencer was a really nice guy and if she hadn't met John first, she might have been more interested in him. And he wasn't afraid of children like she was. Maybe there was a reason to all this madness after all. But she would have to think more about it after a good night's rest. After a quick prayer for safety on their trip, Kate went to bed with a mild headache and a major heartache.

Chapter 13

When Spencer got home after getting Kate's bags packed in his trunk, he finished his last-minute packing, adding his cell phone charger, his electric razor, and some mail he hadn't taken care of yet. He checked his email one last time and responded to his messages, then shut the machine off and unplugged it. Having lost more than one phone during electrical storms while away from home, he was in the habit of unplugging all his electronics before trips.

He stretched out on his sofa and channel surfed, not really paying attention to what played on the square box. His thoughts were on Kate and how she would handle the instant motherhood thing. Spencer was ready to help, but didn't know how much she would accept.

Spencer wished now that he would have pressed John harder to tell Kate about Sarah and then things would have been a lot different and less stressful. He almost overstepped his bounds, but knew John would have told Kate eventually. Sighing, Spencer tuned into a James Bond film.

The next morning Spencer showered and arrived at Kate's by quarter to seven. The day was sunny and warm, perfect for a trip. It would be a long drive though. Spencer didn't have to knock on Kate's door as she was ready and waiting. She held a bigger purse and by the door was a tote bag filled with reading materials.

Spencer could hear Buttons whining from inside. "Is he okay?" Spencer gestured toward the noise. Kate looked back toward the living room. "Yeah, he'll get used to it. He's in his kennel until Jen comes at lunch time to play with him. She's actually able to stay here and watch him while we're gone."

"That's nice and he's a lucky dog."

"Yeah." Kate locked her door.

"Are you ready?"

"As ready as I'm going to be." Spencer reached for her bag and asked if she wanted it up front.

"Please."

They lived near a whole network of Interstates, from 55 to 64 to 70 to 270 and a few others. He adjusted the air flow before heading toward Interstate 64 which he would take until connecting to I-70 west and beyond.

After settling in the car, Kate asked if he wanted her to drive any.

"If you don't mind. I start to get sleepy after about five or six hours, so that would be great."

"Sure. Mind if I read for a while?"

"Go for it. What are you reading?" Spencer asked, eying her book.

"The latest John Grisham."

"I like him too."

"I bought it at Barnes & Noble last week. I had to get something suspenseful and intriguing to help get my mind off of John. Haven't had much time to read it though."

Spencer nodded. "I understand, sorry."

"You can stop apologizing now. It's not your fault. Completely."

"Thanks. As a matter of fact, I came close several times to spilling the news, but I just couldn't do that to John with him so far away and in harm's way. But I wanted to. I really did." He swallowed quickly, forcing a lump down his throat.

Kate put her hand on his arm. "I know. I realized that last night when I couldn't sleep. I thought about it, and figured that was what had been on your mind." She looked out her window for a minute before continuing. "I forgive you. John, on the other hand, not so much."

"You need to, you know."

"I know; I'm still too angry right now."

Spencer nodded, though he didn't agree. He drove in silence for a few minutes before asking her, "You warm, cool, just right?" He switched lanes to pass a semi.

"I'm fine. I like it a little cool."

He waited before getting in front of the semi before speaking again. "By the way," he gestured to the back seat with his right thumb, "I have snacks and drinks in the cooler, help yourself."

"Thanks." Kate settled in with her book and occasionally looked out the window at the flashing scenery.

Spencer drove several hours before they agreed to eat at Arby's after refueling the car. With both humans and automobile refueled satisfactorily, Kate and Spencer returned to the car where Spencer fiddled with the radio and found an oldies station before getting back on the highway. They heard the tail end of a weather report mentioning something about snow, but they weren't sure where the station was located and didn't worry about it. Although Kate commented, "Isn't it a little early for snow except way up north?"

"I would think so, but you never know. The weather seems to have gotten weirder over the last few years." He got up to speed again and smoothly transitioned into the right lane of traffic. It was now mid-afternoon and they decided over their cheddar melts that Kate would drive in a few hours and keep the wheel until they stopped for the night.

When they reached the point for Kate to take over, Spencer pulled into a rest area. "It's getting windy; do you still want to drive?" he asked, while stretching next to the car.

Kate looked around at the sky. It was looking a little gloomy and much cloudier than it had been back home. She brushed hair from her cheek, to no avail in the breeze. "I think so. Storms don't scare me. Just idiotic drivers."

Spencer grinned at her. "I second that. Though I haven't seen too many on this journey yet. I'm going to walk around for a bit, should I lock the car?"

"Yes, I'll be back in a few minutes."

Spencer hit the lock button on his key fob and watched Kate head to the restroom. He started power walking on the trail surrounding the rest area. Large oaks and maples were just shedding their rust, gold and plum-colored leaves. He took a deep breath of fresh air. It felt good to stretch after sitting so long. He wondered how Kate was doing. So far she had been pretty quiet, hiding behind her book. At lunch she didn't say much, besides ordering her food and insisting on paying for it. Spencer gladly offered to pick up the tab, but he let her have her way. He knew she had a lot on her mind.

He moved into a slow jog and went around the trail again. For mid-October, he felt it was chillier than it should be. He almost wished he had a jacket and normally it took quite a chill before he needed one. As he came back around, he saw Kate waiting at the car, so he jogged a little faster the rest of the way back.

"It's getting cold," Kate commented, rubbing her arms.

"I know, I wonder if a storm's coming. I wish I knew the local stations as we travel west."

"Can I get into my bag? I have a sweatshirt in it."

"Sure," he unlocked the trunk for her and while she got out her sweatshirt, he dug through his own bag and got out his gray sweatshirt with the blue air force emblem embroidered across the chest, tossing it to the back seat if he needed it later. Then he got in on the passenger side. He put the key in the ignition and took out a magazine from the back seat.

They took off after Kate adjusted the seat and mirrors. "Smooth," she said after sliding into traffic.

"She's a good car."

"I'll need a new car soon so I can get a car seat in it easier."

"If you want help, let me know."

"That would be great. I'm not exactly mechanically inclined."

Spencer thought about their possible car shopping trip. *If I help her buy a car, maybe she's warming up to me. And then again, maybe she's using my offer because she just wants my help.* Maybe in time, when they were both over their grief, they could get serious and eventually become a family.

He had wanted to get married for several years, but with his constant traveling and moves across the country, he had a hard time getting serious with anyone. This was the longest time he'd been stationed at a base so far and he fell in love with a girl who fell in love with his best friend. He couldn't have made up this scenario in a hundred years if he tried. He went back to his car magazine before he got depressed thinking about his love life—or lack thereof.

****

Kate drove for a while in silence, and Spencer eventually fell asleep. They were still an hour or so from the Nebraska/Iowa border and several miles northwest of Kansas City when she noticed white flakes floating around the car.

"Spencer, wake up. What are these white things?" Kate knew exactly what they were, of course, but she needed confirmation as they certainly caught her off guard. It was way too early in the year to see white flakes drifting to the ground. And accumulating; coming down fast. She turned the wipers on high.

"Huh?" Spencer sat up, rubbing the sleep from his eyes. Kate repeated her question.

He looked out the windshield and at the sky. "Snow? Oh, man." He looked at Kate who gave him a quick glance. "I don't have a good feeling about this," he added. "There was one thing I forgot to do that I *always* do before leaving on a trip, except this one. Check the weather. Dang!"

"I didn't either, didn't even cross my mind."

"Where are we?" Spencer fiddled with the radio and found a station with weather bulletins.

"Northwest of Kansas City, almost into Iowa."

Spencer stopped on a radio station talking about the weather. "...and for Clay County, a winter storm watch is in effect until midnight tomorrow. This unexpected blizzard will bring high winds and heavy snow...stay tuned for further details. Now back to your regular programming."

Spencer pulled out the atlas he kept stored under the passenger seat. "You okay to drive for a few minutes while I figure out where we are?" He was flipping to the Missouri page, so she gave an audible yes.

He studied their route directions, thinking. What he heard on the radio did not sit well with him. He silently berated himself for not checking the weather. How could he have forgotten? Because he had let his heart get ahead of his brain.

Kate shivered. "Figuring anything out?" She switched the temperature dial over to low heat. "This doesn't look good." The snow was coming down fast and furious and the wipers were having a hard time keeping up.

"Why don't we get off at the next decent exit and I'll assess what we need to do."

Kate drove a few more miles before pulling into a gas station. She grabbed her sweatshirt and slid it on over her top. At least she had packed some long pants, but she wasn't prepared for snow of any kind, let alone a blizzard.

"What was the name of that county?" Spencer ran his finger across Missouri and up into Iowa, along their route. Kate had pulled the car off to the side away from the gas pumps. "Carson? Carter? Something with a 'c'." Kate leaned over to see the map.

"Here it is, Clay County. Hmm. I think it's coming from the northwest. Let's see how far we can get before stopping for the night. Do you mind if I take over early?"

"Nope. I'm going to get a hot chocolate at the station, want anything?"

"A black coffee."

Kate stopped to stare at him. "Coffee?"

He was still looking at the map. He nodded, tapping his fingers on the map and thinking.

He's worried; now I'm worried. She knew Spencer didn't drink coffee unless he was under stress. She left the car, power walked toward the station, used the restroom and bought their drinks, rushing back to the car as fast as she could while holding the two hot cups. Spencer had pulled the car up to the front. Kate noticed he was now wearing his sweatshirt.

"Ready?" he asked, taking his coffee.

She nodded, while buckling in.

"Thanks," he took few sips from his cup before backing out. "Let's get going. We've got a full tank, clear windows, and the oil still looks good."

He pulled into traffic and they were on their way. They drove on, with more flakes coming down in swirls. It was starting to collect at the sides of the roads. He once again chided himself for neglecting to check the weather.

"How do you feel if I keep going until either the roads close or I fall asleep?"

"What do you mean?"

"I think we should get as far as we can get before stopping for the night." His serious tone matched his expression.

"What are you thinking?" She twisted the cardboard wrapper around her cup while listening to Spencer's idea.

"That we're in the middle of a blizzard, in the middle of October, in the middle of the country." He gave her a quick smirk.

"I see." Kate shivered again. It was so strange to feel so cold after leaving home that morning. The skies were grayer and the white stuff was getting thicker. Spencer had the wipers on high to keep the windshield clear. "Aren't you cold?"

"I am." He turned up the heat a little bit.

They drove in silence for quite a while until the roads became nearly impassible. It had gotten too dark for Kate to read and she kept an eye on the weather and the roads.

After a couple of hours, Spencer said, "Start looking for an exit with decent hotels." They were only going about forty miles an hour. Traffic in the area had slacked off considerably.

"I'm looking." Kate turned the heat up again and packed her book and parenting magazines away. They had been discussing how Kate's life would change after this trip while they snacked on grapes and granola bars, not sure what they would be able to eat later.

"How are you doing?" she asked.

"Good. But I'm peeved at myself for not making more thorough preparations by checking the weather. I feel like an idiot." Traveling with Kate on this personal journey was messing with his mind and his heart. *Oh, well. There's nothing I can do about it now.* He grimaced at Kate briefly before turning back to the snowy roads.

Kate put her hand on his arm. "You're not the only adult here. I could've easily checked myself. And I haven't exactly packed snow boots and sweaters, either."

"Still. I should have known better." Spencer sighed.

"Never mind." She was quiet a minute before she noticed the blue sign listing hotels up ahead. "There's a Hampton Inn at the next exit five miles further."

"Perfect. Here we come; pray they have a room or two."

Kate glanced his way. "Preferably two."

He gave her a quick look. "If we're lucky."

"True."

"You can have the bed."

"How gallant of you."

"Naturally." He gave her a quick grin before turning off at the exit and took a right toward the hotel. They both knew they were trying to lighten the mood in a tense situation. Somehow, they would get through it. "The parking lot looks full, but I'll run in and check."

Chapter 14

"We're in. Took the last room." He handed her a key card.

"That's a relief. How much snow is on the ground already?" Kate looked around the parking lot.

"At least a foot and it doesn't look like it's stopping any time soon. Let's get our bags, unpack and I'll park the car later." He popped the trunk and got their bags.

"I can get mine," Kate protested.

"Your hands are full. I got it." He led the way inside and to the elevator. "We have a two-room suite."

"Perfect. As can be."

"It's all they had. I figure if we split the bill, it would be close enough to the cost of a regular room, so I took it."

"Good thinking." Kate followed Spencer down the hall after getting off on the third floor. Although paying for their room was the least of her worries at this point.

"Here we are," he said, dropping his bag. He took out the card key from his pants pocket and let them in.

Kate reached for a light switch. "Very nice," she said, walking over to the window. She closed the curtains and turned the heater on to medium. She took in the sofa, queen bed, and flat screen television resting on a large dresser. The décor was tan and maroon, which wasn't too bad. "What's in the next room?"

"Pretty much the same with a bed, dresser, and television looks like." He peeked through the door. "Which one do you want? You pick." He set his bag down on the luggage rack next to the dresser and stretched out his arms over his head. He rubbed his arms, trying to get warm.

"I'll let you know."

Spencer watched with amusement as she first stretched out on one bed and curled up into a ball, then moved to the other. He walked to the doorway of the adjoining room to see if she did the same thing. "Well, what are the official results?" he teased.

"I like this one. You can have the other."

"Thanks, doesn't matter to me. I'm grateful to be out of the car for a while after all that sitting."

"I know. Do you know if there's a gym?" She walked over to the desk and opened the drawers searching for an amenities book. She answered her own question. "Yep, first floor across from the pool. I brought some sweats, you?"

"Always."

She had only seen him in sweats a time or two, as he seemed to be warm blooded. Today he wore a nice button-up shirt with jeans and looked pretty good, with his clean-shaven face. She smiled as she thought about it; he was on leave but had shaved this morning anyway. She wondered if it was a personal preference or if he'd shaved out of habit. But she certainly wasn't going to ask.

To get her mind off his appearance and habits, she said, "I can change in my room; let me unpack a few things first."

"I'll be here." He took his own bag and lifted it to the bed and unzipped it.

Kate rolled her bag into the adjoining room and unpacked part of it, not knowing how long they would be stuck. She imagined after their workout, they would watch the news and see what they could find out. Pulling out sweat shorts and a T-shirt, she changed into them, then brushed fingers through her hair and put on her tennis shoes.

"Are you decent?" she called through the door.

"Yeah. Come on in." He was stretching and doing knee bends at the side of the bed by the window.

"Starting already?"

"You know how small hotel gyms usually are."

"Good point. I guess I can stretch on this side as long as I don't hit the bathroom wall." She looked around and got situated in a way so she could stretch also. There was one good thing she liked about being active duty, and that was being forced to stay fit. Their physical tests once a year were grueling, but it kept her motivated to keep in shape year round. She did some knee bends, squats, lifts and jumping jacks. She tried to ignore Spencer's grin. She didn't know what he saw that was so funny. "What?"

"Nothing." He kept up with his jumping jacks.

Kate stopped moving. "Nothing, my foot."

He grinned even broader and stopped to talk. "It's just that here we are on leave, in the middle of a blizzard in the middle of the country and we're still worried about staying fit for the air force."

"What's so silly about that?"

"I think we'll have more important things to worry about over the next few days like how to dig ourselves out."

"Next few days?" Kate squeaked. She stared at Spencer.

"From what I heard downstairs while checking in, this is only the beginning. They think it might snow a few feet before it moves out."

Kate plopped on his bed and groaned.

"I can think of worse things that could happen to us." He started some lunges and Kate watched his fluid movements. He was a strong, well-muscled guy, with a sweet personality.

I better watch myself. She took the bait. "Like what?"

"Like getting in trouble going AWOL and not being able to use the phones, not having any electricity, running out of food, you know being stuck in the woods with bears…"

"Stop, I get it. But could we get stuck here? Should we call in?"

"Nah, we're good."

"Are you sure?" Kate wasn't as confident. The air force had rules whether you were on leave or not.

"What can they do about it anyway? Send in a helicopter in this blizzard? We might as well make the best of it. Besides, this is only the first day of our leave; we'll worry about it if we're still stuck on the *last* day of leave. We're fine until then." He turned sideways, parallel between the bed and the wall and did toe touches in rapid succession.

He stopped and turned to her and added, "I noticed a gas station about half-a-mile down the road, I say after our workout, or maybe before, we should stock up on more food. The snacks we have were only for the drive. As a matter of fact, let's do that first." He looked at Kate in her shorts.

She looked like she would be ill. "Are you serious?"

"Yes. I'll take the car and be back as soon as I can. You have my number if you need me."

"I'm getting nervous." She shivered.

Spencer walked over and sat next to her on the bed. He wrapped his arm around her shoulders in a reassuring hug. "We'll be fine. It will just take longer to get Sarah." He gave her another squeeze and got up. He slipped his jeans back on, over his shorts and put on an extra sweatshirt, this one with a hood. "This is the best I've got. I'll be back as soon as I can." He shivered from a chill.

Kate got up and walked him to the door. "Be careful and come right back." She gave him a quick impulsive hug.

He hugged her back, "I will. Stay here and try not to worry." He left and she stood there for a minute, not sure what to do. She decided she might as well go down to use the gym since she was dressed for it and didn't have anything better to do than worry.

She worked out in the small gym where only one other guest was using a treadmill. Kate gave him a brief smile and then adjusted a stair stepper for her speed. When the man left, she moved to a treadmill and walked for twenty minutes. After she wiped it down, she went back upstairs.

Spencer wasn't back yet, so she took out everything for a shower and waited a few minutes to see if he would come back. He didn't, so she hopped in, keeping her clothes in the bathroom in case he returned. Afterward Kate dressed quickly, slung her towel over the curtain rod and removed her belongings except for her toiletries.

Kate stored her clothes neatly in a dresser drawer. She walked into the other room and switched on the television after finding the local channels listed on a card next to it.

"We're on generator power here at the station, and power is out all across the area with trees down, power lines dangling and—" the lights and television went black.

"No!" Kate yelled.

"No, no, no." She stumbled to the window and opened the curtains for light. She looked at her watch. It was 10:30. "Oh, where is Spencer?" she asked. "Please, please get here soon." Just then there was a knock at the door. Kate quickly crossed to the door and looked through the peephole. It was Spencer, holding a couple of paper bags. *Thank God.*

"Oh, thank goodness. Except now, we don't have the refrigerator power for anything." She took a bag from him, while holding the door with a foot.

"I got here just as the lights went out, and took the stairs. The office staff is trying to get the generators going."

"That's good." She closed the door and set her bag on the dresser. "What do we have?"

"Some yogurt, carrots, more grapes, sub sandwiches, soup-in case we have access to a microwave, beef jerky for me, and some dark chocolate for the lady," which he held up with a grin.

"You're a dear! And I got my workout in, so I can enjoy some without guilt." She held out her hand and Spencer dropped the bag into it. "Want some?"

"I need to shower and get into dry clothes first," he chattered.

"Oh, gosh, of course! How will you—"

"I'll manage. I have a small flashlight in my bag and I'll have to leave the door open for what little light there is." He looked at her, waiting for her response.

Her face felt warm. "Sure. I'll just hang out in my room. Eating chocolate. In the dark." She took one grocery bag though and unpacked it first. She watched Spencer out of the corner of her eye, as he took off his shoes and wet socks. "I'll be next door."

Spencer dug out clean dry clothes and took a quick shower, letting the hot water warm him up before it ran out. He stepped out and dried off in the semi-darkness, towel drying his hair. It was a good thing it didn't take long to dry. He put on a T-shirt under his sweatshirt and sweatpants and dry socks. He found an extra blanket in the closet and wrapped himself in that.

"You can come in now," he tapped on her door.

"Are you okay?" Kate was alarmed. His voice sounded weak and he still looked cold.

"Just trying to get warm." He went to the bed and stretched out, pulling the covers over him. Kate sat down at the small table watching him, worried he was now coming down with pneumonia. "Should I go down to the lobby and see if they have any coffee or hot water?"

He nodded without saying a word. He was still shivering. Kate got up and left, getting worried. *Surely he wasn't getting sick on me. I have to lean on him, to get through this latest trauma in my life. He has to be strong for me. Did I just think that? Maybe I'm falling harder than I*

*thought, and John barely cold. But I don't have time to an-
alyze these thoughts right now, I need action. Spencer
can't get sick. Not now.*

Kate propped the door open on the metal latch, hurried
to the stairs and ran down to the lobby. In the dim light
from the sky lights in the ceiling, she stumbled her way to
the café area and found a large coffee pot and cups. She
poured what little was left and hoped it did the trick.

Conversation behind the check-in desk was tense and
loud. Apparently one of the generators wasn't working, but
the staff was working on it in another area of the hotel
from what Kate could understand. She made her way back
upstairs, armed with additional blankets from a flustered
desk clerk and the coffee. She pushed her back against
their room door and slid in, trying not to spill the coffee.

Spencer still leaned on pillows, wrapped up in the blanket like a cocoon. "You don't look so good," she said,
entering the room. She dumped the blankets on the bed and
watched Spencer shudder. "Don't feel so good." He unrav-
eled from the cocoon, crawled into the bed, and with the
extra blankets, recovered himself. He left one arm out and
reached for the coffee. "Maybe this will help," he took a
sip, trying not to spill the hot drink while still shaking.

"From what I heard downstairs, the employees are
working on the generators—" just then the lights and the
television came on. "Oh, good!" Kate jumped up and
clicked the channel to a weather report. She sat in the chair
next to Spencer's bed after turning the heat up.

"Please, do not go out on the roads unless it is an emergency. The road crews are doing all they can to clear and
salt the roads. Only those who are still getting home from

their work day and emergency personnel should be out right now. I'm told by Missouri Department of Transportation that they'll be up all-night working. We're also getting numerous reports of schools closed for tomorrow. Back to you, Steve, for the latest forecast."

"Thanks, Ron. We're still in a severe winter storm watch, with as much as two feet of snow expected in most of our viewing area. We know that KCI is shut down and many flights grounded, causing major headaches at local hotels and the airport. Tonight and tomorrow expect blowing snow with temperatures in the low twenties. Accumulations from the western area to east of us will range from twenty inches to twenty-four or more..." Kate clicked the machine off and leaned back in the chair. At least they could see and stay warm.

"I'll be better tomorrow," Spencer said, finishing his coffee.

"I don't know what you're talking about," Kate replied. "You look like death and anyhow, we aren't going anywhere tomorrow. Did you see that mess we're in?" She gestured toward the silent television.

"Nothing we can do about it, but I'll be fine after a good night's sleep." He coughed, rolled over and promptly fell asleep.

Kate stared at her traveling companion and shook her head. *What a disaster.* She took out her book and read for an hour before calling it a night. Before turning out the light, she prayed, *Lord, help.* It was all she had, but she hoped it was enough.

Chapter 15

Noises from neighboring guests woke Kate the next morning. She shivered and snuggled back under the covers after peeking at the alarm clock. She didn't hear anything from next door, so she figured Spencer still slept.

She woke again an hour later when she heard a soft knock on her door. She sat upright and answered, "Yes?"

"You up?"

Kate couldn't believe the strength she heard in Spencer's voice. Was that really him at her door or someone else? She pulled the blankets up around her, before saying, "You can come in."

The door slowly swung open and Spencer stuck his head in. "What are you still doing in bed, sleepyhead?"

"What? Why? Do we have somewhere to go?"

"No, not really. Just checking on you." Seeing her astonished look, he gave her one of his characteristic grins. "Told you I'd be better."

"You weren't kidding. Did you get the car uncovered and cell phones working, too?"

"I'm good, but that not good. I've had my prayer time, and I'm starving. How soon will you be ready for breakfast?"

Prayer time? He had prayer time? Aloud, she said, "Give me a few."

"Sure." He closed her door and she slid out of bed, grateful at least that Spencer wasn't dying after all. One less thing to worry about. She opened the window curtains and immediately felt like closing them. A white wonderland and blowing snow was all she could see. The shapes under all the snow barely resembled the cars parked there.

She quickly got dressed and walked into Spencer's room.

"You pray?" Kate held a hairbrush in her hand.

"Don't you?" Without waiting for her to answer, he went on, "I read a portion of the Bible and say my prayers for the day."

This sounded like something she needed to learn more about. "Well, what part do you read and what do you pray about?" Kate brushed her hair and then tossed the brush to the bed in her room.

Spencer leaned on the dresser. "Right now I'm reading through the book of Psalms. Reading about David's praise one moment and questioning God the next. He seems to go back and forth like we still do today."

"I need to read that book. Except, I'm questioning more than praising, that's for sure."

"It will come. Baby steps."

"I hope so. 'Cause this whole parenting and home-schooling thing has got me in a tizzy."

"Let's go eat; we can talk more over waffles."

Kate followed him out the door, wondering how Spencer could put away so much food, still amazed that he was better.

Kate and Spencer sat down with waffles, eggs and juice in the mini eating area. Apparently they were the only guests hungry at the moment. Spencer said a brief prayer of thanks for their food and electricity which brought a smile to Kate's tired face. After a few bites of her waffle, Kate asked, "You go to church, right?" When Spencer nodded, she asked, "Which one?"

"Sometimes the chapel on base, depending on my schedule that week. But if Mrs. Pettigrew needs a ride, I drive her and attend hers. She goes to Community Bible."

Kate nodded. "Could I go with you sometime? Actually, make that we?"

Spencer put down his fork and wiped his mouth. "Of course. Let me know when you're ready."

"I don't know when that will be." Kate pushed her plate away, suddenly feeling full.

"I understand. Get Sarah settled and get into a routine. We'll all go together." Spencer put his hand on Kate's arm and gave her a soft squeeze.

"Thanks."

They finished their juice and coffee while talking. Spencer answered her other questions about the Bible and seemed happy to do so. Kate tried her cell phone again, but with no luck.

"I wish I could get a hold of the orphanage. But they must know about this ridiculous weather we're stuck in."

"I'm sure they do. Don't worry."

But that's all Kate seemed to do lately.

****

The next day, Kate woke up to a loud scraping outside her hotel window. She hoped it was a snow plow finally clearing the parking lot. She slid out of bed and opened her curtains. Sunshine radiated off the snow, causing a sharp glare. Hope surged in Kate at the sight of the plow moving great mounds of snow around the parked cars. Maybe they could finish their journey today.

Kate quickly got dressed, excited at the prospect of getting out of the hotel. Then she knocked on the connecting door to see if Spencer was up. He answered, "Come in."

"Good morning. I hear hopeful sounds outside in the parking lot." Spencer was stretched out on the bed, watching the news. Kate noticed a Bible on the nightstand. She was so used to seeing him in the dull green air force uniform, that it always startled her a little to see him in jeans. They looked good on him, especially in the navy knit shirt he wore. And he skipped shaving. *Why am I noticing that? What's wrong with me?*

"That's great. I've been watching the news to see if we can travel north. Looks like things are a go from here to there."

"Oh, good. Should we have breakfast and head out?"

"Sounds like a plan."

After they ate, they walked back to the room and packed. Kate was glad the sun shone, already melting some snow from what she saw through the lobby windows. Spencer loaded the cart with their baggage and pushed it outside to the parking lot with Kate right behind him. She nearly ran into him when he stopped at his car. Or rather where his car should be.

But wasn't.

Now puzzled, Kate and Spencer left the cart near the front door and walked around the parking lot but didn't find his Honda anywhere.

"Well this is interesting. Where in the world is your car?"

Spencer frowned. "Didn't I park it there when I got back from the store the other night?" He pointed to an empty parking space to the left of a side entrance door.

"I'm not sure, since it was dark. But it's got to be here somewhere."

"This is strange." Spencer's forehead wrinkled in puzzlement.

Kate followed Spencer with the cart back inside to the front desk. "Excuse me; I'm looking for my Honda that was parked out there. Any idea what might have happened to it?"

The clerk behind the desk stared at Spencer like he had spoken in Swahili. "Sir?"

"I parked my car out there the night of the blizzard and now it's gone." Spencer stared the young guy down. "I'd really like to know where it is. Please." Spencer drummed the counter with his fingers.

"Uh, uh...just a moment, please." Randy, according to his name tag, disappeared into a small office behind the reception desk.

"What on earth?" Kate asked. Exasperated, she leaned on the counter. *Will we ever get to Sarah?*

Spencer glanced at Kate, agitation on his face. "I have no idea, but now I'm frustrated." He leaned his elbows on the counter waiting until he found out where his car was.

Kate shook her head in disbelief. *Where on earth could his car be? And how could it go missing in the middle of a blizzard of all things?* Kate removed their belongings from the cart to free it up for someone who had a better use for it. Then she rolled their bags near a club chair in the small lobby where she plopped down in utter frustration. She leaned her head on her hand, not knowing what to do.

A minute later, a manager came out to the desk and spoke with Spencer. Kate heard their voices, but not what they said. Then she heard Spencer speak up, "I would appreciate that. We have people counting on us."

Spencer stood to his full height and ticked off items on his fingers, though Kate could no longer hear him. She had never seen Spencer act this way, but it made her feel good that he was in her corner. Naturally, he had a major stake in the situation as the car owner.

This was the first time in a long time that Kate needed someone to come to her aid as she thought about their latest trouble. Normally, she was in control as much as possible and took care of herself. But it was Spencer's car and she was relieved he had to deal with it, because what little energy she had left waned along with her sanity. Her emotions were stretched too thin.

Spencer left the desk flustered and turned to find Kate. He saw her resting her head on the back of the chair and wished he could ease her irritation. He dropped into the chair next to her and said, "Well, let's just say they're on it. Perhaps it was a disgruntled guest, getting stuck here like us. They don't know who had it towed, why or when. They just know that it was."

Kate looked up. "Really? That helps a lot."

"I know. It's really odd." He glanced at Kate and shrugged. "What can we do?"

Kate looked at Spencer and answered, "I just feel like crying."

Spencer's gut wrenched at her unhappy outlook. "Come on," Spencer held out his hand for her to take. She took it so he could help her up. She was too weak. Then he let go of her hand so he could give her a quick hug.

"I know we seem to be having a rough time, but honestly, there's not much we can do at this point. Management is going to call the impound lot and have the car returned at the hotel's expense." He squeezed Kate's back and reluctantly let go. "Let's see what we can find to do." Spencer looked down at Kate's vulnerable face and a rush of compassion overtook him so strong, he shivered. *I better be careful.*

She asked in a voice near tears, "Like what?"

"First, let's take our stuff back to our room, they unchecked us out—if you've ever heard of such a thing—and make a plan." Spencer interlocked his fingers with Kate's and when she didn't let go, warmth soared through him.

"I don't know what I would do without you, Spencer. I'm at my wit's end."

"I'm afraid it's going to get worse before it gets better."

"Why? How?" Kate stopped walking, but didn't let go of Spencer's hand, afraid she might sink to the floor when she heard his answer.

"I'm not sure when the car will get returned, possibly not before four o'clock this afternoon."

"What?" Kate stared at Spencer in disbelief.

"I know, I know." He gently tightened his hold on her hand. "So we need to refigure our plans for the rest of today and tomorrow. I'm sorry, but I don't think we'll get out of here until tomorrow morning. But the hotel is taking care of our bill," he rushed to add.

"That's generous." Kate ran her free hand through her hair, puffing out her bangs.

Kate knew she should let go of Spencer's hand as they made their way back to their room, but she was too confused and disappointed to care. And right now, she could barely put one foot in front of the other. His strength somehow kept her going. She trudged along beside Spencer who pushed the reloaded cart with his other hand until they got back on the elevator to their floor. She leaned on the elevator wall and sighed. *When would all these aggravations and surprises ever end?*

Once back in their room, they unloaded the cart again and Spencer left to return it to the lobby. Kate wandered around the room, unpacking a few things she would need for the night. She laid down on the bed, stacking up the pillows under her chin. In child-like fashion she bounced her legs in frustration.

Spencer returned, found her kicking away her annoyance and sat beside her and asked, "Now what?"

"Good question. Can I scream?" She turned toward him, bending her legs behind her so she could see his face.

"Sure. Hand me all your pillows."

Kate looked at him as if he was crazy.

"Seriously. Hand 'em here." He held out his hands.

Kate gathered the pile and handed them over. Spencer held them all in front of his chest. "Let it rip."

Kate looked at Spencer as if he had lost his mind.

"If it makes you feel better, yes. Right here," he pointed to the middle of the pile. He was willing to do almost anything to help her.

"That's ok; it wouldn't help anyway." Kate looked toward the window, wanting to do something, but with Spencer around, she didn't know what. She couldn't exactly have a tantrum with an audience.

"Are you sure? You want to beat me up instead?"

Kate gave him a tiny smile. "Tempting, but it's not your fault and no, that won't help either."

"What will? I'm at your service." He tossed the pillows back against the headboard. Kate sat up with her legs so near his own, that their closeness caused an intense longing to hold and kiss her or anything to ease her pain. He got up and stood by the window, looking through the grimy glass.

"No idea. Now that I'm trying to get Sarah, it seems like I keep hitting brick walls." She punched the pillows Spencer tossed back on the bed.

Spencer nodded but didn't turn around. He didn't trust himself to speak at the moment. He knew Kate was stressed from the trip and concerned about Sarah. Holding Kate's hand earlier felt so right to him. But he didn't want to hurt her by moving too fast too soon. That was the last thing he wanted to do.

Lost in his thoughts, Spencer didn't hear Kate get up and walk over to him. He felt her touch his arm and turned toward her. She looked as if she was about to cry after all. She asked in a tearful voice, "Can I get hug? Please?"

"Oh, Kate." Spencer turned so he could accommodate her request. With compassion he eased her head against his chest, hoping she couldn't hear or feel his rapid heartbeat. He gently ran his fingers through her hair. Then she began to sob. "Kate, I'm so sorry all this is happening. I know you're exasperated."

"I'm exhausted. I can't do this anymore." She continued to cry and Spencer consoled her the best he could. He rested his chin on her head, breathing in her light flowery scent. They stood there for several minutes while she cried out her pent up aggravation.

He whispered, "I'm here, Kate. I'm here."

Chapter 16

After Kate took a much needed nap, she and Spencer rode the hotel shuttle to a nearby mall. Spencer held the door for Kate in his customary fashion and walked in behind her.

Spencer said, "I know you're going stir crazy being stuck in the hotel. Let's see if we can get your mind off of things for a while." Kate was a do-it-now kind of person and Spencer could tell she was nearly at the end of her rope.

"Might as well, I guess. I'll look for a heavier jacket. If I believed in retail therapy, this would be a good time to try it." She gave Spencer a small smile.

"That's the spirit."

At least they could forget about the mountain of snow outside for a few hours.

Spencer wandered behind her wherever she went. After a while, Kate asked him, "Is there anything you want to look for?" She didn't mind him being around, but didn't want to deny him time to look for anything.

"Not really. If you want me to wander off though, I can." He half-heartedly offered to leave her alone, hoping she'd say no.

"No, no. I just didn't know if there was anything you wanted to look for."

"Actually, there is one thing I want to look at." He remembered he wanted to get her a new robe. This was as good a time as any. He pointed to a jacket in her hand and commented, "I like that one better if you can't decide."

Kate looked at the navy poplin jacket with hood attached and then at him. "You think so? Better than this one?" She pulled another choice off the rack in a shade of green.

"Yes, it's more your color."

"I think you're right. Thanks." She folded it over her arm.

"I'll be in shoes."

"Ok, I'll meet you there in a little bit." He found the ladies nightwear department and searched through the robes. He saw one in a soft fabric in light blue that she would probably like. He paid for it and then went to the shoe section.

"All done?" Kate asked when she saw him carrying a bag.

"Yep, how about you?"

"I found a new pair of boots and a new pair of slippers."

"Oh?" He wondered what color the slippers were, but hopefully it didn't matter.

"Yeah, so maybe there's something to retail therapy after all."

"Maybe. How about dinner?"

"I could eat. What are you in the mood for?"

"Anything that doesn't involve unwrapping plastic packaging."

She chuckled. For several of their lunches, they'd been eating their snacks and the food Spencer bought at the store the first night. They both wanted something more substantial.

They found a barbeque joint attached to the mall, both looking forward to a good meal before heading back to their temporary prison. They both ordered the burnt ends, small chunks of brisket smoked for several hours and then marinated in a tangy barbeque sauce.

"This is some of the best barbeque I've ever had." Kate used her napkin and wiped sauce from her mouth.

Sounds of agreement came from Spencer and he nodded. "It's definitely some of the best I've ever had."

Kate seemed in better spirits, but Spencer sensed something still bothered her. They finished eating and Kate fidgeted with her cloth napkin on the table. The server brought their check and Kate snatched it up before Spencer could take it. "My turn," she said. Earlier, Spencer had paid for their fast food lunch.

"Why?" Spencer asked.

"Why not?" Kate countered. She pulled out her wallet and put down the money including a generous tip for the great service.

Spencer tilted his head. He knew he couldn't say because 'he was the man'. *As much as I'd like to say because we're on a date, she would balk at that idea. And I certainly can't say, because I wished it was a date and it was my privilege to pay the bill.* Finally, he answered, "You got me this time."

"Spencer," Kate's voice was less forceful now, "do you realize that in the last two months," she listed items on her fingers, "you have saved my life, kept my stupid mistake a secret, flown hundreds of miles to attend a funeral at your own expense, changed my oil, absorbed my anger more than once, traveled through a blizzard, and had your car towed," when she mentioned the car, her voice cracked, "all for me?"

He looked her right in the eye. "Yes. And I would do it all again." *In a heartbeat.*

"Why?"

"What do you mean, why? We were both friends of John. That's what friends do. I don't understand why you're asking." Spencer looked upset.

"It's more than that. Spencer, you have gone over the top in every way possible to help me through this mess. I don't know how to thank you and simply paying for your dinner is never going to be enough."

"Enough?" Spencer leaned in toward her. "Kate, I'm hurt you even think you have to repay me. That's not how friends operate. If we always expected payment from the human race, we'd either never do the right thing or be disappointed by not getting repaid. That's no way to live."

"I'm up to my eyeballs in debt to you, Spencer. Yes, I have to repay you." Kate didn't understand Spencer's argument.

"Kate, you can never repay me. It's a gift. They call it friendship." Spencer swallowed hard, wounded by her way of thinking.

"No, Spencer, it isn't. It's all too much," and she wiped away sudden tears with her napkin. She sat in silence, tears running down her cheeks. *Why is he being so difficult all of a sudden?*

Spencer was crushed. He fell back against his chair, in disbelief, feeling helpless as he watched her cry. It never occurred to him that Kate would take things this way. *How am I going to convince her no payment was expected without saying too much? I know that even without any feelings for her that I would help anyway.* Hurt and bewildered, he felt a headache coming on.

The server came by to get their payment and told them to have a good night. Spencer wasn't sure either of them would.

****

The two shoppers returned in silence, each in their own world. But once they arrived back at the hotel, Spencer told Kate he wanted to check on his car before going inside. She waited in the lobby. Spencer walked around to the side of the building to make sure it had been returned, and sure enough it was. Except for some extra snow on the tires and the body, it looked the same. He was relieved.

Together, they rode in the elevator in silence. After returning to their room, Kate dropped her purchases on her bed and then walked into Spencer's room. She continued their previous conversation. "Yes, I do have to repay you, Spencer. And I will, as soon as I get my act together." She tossed her shoes toward her door and plopped on his bed. "If we ever get out of here."

Spencer leaned on the wall by the dresser and crossed his arms. "Kate, if I hear you say that one more time, I'll throttle you." He raised his voice slightly and continued, "You. Are. Not. Going. To. Repay. Me. Ever. And that subject is closed." Spencer squeezed his eyes shut and rubbed his forehead with one hand.

"Spencer, if I have to cook dinner for you for the rest of my life and wash your car, or whatever else, I'll do it. And you can't stop me."

Spencer took a deep breath before saying through clenched teeth, "The discussion is closed. I'm getting a headache." He didn't know what hurt more, his head or his heart.

"Sorry! Do you need something?" She got up and rummaged through her bag. "Here, I have some Tylenol." She opened the bottle and dropped two tablets in his hand. Their hands touched and a spark shot through her arm. She glanced at Spencer to see if he'd felt it too. He had.

They stared at each other for a moment before he said, "Thanks," and left to get water in the bathroom.

He walked back into the room, ignoring Kate. He couldn't look at her right now knowing how she saw things. He slid off his shoes and sat on the bed facing the wall.

Kate got the feeling he wanted to be alone. "I'll read in my room before turning in. Good night."

He simply nodded and waited for her to shut the door. Spencer dropped his head in his hands and thought over their stupid argument. *How could she possibly think she had to repay me? For being myself?* If this situation happened to Jen or Kelly, he would help them in the same way. The only difference was that he was in love with Kate and couldn't tell her.

On the other side of the door, Kate reached for her pajamas. She was completely bewildered by Spencer's attitude. *How can I not repay him after all he's done for me?* He had gone out of his way numerous times to help her, going beyond what any normal human being would do. And why did he think it so strange for her to offer repayment? He seemed to get angry at the very idea. He was even using his own vacation time to help her bring Sarah home. *Who does that?*

Frustrated about their impasse, she turned to her book and read before turning in.

****

Spencer refilled his water glass with ice from the machine down the hall. He sipped on root beer from the cooler while trying to figure out Kate. Crunching on the ice, he asked himself why was she being so adamant about paying him back for doing things he would do for almost anyone? *Did she think he expected something in return? She couldn't be more mistaken.*

He rattled the ice in his glass and poured the rest of the soda from the can. He felt like hurtling the can across the room. Instead he crushed it in his hand and tossed it to the trash can near the desk.

Giving up on finding answers to his questions, he channel surfed trying to get his mind off of Kate and her stubbornness. He found a basketball game, but was so distracted, he couldn't tell anyone if they asked, who the teams were or who won. He was still miffed.

Finally, he got ready for bed. In the dark, he stared toward the ceiling talking to God about the difficulties he was having with Kate and prayed for safety on the rest of their journey. He did feel optimistic about one thing though. At least she was willing to try church.

****

The next morning after a rerun of the same breakfast, which Kate and Spencer were both seriously tired of, they returned to their room. Spencer asked Kate, "Are you okay?" Kate had been pretty quiet all morning.

Kate didn't answer right away. She hadn't slept well the night before, contemplating their conversations from the day before. She looked at him, trying to find the words to explain it all.

How could she thank Spencer for getting her through some of the toughest moments in her life? Especially when he didn't seem to want it?

"No. But I will be. Thank you." She went to her room and shut the door.

A few minutes later she came out with her suitcase. Spencer had the cart again, and they loaded their luggage on it.

"I'm getting tired of doing this." She threw her bag of reading materials on top of her suitcase.

"That makes two of us. But we'll finally be on our way shortly."

Just then Kate heard something ringing from her room. "That's my phone!" She ran into her room and picked it up off the nightstand. "Hello?" Kate plopped onto her unmade bed.

"Oh, Jen! It's so good to talk to you! How are things there?"

"We have a little snow—about two feet of it. The base has been shut down for a few days, but more importantly, how are you? Are you okay? We've been worried about you guys and haven't been able to contact you."

"You wouldn't believe it. We have mountains of snow, had no electricity in the hotel for hours, I thought Spencer was dying, and then his car was towed!"

"You're kidding! Why?"

"No idea. But they returned it late yesterday afternoon and we're leaving as soon as we finish packing and check out—again. We'll finally finish the first half of our trip today. Jen, I'm so nervous; I just want this to be over with. What if Sarah doesn't like me?"

"She'll like you just fine and I'm sure she'll be like any normal two-year-old. Don't put the cart before the horse. One thing at a time."

"I just don't know if I can do this. I'm so afraid of screwing it up."

"Kate, that's what God is for. He'll give you what you need when you need it. There's a verse in the Bible that says with God all things are possible."

"I sure hope so. 'Cause to me it looks impossible."

"How's it going with Spencer? You two behaving yourselves?"

Kate wasn't sure how to answer that. "Oh, gosh. First Spencer was sick, then he got better, then he was like my knight in shining armor about his car getting towed, and then…"

"Yes?"

"I don't know what to think." Kate shut her door since Spencer was also on his phone and she didn't want Spencer to hear what she said.

"What do you mean? You aren't—"

"No! But I think I could…eventually."

"You mean you're starting to have feelings for Spencer and you feel guilty because you loved John?"

Kate pulled the phone away from her ear and stared at it. Then she put it back and asked, "How did you know?"

"First of all, Kate, you're under enormous stress right now. And almost any time a guy and a girl are together for lengths of time in stressful circumstances, it's inevitable for there to be feelings between them. Spencer is a straight-up guy; moral, honest, and trustworthy. You're vulnerable right now. Throw in a blizzard, your anxiety, the close quarters, etc. and it's like a bomb about to go off. Do you think Spencer likes you?"

"Possibly. But maybe he's afraid to say something, thinking I'm still not over John's death, which I'm not. I don't know!" Kate fluffed her pillows and leaned against them. "Do you think it's okay to like Spencer? How do I know when it's time to date again?"

"Everybody's different. Yes, you and Spencer make a great couple. Take things slow. Let him know you're interested, but you're not ready. Be honest. If he's the one for you, Kate, he'll wait. But not forever."

Kate was silent a minute before speaking again. "How should I do that? I've always liked Spencer as a friend and coworker, but I was dating John."

"If he asks, tell him you like him, but it's too soon for anything right now. Don't leave him hanging or confuse him."

"Right now we're sort of at an impasse."

"Oh?"

Kate settled into a more comfortable sitting arrangement on the bed before explaining. "Yeah...we had an argument last night about me repaying him for all he's done for me. He thinks that I shouldn't even try because it was out of friendship and blah, blah, blah." She pounded the extra pillows for emphasis.

"You know Spencer; he's always the southern gentleman. He probably does resent you thinking you have to repay him. Just make him dinner when you get home."

"You think that's all? He's done—"

"Kate, if you force the issue, you'll just make him mad. Let it go."

"Are you sure?"

"Kate...." Jen drew out her name, like she was being difficult.

"Yes?"

"Let. It. Go."

Kate sighed. "I'm having a hard time with that."

"Really?" Jen laughed.

"My stubbornness is showing again, isn't it?"

"Yep."

"I'll just offer to make him dinner sometime after we get back, and that's enough?"

"Perfect. I'm praying for you guys and for a safe trip home."

"Thanks, we apparently need it. How's Buttons?" Kate was glad to change the subject.

"He's looking for you, but he's eating, drinking, peeing and pooping. I come in and he runs to the door, sees me and stops in his tracks. Then he thinks for a second and then runs for a toy or ball. I guess he thinks I'll do."

Kate laughed. "I'm glad he's being good. I miss him."

"All right, you two make the most of it and we'll see you in a few days. Take care, Kate."

"Thanks, Jen. Talk to you later." Kate disconnected the call and saw that she had other missed calls. She took care of those and then packed what little she had left so they could get out of there. As she finished up, she could hear Spencer talking on the other side of the connecting door, but couldn't make out the words. Kate passed through to the bathroom and packed her makeup.

Kate walked back into Spencer's room and saw that he was off the phone. "It's great to be in touch again, isn't it?"

"Yes, it is. I'm almost ready."

"Good, I'll gather the snacks that are left."

Spencer packed his things from the bathroom, and while cleaning out the mini fridge, Kate thought about her phone conversation with Jen. Kate knew Spencer long enough to know that he was definitely a great guy, but how long would he wait? She sighed, not knowing the answer. But at least they were finally getting out of there.

****

"I don't know about you, but I'm happy to leave that hotel behind us." Spencer drove them to the west I-70 ramp.

"I don't think I've ever wanted to leave a place so badly," Kate agreed. The day was cloudy and so breezy she was glad Spencer kept them in their lane against the strong north wind. But even so, it wasn't nearly as awful as the blizzard that forced them to stop a few days ago.

"In a few hours we'll be at the children's home. Are you ready?"

"Not in the least. But I wouldn't be a hundred years from now, either."

"You'll do fine, Kate. I know you will."

"Thanks. No turning back now, especially after the frustration of the last few days."

"No kidding. You want to stop for a waffle, eggs and sausage?" Spencer asked before giving Kate a big grin.

"If I don't see that exact breakfast again for twenty years, it wouldn't be long enough."

Spencer laughed. "Ditto."

Kate pulled out one of her magazines and scanned an article or two. She didn't really feel like reading, but she didn't feel like talking, either. If Jen hadn't called earlier, Kate thought there might still be tension between her and Spencer. The feeling of being reconnected to normal life helped.

Was Jen right by saying making dinner for Spencer was enough? How can it be after all he's done for me? She still wasn't convinced. What she did know was that he was always generous and helping people, it was his nature.

Perhaps repayment was the wrong word. Maybe thanks was better. Was that what bothered him? That he had taken things the wrong way?

This definitely needs more thought, but not right now. Her mind was full with so many major changes in her life, she could barely keep up. She sighed silently as she stared out the window, noticing less cold white stuff on the ground, which was a relief.

Spencer's radio was set to a country music station, but she tried tuning it out. She decided to take a nap. Spencer seemed to have the driving under control anyway.

Chapter 17

It was now mid-afternoon and sunny, but the northern wind made it very chilly. Spencer pulled into the parking lot of the children's home. Kate took a deep breath. Her lunch still sat like a watermelon in her stomach.

Spencer stretched his arms before opening his door. "Kate, don't worry. This is what the trip was all about."

Kate quickly checked her hair in the rearview mirror and took another deep breath. She slowly got out of the car and headed for the front door, with Spencer right behind her. The building wasn't much to look at, but looked well-taken care of. The two-story brick building had a fenced in area with slides and swings on the right side of the building. They walked through the double doors and up to the front desk.

A welcoming receptionist with short brown hair in a floral print dress smiled and asked, "May I help you?"

Kate swallowed nervously before answering, "Yes, my name is Kate Langston and I'm here to pick up Sarah Warner."

The receptionist, Mary Carpenter, according to her name plate, paused for a moment as if trying to recall something. Then she gave a soft gasp, and looking right at Kate said, "I'm sorry for your loss."

Kate was caught off guard but managed to get out a "Thank you."

"We're glad you finally got through that snowy mess. Was it bad?" Mary was so thoughtful, giving Kate much needed reassurance and a chance to regain her composure.

"A little." She looked at Spencer standing beside her, who gave her a small smile.

"Of course. I'm glad you have a friend with you. Sarah is a darling from what I hear. You'll be great with her, I'm sure." She turned away to look at her computer screen.

"We got your message about the delay, so don't worry." Her bangs shook on her forehead as she pulled out a folder from a stack on a nearby shelf and said, "Mr. Miller will be with you in a moment. I'll let him know you're here. And Mr. Carson is on his way also, he just left court."

"Oh, good, thank you." Kate wasn't sure if the lawyer would be able to come since her arrival was delayed. Relieved, Kate and Spencer sat down in the waiting area.

"You okay?" he asked.

Kate nodded. "As good as I'm going to be." She took a deep breath. Mary had been so kind, it helped Kate's nerves settle a little.

"Kate, I know that this is stressful for you and not what you expected in your life, but you'll do fine. And Jen, Kelly and I will help you as much as you need. Okay?"

"If you think so," she said doubtfully.

"I know so. Want a magazine?"

Kate shook her head. Spencer reached his arm around her shoulders for a reassuring hug before he turned to a magazine about cars. They sat in plastic yellow chairs, against a wall near a table displaying family and parenting magazines and a leafy plant in a glazed container. She could almost see her reflection in the shiny leaves. Their feet rested on a deep forest green carpet. Prints of exotic flowers adorned the tan walls.

Kate stared into space, lost in thought. Her knees jiggled and she wiped her hands up and down her legs. Motherhood was just a few minutes away. Her life would change dramatically. She looked toward the ceiling as if she could see God above it. *Help, Lord, help.*

She could hear children's voices down the hall and overhead a Mozart piece playing through the speakers. A door opened to the left of the reception area and a tall gray haired man called for Kate.

"Hello, Miss Langston. I'm Mr. Miller, the director here." He held out his hand and Kate shook it. His grip was solid without being too strong. "Come on in and have a seat." Kate turned back to Spencer for a moment and saw him nod before she followed Mr. Miller into his inner sanctum. Mr. Miller walked back into his office and stood behind the desk, gesturing to one of the upholstered chairs for visitors before sitting in his own. He looked a little like Sean Connery and his manner reminded her of a favorite uncle, which made Kate feel at ease.

Other than a business phone, notepad, and pencil cup, there was a single stack of papers and folders on one corner. Kate relaxed when Mr. Miller smiled.

"I understand you're probably nervous. It's okay. We'd rather see that than someone who thinks they've got everything under control. Parenting is never easy, you know."

Kate nodded in agreement. *You can say that again,* she thought. "When Mr. Carson gets here, we can get to business, but for now, I can get copies of your identification and give you some background. I need two forms of ID for Mary to copy and then we can get started."

Kate pulled out her driver's license and her military ID and handed them over.

Mr. Miller glanced at them quickly and said, "I'll get these back to you in just a few minutes." He opened his door and Kate could hear him ask Mary to make copies. He returned a minute later and sat down again.

"We have some paperwork for you and because you're adopting a ward of the state, you will receive a monthly stipend for Sarah's care. Here are the forms." He handed her several sheets of paper from one of the folders on his desk and pulled out a clipboard from a drawer.

Kate took the forms and read them over before signing. Kate started filling in the first page.

Mr. Miller's phone buzzed and he answered it, "Thank you; send him in." He returned the receiver and said, "Mr. Carson is here now." He stood up to open the door.

"Mr. Carson, I'm Mr. Miller and this is Miss Langston. She's the legal guardian for Sarah Kern/Warner."

Mr. Carson was short and with square-rimmed glasses sitting on a small nose. He was in an expensive-looking suit and seemed to be all business.

"Mr. Miller, Miss Langston," he shook hands with them and said, "Let's get to it then. It's all simple and straight-forward." He quickly sat in the chair next to Kate, put his briefcase on his lap, snapped it open, and pulled out a file folder. He handed Kate some forms and said, "These are the forms for legal guardianship and a copy of John's will."

He paused for a moment and gave her a brief sympathetic look.

"You can call me Kate." She took the forms and flipped through them before signing anything. She added them to the pile from Mr. Miller. She thought she might be leaving with a mild case of carpel tunnel by the time she finished signing them all.

Several minutes later Mr. Miller took the forms from her and set them on the desk. "I'll take you down to the toddler wing and you can interact with Sarah. She has a gentle nature and you'll bond with her quickly, I think. She's a sweetheart and though she hasn't been with us too long, we'll miss her."

Kate nodded, listening. *This is it.* They walked out of Mr. Miller's office and passed Spencer who gave her a quick wink when he saw them. She gave him a nervous smile before following her guide down a long hallway through double doors that led into a large rectangular room painted in red, yellow and blue. Short built-in shelves along two walls held many toys, books and games.

Several girls in coordinated outfits were having a tea party with bears at a little table. Kate smiled, remembering her own days having tea with her bear. The children all seemed happy and were playing with a variety of toys. Some were working tray puzzles, some coloring, others watching a video.

"Sarah is having tea over there," Mr. Miller pointed, "she's in the pink and white polka dot outfit."

Kate looked toward the group of girls playing and saw the girl he indicated. Kate stared at the little girl and sucked in her breath. If he hadn't told her which little girl was Sarah, Kate would have known instantly, for she had John's eyes and nose. Kate hadn't considered the possibility of Sarah looking like John. Kate pushed back a wave of grief and tried to smile as she watched Sarah toddle about with her stuffed puppy which was almost as big as she was.

Kate trailed behind Mr. Miller as he bent down and approached Sarah. "Sarah, this is Kate. She's going to take you to your new home."

Sarah looked up and promptly said, "No. I stay here."

He smiled at Kate. "Even here, one of their first words is 'no'. I don't think you can even teach it to them."

Kate bent down and said, "Hi Sarah. Do you like playing with puppies?"

Sarah nodded, squeezing hers tighter. "Mine."

Kate gave her a smile before standing up. "Does she have much to pack?" she asked Mr. Miller.

"She has her puppy, some clothes and diapers. And a car seat, which we'll help you install."

"Thanks."

"I'll let you stay here and get acquainted while Carol packs her things. I'll have them at the front desk for you." Mr. Miller pointed out the various staff workers around the room if she had questions.

"I appreciate that. She does seem sweet. Does she have any routines or allergies I should know about?" Kate watched Sarah playing; still shocked this was all happening.

"Carol will know more; she works in the toddler wing daily and probably knows all their quirks by heart. I'll have her leave some notes with her bags. There will be copies of her file for you also. I know her medical records from her mother are included."

"Thank you." Kate sat down next to Sarah and her puppy and asked what his name was. Mr. Miller left to interact with another group of children who were playing a board game. Kate smiled to herself when she watched him get down on his knees and helped some toddlers with their wooden puzzles. It was comforting to know he wasn't above playing with the children in the home.

Kate turned her attention to Sarah. "Bo Bo, mine."

"Bo Bo? That's a nice name. Is he thirsty?"

Sarah nodded and poured some tea in his cup.

"May I have some?" Kate asked her.

She nodded again and took another cup from the nearby shelf. The other girls ignored the two of them as they left to watch cartoons. "Why thank you; it's good tea," Kate pretended to sip. "Does it have sugar?"

"Uh uh." Sarah sat down on Kate's lap while holding her puppy. Kate was surprised, but relieved too. "What do you like to play with besides Bo-Bo?"

Sarah didn't answer, but pretended to give puppy some tea. Then she got up and took a plate and pretended to pass him something. "What's that?" Kate asked.

"Cookies," she answered. "Want one?"

"Sure, I love cookies. What kinds do you like?"

"Choc-chip."

"Chocolate chip?"

Sarah nodded.

Kate watched her play a minute longer and then got up the courage to ask, "Are you ready to go to a new home and stay with me?"

Sarah dropped her dishes and looked at her. "Why I go you?"

"Well...because you need a new place to live and...I'll be your mommy now." Kate struggled with her answer, not knowing how much to say or what Sarah would understand.

"Okay. I go."

Kate sighed with relief. Hopefully someday Sarah would understand the whole story. She wondered if the staff had mentioned Kate's coming as a way of preparation for Sarah.

Sarah stacked up all the dishes on the table and picked up Bo-Bo. "I ready. Can I say bye-bye?" Sarah asked.

"Of course. I'll wait right here." Kate stood near the door, fiddling with her jacket string while she waited. The adventure was just beginning. She felt swirls in her stomach and her hands started to sweat. *One hour at a time.*

Chapter 18

Kate walked back to the lobby area with Sarah toddling alongside her, holding her puppy. Spencer stood up as soon as he spotted them. Kate looked down at Sarah and said, "Sarah, honey, this man is Spencer, a friend of mine and he came on the trip with me to get you. We live in a different town." Kate looked up at Spencer, who was staring at Sarah. "We're going to stay in a hotel tonight and then take a car ride back to where I live." Her voice wobbled as she spoke.

Spencer took his eyes off Sarah and whispered to Kate, "She looks like John. Are you okay?"

She nodded. She felt so jittery from the stress of the last few days. "Her belongings are being packed. Can you take her for a minute? I need to use the restroom."

"Sure. Take your time." Spencer sat down with Sarah beside him.

Kate bent down to Sarah's level. "Sarah, I'll be right back, okay?"

The little girl simply nodded. They started to chat about her puppy. While Kate was gone, Spencer worried about Kate and this latest development. He didn't think either of them had considered what Sarah would look like. He said a quick prayer for Kate who was having an emotional moment.

A few minutes after Kate came back and sat on the other side of Sarah, a tall woman with red hair and green eyes entered the lobby holding several items, including a pink car seat and a pink diaper bag.

Kate and Spencer both jumped up to help her unload her burdens. "Hi, my name is Carol. You must be Kate?"

"Yes."

"Nice to meet you."

Kate set down a package of diapers and the diaper bag and shook hands. Kate introduced her to Spencer. Then Carol pulled out a file folder and went over the information inside.

Kate took a deep breath and remained calm while listening to her talk about meal schedules, nap times, and shots, before handing Kate the file. Then Carol had Spencer show her where the car was and showed him how to install the car seat while Kate waited indoors with Sarah.

When Carol returned, she bent down in front of Sarah, and said, "You'll like your new family. Can I get a good-bye hug?"

Sarah nodded and slid off her chair. She didn't let go of her puppy but accepted the hug. "You take care of Bo Bo, all right?"

Sarah nodded, looking a little nervous. Kate thanked her and they left.

Here goes nothing.

****

Spencer headed back east and drove about three hours. Kate picked a Drury Inn for them to stay in. After they checked in, the trio met in the dining area for dinner.

They settled at their table, with Sarah in a wooden high chair. Spencer said a quick prayer and Kate peeked at Sarah, who didn't close her eyes. The poor thing was probably bewildered.

Kate made a plate of macaroni and cheese and some thin carrot sticks and set it in front of Sarah. Kate handed her a spoon, not sure if she could use one, but she took it and started eating. For herself she got a bowl of cream of broccoli soup and a baked potato.

After a few minutes Spencer asked Kate, "Are you okay? You look like you're arguing with yourself in your head."

"What does that look like?" Kate asked.

Kate turned to Spencer who sat across from her. "Well...you're moving your hands one at a time like your weighing your options, and you're scrunching up your forehead..."

"You're rather observant."

Spencer lifted an eyebrow as if to say, what's new?

In between bites of her hot soup, Kate told Spencer what she'd been thinking about. "Since you brought it up...I'm thinking about what type of music to listen to in the car on the way home. Country music is not exactly...educational. And—"

"Educational?"

She kept going. "I think we need to eat better than McDonald's on the way home. Sarah needs to eat from the five major food—"

"Kate. Slow down." Spencer put down his fork and took a deep breath. "I know you want the best for Sarah, and you want her to be healthy and happy. I get that. But don't get hung up on the details. Don't get worked up over small things that don't matter in the long run."

Kate stared at Spencer. "What do you mean not get hung up on the details? These 'details' matter to a child's growth and development." Kate put her own fork down and curled her fingers on the word 'details' before continuing. "I've done a lot of reading and there's lots of chemicals and garbage in food today. Did you know that most cereals contain colored dyes that cause ADD and ADHD and other problems?" She took a sip of water.

Spencer took the opportunity to ask, "Do you know how adorable you look when you get worked up about something?"

Kate almost spilled her water. She glared at Spencer, at a loss for words. Before she could say anything, Spencer put a hand on her arm and gestured toward Sarah with his eyes.

Looking over at Sarah, Kate saw what Spencer noticed. Sarah was drooping and getting sleepy. "Poor thing. I guess we can discuss the 'details' later," Kate gave Spencer a quick glare. They finished eating and went back to their rooms.

Kate fished out some pajamas with fairies on them for Sarah and put her down in the roll away crib with Bo Bo by her side. Thankfully she was out in minutes.

There wasn't a toothbrush or toothpaste among Sarah's things, so she would have to remedy that soon. She wanted to start Sarah with good habits right away.

Kate tried reading her book but kept thinking about what Spencer said at dinner and wondered if he was right. Was she too worried about technical things and not about the big picture? Maybe it was better to love Sarah the best she could, and not worry about the little things.

Then she thought about his silly comment about her looking adorable. *Really? What was that about?* When she first heard Spencer say that, it made her mad. But now upon further consideration, his observation caused a funny fluttering in her middle. *What did that mean?*

Kate went to bed, her mind whirring in all directions.

****

Spencer flicked on the TV in the room just for noise before he unpacked a few things for the night. He thought about the conversation with Kate earlier and wondered about the impulsive comment he made about her being adorable. *Why did I say that? Maybe because I can. I better take it slow.*

After a quick shower, he pulled on sweatpants and an old air force T-shirt then sat on the bed with his Bible. Spencer read a few chapters of Psalms, picking up where he left off. He put the book away and thought about Kate.

He hoped she wouldn't go overboard about trying to do everything perfect for Sarah. He prayed Kate would find the right balance between being a perfect parent and a loving parent and added prayers for the trip home.

He turned the TV volume up and found a major league baseball game between the Cubs and the Cardinals. He rooted for the Redbirds and went to bed after the St. Louis team pulled from behind and won eleven to two. Spencer took the win as a sign that the rest of the trip would go well.

I certainly hope so.

Chapter 19

When Kate woke up, Sarah still slept in her little bed. Kate smiled at the soft snore she heard. She took a world-record shower, not knowing how much longer Sarah would sleep. She left the bathroom door ajar in case Sarah woke up and wondered where she was.

"Sarah, honey, time to get up." Kate leaned over the little girl and shook her shoulder lightly. "Honey, are you awake?"

Kate leaned over the bed and rubbed Sarah's back. Finally, Sarah opened her eyes. "Are you ready to get up?"

Sarah stared at Kate, and glanced around the room. "Are you alright?" Kate tilted her head, waiting for some indication or response. Slowly, Sarah sat up, holding Bo Bo tight. She rubbed sleep from her eyes with the back of one hand.

"How about a quick bath? Then breakfast?"

Sara nodded.

"Hold on while I get the water going." Kate started running lukewarm water in the tub.

"Let's get you out of your dirty diaper." She took care of that and then put her in the tub. While Sarah splashed happily in the tub, Kate watched her as she blow dried her hair. Once they were both dressed, Kate called Spencer's room and asked if he was ready. They would meet in the breakfast area in five minutes.

"Good morning, ladies," Spencer greeted Kate and Sarah from a table with a high chair already pulled up to it. He wore an untucked striped knit shirt and faded jeans. And he had shaved his whiskers.

"Morning." Kate leaned down to Sarah and asked if she could say good morning or hello to Spencer. She shook her head. Kate picked her up and set her in the chair, and slid a bib over Sarah's head. "Sorry, she's a woman of few words this morning. Hasn't said one at all even to me, though she had fun in the bath."

"That's okay. What do you think she'd like?"

"Good question." Kate looked over at the counter where the food sat. "How about some scrambled eggs, a muffin and milk?"

"Coming right up." Spencer left their table to get Sarah's breakfast, which Kate appreciated. She herself didn't want much, just hot coffee. She sat in the chair next to Sarah and patted her hand. "Ready for your breakfast?"

Sarah looked around bewildered, but didn't answer. She sort of shrugged her shoulders half-heartedly.

"Here we go, one egg and muffin special. With milk." Spencer set the dishes down with a flourish like an Italian chef.

Kate grinned. "Thanks, Spencer."

He nodded and slid in his chair.

Kate found Sarah some silverware and left it on the plate, turning it around for Sarah to reach. But Sarah picked her cup up first and took a long swallow.

"She's thirsty at least," Kate commented. "Have you eaten?" she asked Spencer.

"A little. What would you like?"

"Coffee. A banana I guess."

"That all?"

"I'm not very hungry."

"Coming right up." Spencer got up to get Kate's order, wondering if she was feeling alright. He poured her a cup of coffee and grabbed a banana from the tower of fruit and grabbed an orange for himself.

Sarah picked at her breakfast, but did eat some. And Kate shared her banana with her, which she seemed to like. Kate grabbed another banana for Sarah's snack later.

Spencer and Kate discussed the route home, and were relieved to learn from the TV in the corner of the dining area that the weather should be clear for their trip home. Most of the roads were now cleared and back to normal.

****

A short time later Kate sat with Sarah in the lobby while Spencer loaded the car. Kate pulled Sarah's coat around her and zipped it up. The weather was still cooler for this time of year but at least it wasn't snowing.

Spencer came back in and they walked out to the car. Kate strapped Sarah in and they were on their way. It was a few minutes before Kate noticed Spencer changed the radio to a classical station. When she mentioned it, Spencer replied, "One hour of classical for every two of my choice."

"That's totally fair." Kate grinned as she adjusted her seatbelt. She was glad they were on the final leg of this nightmare and hoped it wasn't as adventurous as the beginning.

Kate took out a notepad and pen from her bag and started jotting down notes. She was a big list maker.

"What's that?" Spencer pointed to her writing.

"A list of things I have to do when I get home." Kate tapped the pad with her pen.

"Like?"

"Put up the plants... move Buttons' food... lower the towel racks in the bathroom... add a non-slip mat to the tub...plug the outlets...put a safety lock on the medicine cabinet—"

"I see. And buy tofu, hummus, and seaweed?" Spencer joked.

"Very funny. McDonald's is not exactly the healthiest fare, you know."

"I know. It's one of those things you do only occasionally, like when traveling."

"I'm not sure it will be rarely in my case."

"Still. But we can do Subway or Panera Bread before getting home."

"Either of those would be fine."

Spencer let Kate get back to her list and let his thoughts wander as he heard notes of Bach, Beethoven and Tchaikovsky playing in the car. To anybody on the street, they looked like a normal family in his car, taking a family trip. He longed for it to be true. But he knew Kate wasn't ready. She still needed time to grieve, and now time to adjust as a new mother. Spencer thought Sarah was cute, with her curly blond hair and tiny round nose. He caught himself peeking at her often in the mirror as he drove.

His car had been overtaken with pink stuff. Pink car seat, pink diaper bag, pink clothes in pink tote bags, pink blanket around Sarah who was wearing a coat...in pink.

Sarah was pretty quiet so far, probably because she was with total strangers. Kate asked her a few questions, trying to get her to talk, but she didn't really answer.

Spencer didn't expect the drive back to be this quiet, but it seemed that his passengers were exhausted. He could understand why Kate was worn out after all the events over the last few months. Instead of being awake and making plans, Kate was more like a wilting flower. After her list making, she had gone to sleep against the car window.

Chapter 20

Spencer pulled off the highway and into a gas station. Kate woke up and asked, "Where are we?"

"Still a few hours northwest of St. Louis. Do you need anything?"

After a yawn and a stretch, she answered, "I need to use the restroom and check Sarah's diaper."

"Okay, I'll fill up while you do that." He turned to slide out of the car, then thought he better ask if she needed help.

"I'm good, thanks." Kate got out of the car and took Sarah inside, hoping the bathroom was decent enough to use, and to change a diaper. Stacks of soda and beer were on her right and she looked past them for the restroom sign and headed that way. Kate noticed that some gas stations were dirtier and less kept up than others.

"Sweetie, let's get you changed and then I'll go....potty." Kate hefted Sarah up to the changing table after spraying it down with Lysol from the bag. She changed Sarah's wet diaper and finished up in the bathroom. She had to get used to carrying a diaper bag and keeping an eye one a toddler. She yawned several times since she hadn't slept well in the hotel.

Kate saw Spencer right outside the doorway and he wrapped his arm around her and whispered, "There are some interesting characters here. Are you ready to go to the car, or did you want anything to eat or drink?"

Kate frowned. "I'm fine, but I should fill her cup with water." She fished a pink plastic cup with yellow flowers on it from the diaper bag.

"You take her to the car and I'll get the water."

"Okay. Come on Sarah, let's get buckled in."

They took off a few minutes later.

****

The rest of the trip went without incident and they pulled into Kate's apartment complex around eight o'clock. "Home, sweet, home." Spencer turned the engine off and stretched.

"Finally. I can't wait to see Buttons. I missed him." Kate unlocked her seatbelt and twisted her neck back and forth. She glanced at Sarah, who had a glazed look.

"I bet. I'll help you get unloaded. We can probably use the stroller to hold quite a bit of this pink stuff."

"Good idea. I'll carry Sarah if you don't mind bringing the rest."

Spencer got out and popped the trunk open. He took out the stroller, loaded it up with diapers, toys and clothes and followed Kate. The two adults hadn't talked much as Kate had slept most of the way.

They made their way to Kate's door, making a lot of bumping noises. Thankfully it wasn't too late at night, televisions and voices could be heard from neighboring apartments. Kate fished out her keys after putting down the diaper bag and handing Sarah to Spencer. Before she could get the door open, she could hear Buttons barking.

To Sarah, she said, "I have a puppy, too. He'll like playing with you." Kate talked to Sarah in a childish tone, which made Spencer smile. Kate opened the door, took Sarah back and set her down inside. "Sweetie, this is your new home." Kate let Spencer by and watched Sarah's reaction.

Sarah looked around and headed down the hall. Spencer said he'd be right back. Kate followed Sarah and watched her.

Then Kate let Buttons out of his kennel. "Hi, boy!" Kate gave him a tight squeeze, but Buttons wanted down to investigate their guests.

Kate asked Sarah, "Do you like puppies?"

Sarah nodded, and hugged Bo-Bo tighter.

"Buttons, settle down. Come here, boy." Buttons kept jumping on Kate's legs. She scooped him up and knelt down on her knees so the dog could check out Sarah and she could pet him if she wanted.

Sarah tentatively put out a hand and patted Buttons on the head.

"There you go, nice and gentle." Kate smiled at Sarah.

Spencer came in with another load. "Where do you want the diapers and clothes?" he asked.

"Good question." Kate looked around her living space while considering his question. "In the linen closet for now. I'll get her a dresser eventually. At least my room is big enough for a small bed and dresser."

Kate turned to Sarah. "Would you like to read or watch TV?"

Sarah nodded, climbing up on the sofa. Kate unzipped Sarah's coat and pulled it off, tossing it to the other end of the sofa.

"Here are some books I thought you might like." Kate took a pile of new board books from the entertainment shelf and handed them to her. Sarah had slept so much in the car, Kate wasn't sure she would be ready for bed in a strange place yet. Kate stifled another yawn.

"Tank you," Sarah replied in a soft voice, taking the books.

"You're welcome. I'm going to help Spencer with your things, but I'll be close by."

Sarah nodded, but didn't say anything.

Kate gestured to Spencer to meet her in the dining room. "What do you think?" Kate asked.

"I think she'll be fine. She needs time to adjust and then I'm sure she'll trust and love you." *I do.*

"I hope so. This weekend I want to find her some furniture."

"Need help?"

Kate looked at him and shrugged. "Probably. I'm sure you could find better things to do though."

"Not really. I've had enough interesting for a while."

Kate laughed, and said, "No kidding. Want something to drink?"

"What have you got?"

"Good question. I don't remember. I better get some milk, cereal and snacks soon," she said heading to the kitchen.

Spencer came up behind her and said, "We can do that."

Kate turned around and almost bumped into him. "Sorry." She backed up. "We?"

"You know Kate, I feel slightly responsible for Sarah too, even though you may not feel that way. I can't help it. I wanted to tell you so many times, but I didn't want to break my promise to John." Spencer looked at the floor. "I wished I could have convinced him to tell you. Lord knows I tried." He looked at Kate, regret in his eyes.

Kate walked over and put her hand on his shoulder. "Don't worry about it. It's done now. Thanks for helping me and being there for me. This trip would have been much more traumatizing without you."

Spencer pulled her close and hugged her, suddenly emotional. "I miss him, too," he whispered. Kate rested in Spencer's arms, from sheer exhaustion and the need for his comfort and strength.

After a few minutes when Kate didn't move away, Spencer pulled her away from him and looked her in the face. "Are you all right?"

She couldn't trust her voice, so she shook her head. He pulled her back close and rubbed her back, wishing he could do this every day.

"New Mommy? I thirsty." They turned to see Sarah toddling in.

"He my new daddy?" Sarah looked at Spencer.

Kate and Spencer quickly pulled apart and Spencer started to say, "Not yet—"

Kate quickly wiped her wet eyes. "No, Honey, he's a good friend of your daddy. You probably don't remember him." Kate knelt down to her level and pulled her close. Just then the words Spencer said dawned on her. She picked up Sarah and looked at Spencer. "What did you say?"

"When?"

"Just now when she asked if you were her daddy?"

"Oh, nothing." He headed to the living room. Kate was right behind him.

"Do we need to talk?" Kate found a cup of water in the diaper bag and handed it to Sara.

"Who us?" Spencer sat down on the sofa and picked up the book *Are You My Mother?* Kate held Sarah on her lap and sat down right beside him, close. She watched Sarah drinking from her cup, but she looked like she was fading. She turned to Spencer, "Yeah, us."

"Not now. Maybe some other time." Spencer shouldn't have said anything; he was afraid Kate might get irritated with him.

"I have a little girl to put to bed."

Spencer took the out. Didn't have to tell him twice. "Right. I'll get those drinks from the kitchen." He turned to Sarah, bent down and said, "Sleep tight."

Sarah simply nodded.

While Spencer was searching in her kitchen for something to drink, Kate pulled out pajamas from the bag the orphanage gave them. Later Kate would have to sort through her belongings and see what she might have to add.

Kate took the diaper bag to the bedroom and Sarah followed. "I'll make you a little bed on the floor next to mine, how's that?"

Sarah nodded again, almost asleep. Kate put down some blankets and a small pillow she had purchased before the trip and made a simple pallet on the floor. She changed Sarah's diaper, put her in pink pajamas and laid her down. She was out in minutes, hugging her puppy.

"She okay?" Spencer asked. He sat on the sofa after pouring them each a glass of sparkling water.

"She's already out." Kate plopped on the sofa next to him. She was really tired. She took a couple sips of her water. "Thanks, Spencer, for driving us home. I don't think I could've done it." She yawned again.

"You're welcome. Glad I could do it. Would you like me to run to the store and get you a few things so you don't have to take Sarah?"

Normally Kate would balk at the idea, but she already felt out of her league and exhausted. She replied, "That would be great. I'll make you a list." She found a tablet from the kitchen and wrote the things down she needed. She tore it off and handed it to Spencer. Then she reached for her suitcase. "Do you mind if I go to bed?"

"Not at all, I'll just let myself out when I get back. I'll also take Buttons for a quick walk. Are you sure you're okay?"

"No, but I'm too tired to think about it. See you tomorrow." She dragged her bag behind her and shut her bedroom door. She was in bed in minutes and fell asleep as quickly as Sarah.

****

Spencer left with Kate's list and drove to the nearest grocery store. After noticing what little Kate had in her refrigerator, which was understandable after a trip, he added some things to the list. *Whew, I'm glad Kate didn't make a big deal about what I said earlier. Why do I keep saying things like that? I'm going to have to watch myself from now on.* He pushed the cart toward the dairy and got the milk and eggs and turned toward the floral department. He added a small bouquet of daisies.

When Spencer returned to Kate's apartment, he brought in the groceries and put the cold items away. He found a vase above the refrigerator and filled it with water for the flowers he bought impulsively, and did his best arranging them. He set the vase on the counter with a short note on the tablet Kate used earlier.

> *Kate,*
> *Glad we made it home. Sleep well and talk to you soon. Enjoy the flowers.*
> *Spencer*

After taking Buttons for a short walk, he took Kate's car keys off the rack by the door installed Sarah's safety seat in Kate's car. That was one less thing Kate had to do. He returned her keys and locked the apartment door.

Back at home, he unpacked his suitcase. He plugged in his cell phone, took a quick shower and went to bed. He prayed for wisdom for Kate and himself and fell asleep.

Chapter 21

The next morning, Kate still felt tired. She walked out to the kitchen and saw bags of groceries on the counter. *Bless that man.* Also sitting on the counter were some lovely flowers in a vase. The sight didn't surprise her as much as it should. She took a quick sniff before she heard the phone ring.

"Good morning, how are you two?" Spencer asked.

"I'm still tired, and she's still asleep." Kate yawned before adding, "And thanks for the groceries. What do I owe you? I haven't found the receipt yet." She glanced around the bags but didn't see it.

"I know the trip didn't go as planned, so don't worry about it."

"And the flowers are lovely, thank you."

"You're welcome; I hope they cheer you up a little."

"They do. So, the receipt?" Holding the phone on her shoulder, she put away boxes of macaroni and cheese, and packages of single serve apple sauce, both presumably for Sarah.

"Already paid."

Kate leaned on the counter, holding an empty sack. "Don't start that again."

"Start what again? It was only a few bucks; I don't see the big deal."

Kate yawned yet again, before she could reply. "I'm too tired to argue. I feel like I need to go back to bed. And I should check on Sarah." She turned her head toward the hall as if she could hear Sarah.

"Why don't I pick up some muffins or something and watch Sarah since you're so tired. I can even put the rest of the groceries away if you haven't yet." Spencer tried to keep concern out of his voice, but wasn't sure Kate noticed it or not.

Kate grunted a "Sure," and hung up.

Kate was too tired to even make coffee. She checked Buttons' bowls, saw they were filled, put him out on the patio a minute, and padded back to the bedroom. She put the back of her hand on Sarah's forehead which felt a little warm but not alarmingly so. She kicked off her house shoes, wiggled out of her robe, tossing it to the end of the bed, and crawled back under the covers, thinking Spencer could let himself in and do whatever he liked.

****

Spencer was surprised at Kate's abrupt hang up. He was already dressed and had eaten a bagel with juice purchased the night before along with Kate's groceries. He slid his feet into his shoes, grabbed his keys and drove to the nearest store. Spencer picked up muffins, bagels, and juice.

He let himself in with his key when Kate didn't answer the door. Buttons came running over, his tail wagging. "Hi Buddy, how ya doing?" Spencer whispered to the dog. He gave him a quick pat and searched for Kate when he saw that the blinds were all still closed and he heard no activity.

Kate was still in bed, in a deep sleep. He tore himself away from Kate's direction to check on Sarah. She was still asleep too. They must be worn out from the trip.

He figured Sarah needed a diaper change. Back in the hall bathroom in search of a wash cloth, Spencer tried not to remember that awful night with Kate. But seeing the addition of new hooded towels hanging up and the rubber ducks and sponge letters in the tub made him smile.

He found what he needed and lifted Sarah to the bed on the other side of Kate. He washed Sarah's face and hands and changed her diaper with the items he found sitting on the dresser.

Spencer laid the toddler back down, who hardly stirred. He tiptoed out and went to the kitchen. He saw that some of the groceries had been unpacked but not all of them. He saw the sack with the Dove chocolates still inside. *Rats, she hasn't seen them. Oh, well, time for those later.* He was glad she liked the flowers.

After putting the rest of her groceries away he walked Buttons again. They managed to miss most of the snow piles now mixed with leaves still falling. Broken branches scattered the ground from the heavy snowfall. Spencer shook his head remembering their nightmare.

Spencer walked the track three times around. Then they went back inside. Before he called Kate that morning, Spencer had been by the help desk to get all his leave and insurance paperwork done. That was a hurdle he was glad to be over and it went better than he thought.

Kate's phone rang while Spencer was on his way back to the bedroom so he returned to the kitchen and answered it. Mrs. Kern, John's mom was on the line. "Hi, Mrs. Kern. It's Spencer. How are you?"

"Doing well under the circumstance, I guess. And you?"

"Not too bad. We just got back with Sarah. But both she and Kate seem to be out of it this morning. I'm here to see what's going on."

"Oh, dear. They're probably just exhausted from the trip."

"You're probably right."

"I'm sure you'll take good care of them."

Spencer smiled. "I'm trying."

"The reason I'm calling is because I wanted to talk to Kate about visiting in a few weeks. We have to empty and clean out John's apartment so it can be released for rent. Will you give Kate a message for me?"

"Of course. Did you want Kate to help?"

After a brief silence, Mrs. Kern answered, "Oh…only if she wants to. I totally understand if she's uncomfortable. We'll stay at John's; I already have a key and my daughter-in-law will be with me."

"Good. If you need me for anything, let me know. Still have my number?"

"I do. We'll need help getting his furniture somewhere. Would you be willing to help with that?"

"Of course. Just let me know when. I can probably get a couple guys to help."

"Perfect. I'll cook us a nice lunch."

"You can count me in!" His mouth watered instantly.

Mrs. Kern laughed. "Thanks, Spencer, we'll talk soon. Take care of your patients."

"Yes, ma'am. See you soon." Spencer hung up and grinned. He recalled the Thanksgiving meal he'd had with John and his family one year and a fourth-of-July picnic at their house. If anyone could cook, it was John's mom. She had made everything from the turkey to the pumpkin pie at the feast they'd shared. Spencer rubbed his belly, remembering the aromas and his satisfied stomach.

Sarah's groans brought him back to the present. Spencer walked back to the bedroom and found Sarah sitting up in bed and rubbing her eyes. "Hey, Honey, how are you feeling?" Spencer knelt down to her level and brushed hair out of her eyes.

"I thirsty." Her cheeks were pink and lined from sleep.

"Would you like some juice?"

Sarah nodded and started to get up.

"That's okay, I'll get you some. I'll be right back." He checked on Kate, but she was still asleep. Back in the kitchen, Spencer found a new purple cup with hearts on it. He shook his head. Spencer filled it with half juice, half water for the little girl. He returned a minute later with the cup. "Here you go, Sweetheart."

She took several swallows.

"Would you like to take a bath?"

She shook her head.

"How about some stories?"

Sarah smiled and nodded.

"Let's get you dressed." He found some clothes in a stack on Kate's dresser. Then Spencer picked her up with a couple of the blankets while she held her stuffed puppy. In the living room, he settled her on his lap in the club chair with a pile of books. Sarah sipped her juice as he read her two stories before she fell back asleep. Spencer sat there in the quiet, with only the sounds of a ticking clock and Sarah's breathing. He gently stroked Sarah's hair while he daydreamed.

Will Kate be ready for a relationship any time soon? Or am I setting myself up for disappointment? Did Kate have any interest in me or am I grasping at straws? As he thought about their past trip, he thought maybe Kate had some feelings for him. She seemed to be thankful for his help and willing to let him continue helping with Sarah. But was that just because this was the beginning of her parenting adventure or because she wanted him around?

What he did know was that Kate could be one stubborn woman. And that she had a hard time accepting help. Even now, she wanted to repay him for going with her on their adventurous trip. *Whatever for? Wouldn't anyone else have done the same thing?*

He wished he knew.

He sighed and laid Sarah back down on her makeshift bed and checked on Kate. She was still asleep. He set a glass of water on the night stand in case she woke up.

Buttons needed food and water, so Spencer filled his bowls. Then he sat down at Kate's computer and checked his email. He didn't have anything important, so he surfed random topics and sites for a while and then played several games of Tetris. He grew bored and decided to cook something in the kitchen. He didn't cook a lot, but mostly because it was only him. But he would try to make some comfort food for the girls. He turned on the radio and tuned it to his favorite country station, the one he had tuned in his car. Then he washed his hands and got to work.

Chapter 22

An hour later Spencer took out the baked macaroni. He found an opened jar of apple sauce in the refrigerator and took that out, setting it on the table. He hoped the girls were hungry, his own stomach growled as the scent from the baking casserole taunted him. He set the table for three and poured three waters before checking on his patients.

Sarah sat up in the bedroom playing quietly with her puppy. Spencer thought she looked unsure of what she could or couldn't do in her new environment.

He bent down to her level and asked in a soft voice, "How are you feeling?"

"I hungy." She didn't look up at him.

Spencer smiled. "Do you like macaroni?"

She nodded.

"How about apple sauce?"

"Mmm." She slowly looked up at him with a shy smile.

"Good. Let's get ready to eat." Spencer lifted her to the bed and changed her.

"Can you take your puppy out to the living room and wait for me?"

She nodded and left the room. Spencer sat on the bed and shook Kate's shoulder. She stirred and opened her eyes. "How are you feeling?"

"Wiped. But I'm hungry. What smells so good?"

Before Spencer could answer, Sarah answered, "Roni 'n sauce." Spencer turned to see her standing in the doorway. He stretched out his arm for her to come so she could see Kate. He lifted her up onto his lap. Kate gave her a smile and patted her knee. Kate looked at Spencer with an arched eyebrow. "Interpret, please."

"That would be baked macaroni and apple sauce."

"You cooked? For us?"

"It isn't gourmet but it's ready." Spencer took one arm and helped her to her feet. "Okay?"

"I can take it from here. I won't be late for dinner."

Spencer said, "Come on Sarah. Let's get you to the table and put your bib on." A minute later he set her into the booster seat, buckled her in and pushed her to the table. "How's that?"

She nodded, holding up her plate.

"I guess you're ready, huh?"

Kate joined them and said, "Looks good and smells great." Her voice sounded tired. She sat on one side of Sarah and took a sip of her water.

"Feeling better?" Spencer sat down across from Kate with Sarah between them. He tried not to think about this becoming a daily event. For now, he would enjoy it as often as the girls would let him.

"Yes, thanks."

"Let's get some food and liquids into you and that will help." He cut the macaroni and served them, then passed the apple sauce and cooked peas. He tried giving Sarah some vegetables, but she said, "No geen ones."

"You don't like peas?"

She shook her head. "Just carrots." It sounded like cawots.

"You should try them. They're good for you and they taste good." He placed a small serving on her plate. "How's that?"

"Good, tank you."

"Need help with your macaroni?" he asked.

"Pwease." She pushed her plate to Spencer.

He cut up her serving into bite sized chunks and pushed it back. "Here you go. I hope you like it. It's a very special recipe."

"Really?" Kate asked.

"I made it up, actually."

"It tastes great. I'll have to make it sometime."

****

After Sarah went back to bed, Kate and Spencer stayed up late talking. Kate sipped hot tea. They discussed caring for Sarah.

"I don't even know if I can leave her up here when I do the laundry," Kate gestured with her hand. "And how is she going to react when I have to drop her off at daycare? How do you pick one out? And how did John's parents get my number anyway?" Kate was on a roll.

Spencer had mentioned Mrs. Kern's phone call after he had put Sarah down for the night.

He listened with an amused face. "Is that all?"

"Spencer! I'm dead serious! I'm a mom now." Kate crossed her arms, feeling a little overwhelmed and uptight.

"I know. You're doing fine. It's only been a few days. I can answer the question about John's parents. I talked with them at the funeral luncheon. They told me they knew about Sarah but only found out about her recently. They want to be a part of Sarah's life." Spencer took a swallow of his water before leaning his arms on his knees.

"I don't know about that. She's got enough to deal with right now."

Spencer looked at Kate. "I know, but they want to keep in touch. She's their granddaughter you know."

"True," she admitted. "But I don't want any interference."

Interference? "They just want to be a part of her life, not take over, Kate. I'm sure they're sincere."

"I'll be the judge of that."

"I know them. Besides they're not exactly spring chickens. And they just lost their son." Spencer's volume descended a notch at the sad reminder. He sighed. *How ironic. Kate, who never wanted to be a mother in the first place and now is one, didn't want any help. I shouldn't be all that surprised, since she's acting more like herself— fiercely independent.*

"How well?"

Spencer tuned back in to their conversation. "Oh, how well do I know John's parents?"

Kate nodded. She got up and closed the balcony blinds. She took her empty mug to the kitchen before sitting back down, a little further away than Spencer liked.

"Pretty well, I guess." Spencer resumed their conversation. "We don't send Christmas cards or anything, but I know their character and they did a good job in raising John and his brother, that sort of thing. I've been there for a couple holidays. His mom's a great cook, mmmm. They're grandparent-ly," he added.

"Grandparent-ly?"

"Yeah, you know what I mean. Bake homemade cookies, spoil them rotten and send them home, kind."

"They're too far away," Kate complained.

Spencer glanced at her and saw she was actually serious. "We have these inventions called airplanes these days…"

Kate glared at him. "Not funny."

"Kate, parenting is hard work. I admire your tenacity for the job, but you don't have to do it alone. Which reminds me, for the upcoming exercise at work, I'm working the four-to-midnight shift the first week, so I can watch Sarah when you go back to work if you want me to." He wasn't about to tell her he had volunteered on purpose for that shift when he had turned in his paperwork.

"Oh, really? And then what?"

"We'll work something out. But in the meantime, you'll have more time to get to know each other before you have to drop her off at a stranger's."

"'We'll work something out'? Do you have a mouse in your pocket? Is your name on the adoption papers?" Kate huffed her bangs. She fumed in silence for a minute before continuing, "Hey, did you volunteer for that shift? Nobody likes that shift; it's long and boring." Kate looked at him, her arms crossed again.

Uh, oh. Spencer looked away, trying to see out the blocked patio door, but he knew his face gave him away.

"Spencer! Why?" Her sore throat made her voice crack which made her even angrier. She got up and started pacing around the living room with her hands stuffed in her back pockets and started mumbling to herself.

He let her vent for a few minutes and when she got quiet, he told her the truth. He whispered, "Because I want to help you. And because I love you." He waited for her response. She punched him in the shoulder on her way back to bed.

Worse than I thought.

Spencer let himself out, locking her door. He hoped she slept well.

He probably would not.

****

The next morning, Spencer woke up, feeling bad about leaving Kate and Sarah the night before. But he felt it was the best course of action, though maybe not the one he wanted. Luckily, it was Friday and he could help Kate with Sarah over the weekend. If she would let him. He did some stretches in his room before showering and dressing in his green and black uniform. His black boots always pinched his pinky toes, so he put them on at the last minute before each shift.

That morning, he had a stint at the Belleville gate, checking IDs of all those who drove on base. It was usually pretty boring, but everyone had to take a turn. He hoped Kate could manage until noon. On his lunch hour, he would check on her and Sarah.

After wrapping up his shift at the gate, Spencer returned to the Security Forces building and called Kate.

"How's it going? You two feel any better?" he asked when she answered.

"We're doing okay, I guess."

"Can I get you guys anything? I'm on my lunch break."

"Not really...actually some more orange juice would be great. And dog food for Buttons. It's running low."

"Sure, what kind?"

"Whatever's on sale, he's not picky."

"Ok, I'll stop at the commissary on my way over and see you in a bit. Had lunch?"

"We did; thanks."

They hung up and Spencer left for the items at the store and was at Kate's a few minutes later. Kate thanked Spencer and put the items away.

"You're welcome." Sarah came into the kitchen to see what they were doing and Spencer said hi to her. "Feeling better?"

Sarah nodded. "I sleeped good."

"Good, glad to hear it."

"Come on, Sarah, let's read some of those books before I go back to work." Kate sat at the other end of the couch and listened. She wasn't as tired, but still didn't feel like unpacking or doing any laundry quite yet.

"Thanks for the dog food."

"You're welcome. I'll see you later."

Chapter 23

Later after a slow afternoon of driving around the base and the flight line, Spencer drove home and changed out of his uniform. He slipped on a pair of sweats and an old Tennessee T-shirt. He was heading back to his car, when he saw Mrs. Pettigrew heading to her mailbox with some letters. She wore a red cardigan and tan slacks.

"Hi, young man. Glad to see you made it home."

"Hi, Mrs. P. Yep, we made it through the blizzard all in one piece."

"I prayed for you when I heard about that freak storm." Mrs. P shut her mailbox and joined him on the sidewalk between their driveways.

"We sure do appreciate it. That wasn't the only storm we had, but that's another story. Everything good here?"

"Nothing out of the ordinary. How's the little girl adjusting?" Mrs. P tucked a stray curl behind her ear.

"Sarah? She and Kate are both worn out from the trip especially Kate, after all the events lately."

"That's too bad. I'll pray for them to feel rested and for a good adjustment."

"Thanks. I'm going to fix them some chicken soup unless Kate's doing better."

"Sounds good. Nothing like it for what ails a person."

Spencer leaned on his car door. "How's the hip?"

"Stronger every day. The doctor says I can leave this contraption," she lifted her walker and put it down again, "in another week or so. I'm glad to get rid of it before winter sets in." She chuckled. "I mean, real winter."

"No kidding. Let me know when you want your outdoor chores done. I haven't had any cookies lately." He loved to tease her.

"Now that I think about it, it is almost time for weather stripping and trimming the roses and butterfly bushes." She looked around her yard before adding, "Next week perhaps?"

"You got it." Spencer waved and got in his car.

Spencer arrived at Kate's in short order and entered when Kate called, "Come in." Buttons came running to greet him, so Spencer set the bags down and scooped him up to give him a quick rub from head to tail. Then he slipped off his shoes and left the groceries in the kitchen. After chatting with his neighbor, Spencer had picked up some things at the store.

"We're in here."

Spencer headed for the dimly lit living room, hearing sounds from the TV. "Ah, an old Disney classic." Spencer heard the *beep beep* of Herbie, a car with a mind of his own in the film *Herbie Goes Bananas.*

"I didn't think it would warp her mind too much." Kate lay on the sofa, with a blanket over her. Sarah was on a pile of blankets near the TV, holding her puppy. "Hi, Mr. Daddy," she gave Spencer a quick greeting before turning back to the car's antics.

Kate and Spencer exchanged a look. Spencer shrugged. Kate frowned.

Spencer sat on the chair and slid out of his coat, laying it behind him. "Have you guys eaten?"

"Just movie snacks."

"Are either of you in the mood for chicken soup?"

"Got some?" Kate perked up at the suggestion.

"Not yet. I bought the ingredients."

"Sounds good to me. Have at it if you're so inclined." Kate gestured to the kitchen. "You know where almost everything is. Let me know if you need something."

"Well, I'll see what I can do. One pot of hot chicken soup coming up." Spencer hopped up and rubbed his hands together. What they didn't know, was that Mrs. P gave him the recipe months ago. All he had to do was follow her simple instructions. He already had the broth after boiling the chicken the night before. He turned on the radio, still tuned to his station and got to work washing carrots and celery. He was glad to cook, especially for three. So much easier and more fun than just cooking for one.

Sarah came in after a few minutes out of curiosity. "What you do?" she asked. She was still in her pajamas, a purple set with kittens on them. She held her puppy and a small soft pink blanket.

"I'm making some homemade chicken soup for you and your mom. Do you like soup?"

"Umm...don't know."

"I think you will. I'll make it special."

"I try it."

"Sounds good. Do you want to watch me or your movie?"

"You."

Her answer surprised him, but he went into the living room and let Kate know. She nodded and clicked off the movie.

"Sarah, can you sit on this stool?" Spencer pulled out a low foot stool from the pantry floor. "There you go." He got her settled with her puppy and blanket. "Now I'm going to chop up vegetables for the soup. It might be loud."

Sarah nodded, her eyes wide. She sat very still and watched his every move. She probably hadn't been in a kitchen much, considering where she'd been for the last few months.

Spencer shared each step with her and they talked about vegetables, what they were and how they grew. Sarah seemed to take it all in, storing it in her little mind. Spencer enjoyed chatting with her. He offered her bits of carrot and celery. She scrunched up her face with the celery which made Spencer laugh. "Don't like celery so much, huh?" But she enjoyed the carrots.

Soon he had all the ingredients in the pot with the simmering broth. "Now, we just let it do its magic." Spencer scraped all the scraps in the trash and washed up the utensils and cutting board, leaving them to dry in the dish drainer left by the sink.

Then they rejoined Kate in the living room. "You want to color or read books?" Spencer spoke in a soft voice, so as not to disturb Kate.

"I'm not asleep. Just have my eyes closed."

"Oh." Spencer spoke in a normal voice.

"Color," Sarah answered.

"I can do that." Spencer sat at the end of the coffee table and waited for Sarah to get her coloring things. She had some markers that only color on certain paper. Sarah plopped on Spencer's lap. He was startled for a minute, but quickly recovered and resettled her in a more comfortable place. She pulled off the lid of a blue marker. The picture she chose had Minnie Mouse and some flowers on it. Very girly. *Not a Superman or Batman in sight. I'll have to broaden her horizons.*

"Want me to color a flower?" Spencer asked her. She nodded and handed him a purple marker. "You want some purple flowers, I take it?"

She nodded again, leaning on the table and scribbling on the page.

A few minutes later, they ate the prepared chicken soup with warm French bread. "Absolutely delicious. This hits the spot. Thanks." Kate dipped a piece of bread in her soup.

"Thanks. It's Mrs. Pettigrew's recipe."

"It's fantastic. I'll have to get a copy."

"Sure."

After they ate, Spencer washed up the few dishes and stored the rest of the soup in the fridge for the girls. He put Sarah to bed for Kate and then took Buttons for a short walk. Kate wasn't in the mood for company, and with Sarah in bed, Spencer called it a night.

****

The next morning was sunny and it was supposed to be in the mid-fifties. For October, it was great weather to get things done outside. Spencer figured the girls would be fine for a while, so he checked with Mrs. Pettigrew about getting started on her projects. He thought it would be a good day for it and wanted to take advantage of the warmer temperatures.

After a quick breakfast of cereal, he walked next door. Mrs. Pettigrew was always up with the birds. A few minutes later, Spencer had her husband's loppers in his hands, making his way around the perimeter of her house. He trimmed four butterfly bushes; one with pink flowers, one with purple and two with blue. And three rose bushes; two pink, one red. He gathered up all the scraps and dumped them in the compost bin Mrs. P kept next to the garage. He returned the loppers to their space on the peg board in the garage and pulled out her mower.

When the small yard was cut, he returned the mower and grabbed the rake. After adding the grass clippings to the compost bin, he hung up the rake and knocked on Mrs. P's door.

"Done already?" Mrs. Pettigrew gave Spencer a wide smile. "Wipe your shoes off, young man and come on in. I've just taken the first cookie sheet out of the oven."

Spencer left his shoes on the porch and made sure he didn't have any loose grass on his sweats. He stepped in to the house and the scent of cinnamon and sugar tantalized his nose. "They smell great."

He walked through a living room where a piano sat against one wall and a cuckoo clock hung above it. Across the piano top sat photo frames of different sizes and colors displaying pictures of Mrs. Pettigrew's family. Her son had two daughters and her daughter had two sons, which Mrs. P said always brings a smile to faces of new visitors. Spencer followed his nose and walked through to the kitchen.

"Sit yourself down. You're lucky I had enough eggs. Otherwise you would've made a quick trip to the store first." She winked at him and set a plate down on the table.

"I sure would have if you needed me to. Anything to keep those cookies coming." He washed his hands at her kitchen sink before sitting down. He grabbed two cookies and bit into one. "Ah...now I can keep going."

"Have as many as you need. I don't want to deplete all your energy, you know."

"No danger of that. I'll have another or two and then check your windows."

"That's wonderful. The plastic and other supplies are sitting on the workbench in the garage."

"Got it. Thanks for baking on such short notice."

"I'm glad you asked. The weather was perfect for it; I'm grateful it worked out." She took a cookie for herself and dipped it into her coffee before taking a bite. "How are Kate and Sarah doing now?"

"Doing well. I did make the soup last night and gave you credit for the recipe." At his comment, Mrs. P gave him a smile.

"That's good to hear."

Spencer finished his last cookie and said, "Thanks, Mrs. P. I'll do the windows and then check on Kate."

"That will be fine, Spencer. Thank you so much."

"You're welcome. I'll say goodbye before I leave."

She nodded and picked up the nearly empty plate. "And I'll have a baggie of cookies for Kate and Sarah."

"Great."

Chapter 24

While Spencer worked for his neighbor, Kate turned on her cell phone after finding it in her bag. She had to charge it before she could check messages or read her texts. Most of her friends called her on her cell rather than the apartment phone. She let Buttons out on the patio and fixed Sarah a bowl of sliced fruit and a glass of milk. She made herself some toast and coffee.

She returned a call to both Jen and Kelly while Sarah watched one of the videos Kate had purchased before the trip. Jen already knew about most of the trip, but she filled Kelly in on all that had happened.

Kelly said, "Well, I can't wait to meet her. Especially after your adventurous trip."

"It'll be a few days, after we recover."

"Totally understand that. Take care of yourselves. Toodle-oo."

Kate had bought only a few videos for Sarah, not wanting her to watch too much television. Kate didn't want it to become an automatic babysitter. With the movie last night on TV, and now the video, it was more than Kate preferred she watch. She sighed as she straightened the living room. *Already failing at this parenting thing.*

She went to the bedroom to sort the laundry. She knew Spencer would be by, but didn't know when. She wished she could shower, but didn't want to leave Sarah alone.

Kate felt much better and now felt like cleaning and organizing. Sarah's things were everywhere, and now it was time to put them in their proper place.

Kate phoned Spencer, but had to leave a message. A bag of chocolates sat on the counter, but she couldn't remember asking for them. *Another treat from him?* She added them to her snack stash with a shrug.

She cleaned out the diaper bag, adding more diapers and wipes. She placed it by the door for the next time they had to go somewhere. Then she put dirty Sippy cups and coffee mugs in the dishwasher. She started going through the mail pile that Jen had left. The trip seemed like months ago instead of days. Most of the mail she dropped into her recycle bin under the sink. She added the bills to the organizer on the counter.

Kate felt like she was making progress. She pulled the blankets off the sofa to add them to her laundry pile and pulled out the vacuum.

"Sarah, can you sit up on the couch for me so I can vacuum the floor?" Her video was over and she had been reading her books.

Sarah nodded and complied. She pulled her puppy and pink blanket with her. "Thanks, this will only take a minute. It's kind of noisy, okay?"

She understood and hugged her puppy tight. She watched Kate plug it in and turn the machine on. Kate made quick work of that task and then put the machine away. "That wasn't too bad, was it?"

Sarah shook her head.

"Good. Now how about a bath?"

Sarah grinned. "I like bath."

"Let's get you cleaned up and into some clean clothes. You're feeling better, aren't you?"

She nodded again before they headed to the bedroom. "Me, too. It's time to clean up this mess of an apartment." Kate gave Sarah a bath, letting her play with the bath toys while Kate sat on the commode and flipped through a magazine.

A few minutes later, since it was warm enough, Kate opened the patio door a few inches to let in fresh air. Most of the snow had melted in the warm days after the storm. She gathered the bathroom and kitchen trash, tying it up and placing it by the front door. She swept the floors and dusted the bedroom and living room. Sarah was busy having a tea party with her puppy and a new doll Kate had bought for her.

Kate was relieved that Sarah seemed to like her new home and especially her. So far, Sarah behaved well and was easy going.

Just then there was a knock on the door. Kate brushed her hair behind her ears and wished she could shower and actually get dressed. This certainly wasn't the first time Spencer would see her in her robe though. *Oh, well.* She opened the door to let him in.

"Wow, you're looking better."

"I feel better. I'm finally cleaning up after the trip. Come on in." She shut the door and asked him if he wanted any coffee or tea.

"I'm good, thanks. I brought some of Mrs. P's cookies."

Kate eyed the plate. "Sounds like a perfect treat after straightening things. Thanks." Kate took the plate and took it to the kitchen. She poured a fresh cup of coffee and sat down with a napkin of cookies. "Sure you don't want anything?"

"I'm good. Had enough cookies earlier after working for Mrs. P."

"Ah, keeping the help happy."

"It's a good system." He gave Kate a quick wink.

Kate remembered the candy he bought. "Oh and thanks for the new bag of chocolates by the way, the first bag from the trip is long gone."

"Glad you found them; you're welcome." Spencer sat down on the chair opposite Kate. "Hi, Sarah. How are you?"

She gave Spencer a smile and said, "Good. Have bath."

"I'm glad. You look better, too, like your mommy."

Kate didn't agree, but didn't argue. "Speaking of looking better, would you mind if I took a quick shower while you sat with her?"

"Not at all. Have you started the laundry yet?"

"No...I guess I could throw a load in the washer first if one's free. I'll be right back."

"Take your time. I'm going to have tea with a puppy and a doll."

Kate grinned. "Have fun." She quickly disappeared down the hall. She came back with an overflowing basket, a bottle of laundry soap and a small coin purse. "Sarah, I'm going to throw some clothes in the machine, but I'll be back in a minute, okay?"

Sarah looked up briefly and said, "'K, Mommy. I be here Mr. Daddy."

Kate and Spencer exchanged another look. "Right." Kate left the room.

****

Kate had answered the door in her robe. *I gotta keep my thoughts pure, but oh, how I'd love to see underneath that ratty pink thing.* He was glad he bought her a new one at the mall. He didn't know when he'd give it to her, but he wanted to soon.

Spencer turned his attention to Sarah who was asking if he wanted cookies with his tea. "Absolutely. I never turn down homemade cookies. What kind are they?"

"Choc chip. I make them."

"They're as good as Mrs. Pettigrew's. Thank you."

"Who Miss Pppetgrew?"

Spencer smiled at her attempt to pronounce the name. "Mrs. Pettigrew is my neighbor. And she bakes all kinds of cookies. In fact, I brought some with me. You want one?"

Sarah nodded her head vigorously.

"Come to the table, and I'll get you one. I'm sure your mom won't mind." He sat her in the chair at the table and found a Sippy cup on the counter. "Would you like some milk?" he asked from the kitchen.

"Yes, please."

"One milk-and-cookie special coming right up." He filled her cup and grabbed a napkin with two cookies. "Here you go," he put her snack down and sat at the table with her. "What have you been doing today?"

Sarah had to swallow before she could answer. "Readed books. Watch movie. Pick up toys."

"That's good. It's important to help Mommy clean up and be her helper. Good job."

Sarah smiled around a bite of cookie. "These good." Sarah was making quick work of her snack.

"I'll be sure to let my neighbor know."

Later, after a simple dinner and Sarah had gone to bed, Spencer said to Kate, "Can we talk?" He had enjoyed playing with Sarah while Kate did her laundry and ran some errands.

"Sure, what about?" Kate plopped on the sofa and rested her feet on the table. She closed her eyes for a minute and sighed.

"Little Sarah, as darling as she is, can't keep calling me Mr. Daddy." Spencer hoped this conversation would go well, but he had his doubts. He didn't mind Sarah's name for him at all. As far as he was concerned, he would be thrilled to be her daddy. But, it would be hard to explain her name for him in front of others that didn't know the situation.

"You got that right. How did she come up with that, anyway?" Kate sat up and frowned. "I don't know how she knew that dads went with moms like cake with ice cream, but she seems to think you should be her daddy."

Spencer said, "And what's wrong with that?"

"We're not—I mean you're not—umm. I'll think of something." Kate jumped up, grabbed her mug, and left for the kitchen. Spencer let it go.

"We have to settle this. I mean, this could potentially be embarrassing." Kate came back with a steaming mug and sat back down.

"I know. There's really only one perfect solution, you know." Since Kate continued the conversation to his surprise, he rolled with it.

"And that would be?" Kate looked at Spencer.

Spencer looked at Kate, with her hair fixed and makeup on, though he didn't think she needed it. Even in her yoga pants and oversized air force sweatshirt, she was as beautiful to him now as she was when she first opened the door earlier in her robe. He took a deep breath and admitted his true feelings. "For me to be her daddy of course."

Dead silence.

Kate gulped. "You can't be serious."

Spencer took another deep breath. "I'm dead serious."

Kate continued. "I know you knew John and kept his secret and helped me with getting Sarah here, but still. No need to feel obligated."

"Obligated! Is that what you think?" Spencer nearly choked on his tea.

"Well, of course. You feel like you have to step in for John—"

"Kate Nicole Langston." He enunciated each part of her name as a single sentence as he put his glass down on the table with a thud. "In no way, under any circumstance, do I feel 'obligated.'" He spoke as if obligated were a dirty word. "Did you think I was joking yesterday when I said I loved you?"

He stayed where he was, in the chair across from her, afraid to move any closer. The last time he mentioned his feelings, she punched him in the arm.

"Spencer." Kate said his name rather sternly.

"Yes?" *Here it comes.*

"It's time for you to go." Kate didn't look at him, but at the floor.

Spencer silently let out his breath. He slowly got up from the chair and slid his coat on. "I'll get Mrs. Pettigrew's plate later."

Kate nodded, not making any moves to get up.

Spencer walked past her and let himself out, letting the door close softly behind him. Leaning on the outer side of the door, he sighed. Every time she rebuffed him, a little piece of his heart cracked. He didn't know how much longer it could stay together.

He ambled to his car and unlocked it but didn't get in yet. He looked up at the clear sky, trying to shake his disappointment. Apparently winning Kate's heart would take some time. A star twinkled in the distance, as if to say, "You can do it."

But he wasn't sure if his heart would still be in one piece that long.

Chapter 25

Kate sat stunned on the sofa after Spencer left. *He couldn't love me because he felt partially guilty for not telling me about Sarah, could he?* She swung her legs up on the sofa and pulled down the blanket and wrapped herself in it, confused. *And yet, he said he wasn't obligated. If not, what then? I'm still in love with John, aren't I? Even though he's gone? What should I do now?*

Before going to bed, Kate finally finished unpacking her suitcase. She thought over their trip and how stressful it had been. And then she recalled their conversation about Spencer's daily prayer and Bible time. Even though she had sensed God's presence the day that she remembered going to church as a young girl, she hadn't given God much thought since.

Spencer talked about God like he was real, and somebody to talk to regularly. A somebody who had everything under control. She certainly hoped so, because her life was definitely not under control. At least not anymore.

Kate finished her tea, put her cup in the dishwasher and went to bed with no answers to her questions.

****

The next morning after breakfast, Kate tried returning Mrs. Kern's call, but had to leave a message. Kate realized it was Sunday and they were probably at church.

Since the day was warm, Kate took Sarah and Buttons out for a walk around the apartment complex and showed Sarah the little playground. Sarah wanted to swing, so Kate pulled her out of the stroller and strapped her in the blue bucket swing while Buttons roamed around the stroller. Sarah loved the swing and Kate smiled at her squeals.

"Is this fun?" Kate asked her.

"Yes! More, Mommy."

Kate pushed her a little higher, but not too high. She didn't want to scare her. Kate let the sun warm her face as she kept the swing going. She was glad to be out of the apartment, getting fresh air and exercise, for the first time in several days.

Kate and Sarah talked about the different birds and small animals they saw. Buttons yapped at a squirrel and tried to run after a cardinal. "Nice try, Buttons."

Sarah tired of the swings, so they walked over to the sandbox. "Do you like sand, Sarah?" Kate asked.

Sarah looked up at her with an unsure look on her face. "Maybe another time," Kate said. "How about the little horse over there?" In a small square of wood chips a few metal and plastic animals sat on large springs that bounced back and forth. Kate sat Sarah on a brown horse and showed her how it worked. She held on to her though so Sarah wouldn't slide off the side. "Do you like it?"

Sarah nodded.

Buttons began to bark in a friendly manner and then a voice said, "There you are." Kate turned around to see

Spencer bent over, petting Buttons. Kate stole a glance at him, noticing his appearance. She realized he must have come from church, thus the khakis and button up shirt and tie. Kate's heart lurched. He looked...handsome. When he stood up their eyes locked.

She quickly slid Sarah off the horse before she fell off.

Finally, he said, "Are you okay?"

"Sorry. Didn't expect to see you today." *Or looking so nice.* She gave him another quick glance.

He cleared his throat. "It just so happens that Mrs. Pettigrew had a get together last night and has leftovers for a picnic. It was her suggestion, if you don't have plans." After their conversation last night, he was glad he could give credit to his neighbor for the picnic idea. He had planned to stay home otherwise.

"Sarah and I do not have plans for the rest of the day, actually." Kate answered.

"Hi, Sarah. Having fun?" Spencer was glad to turn to the little girl who gave him a big smile.

"Yes! I love swing." She clapped her hands with excitement. Today, Sarah wore another pink outfit, this one with matching top and pants with pink stripes.

"Me, too. When I can find one big enough." Spencer's statement surprised Kate. "I do too," she added.

"So what kind of leftovers are we talking about?" Kate asked, strapping Sarah back into the stroller. Wordlessly, she handed the dog leash to Spencer.

"Ham. Baked beans. Potato salad. Brownies." Spencer paused between items.

"I see." Kate leaned around the stroller to see Sarah's face. "What do you think, Sarah? Should we have a picnic with Spencer and Buttons outside?"

"Yes, Mommy! I like outside."

"I guess we're going on a picnic." Kate looked at Spencer and he gave her a small smile.

"The food's in my car. I figured you guys were around somewhere since your car hadn't moved."

Kate nodded. She was suddenly nervous and afraid to say too much. Suddenly she felt like she was on a first date. *I'm not dressed for company and skipped my makeup this morning. And the wind has messed my hair up for sure. Nothing I can do about it now so I'll try to enjoy this impromptu picnic anyway.*

****

When Spencer first got to Kate's he wasn't sure about the picnic idea. He didn't know where the girls had gone, but when he saw Kate's car still in the lot, he knew they weren't far. He had taken Mrs. P home and she had handed him the leftovers already packed up. It was her way of thanking him for the work done yesterday and for driving her to church when he was available.

The moment that Kate looked at him at the park seemed surreal. Spencer couldn't quite place the look she had on her face. She seemed a little stunned, but he wasn't sure why. At least she wasn't annoyed that he showed up. After the way she had dismissed him last night, he wasn't sure he would be welcomed.

But he decided when he got home last night that he would just have to woo her the old-fashioned way: with lots of time, attention, and surprises along the way. He was going to enjoy himself for as long as it took. Because he knew deep down in his heart, that Kate was the one for him. And he was going to prove it to her—one day at a time.

Buttons nibbled on the scraps left from their picnic while the three humans sprawled out on the blanket Kate brought. "Mrs. Pettigrew is an excellent cook, Spencer. Please give her my compliments. I feel like I'm going to explode. After eating only comfort food lately, I feel like I've eaten a feast."

"I know. She's an excellent neighbor for a poor helpless airman like me."

Kate rolled over to her side to see Spencer's eyes crinkled in the corners. "Very funny. You're neither of those."

Kate glanced at Sarah, who was throwing a ball for Buttons. There were giggles from her and happy yips from the dog. Kate wasn't sure who was having more fun.

Spencer watched the two playmates. They were having a good time, making each other happy. He chuckled as Buttons trotted back to Sarah and dropped the slobbery ball in her lap.

Sarah picked it up and threw it as far as she could, which wasn't very far. But it was far enough for Buttons to get a little exercise.

Kate leaned toward Spencer, and turned his face toward her with her index finger. She took a deep breath. "Spencer, I'm sorry. I know I hurt your feelings last night. I didn't mean to. I just can't switch from John to you so fast—" Suddenly emotional, Kate put her head down on her hands.

Spencer sucked in his breath. *Now what have I done? Making her cry is the last thing I want to do.* "Kate, I'm sorry. I didn't mean to hurt you." He rubbed the back of her head, regretting his impatience. *What was I thinking?*

Luckily Sarah and Buttons were oblivious to their conversation. Their laughing and barking along with robins and cardinals singing from nearby trees floated around them. Finally Spencer said, "I didn't mean to come on too strong. Please forgive me."

"Spencer? I like you. A lot. I'm just not ready." Kate wiped her face with a napkin before turning back toward him, but she kept her eyes closed.

Spencer swallowed a lump in his throat. "I understand. I'm sorry."

"No forgiveness needed, okay?" With her left hand, she took his right hand, the one rubbing her hair, and squeezed it without letting go. She gave his hand a quick peck and held it under her cheek. His hand was strong and bigger than hers. And yet it was a perfect fit.

In the peaceful sounds of nature, Kate realized something. *Yes, I can love him.*

In time.

Chapter 26

As soon as Kate realized she could love Spencer someday, her phone buzzed. She reluctantly sat up and pulled her phone from the pocket of her pants. "Hi Jen."

"Hey, what are you and Sarah up to?"

Kate looked over at Spencer who also sat up. The quiet mood was over. "We're actually over at the park right now."

"Isn't it a gorgeous day to be outdoors? Listen, Kelly and I wanted to know if we could come over in about an hour and meet Sarah. That okay?"

"Sure, that would be great."

"See you then." Kate disconnected the call and slid the phone back into her pocket. She turned to Spencer. "Jen and Kelly are coming over later to meet Sarah."

Spencer nodded. "That's good."

Kate turned as Buttons jogged over and plopped down at her knees. "Sarah, I think you wore Buttons out. You look a little tired yourself."

"Not tired. I fine." Sarah crossed her arms and stuck out her chin.

Really. "Hmm. Perhaps we should head back." Kate got up and stretched. If Jen hadn't called, Kate could have fallen asleep herself. The fresh air, her conversation with Spencer, and the trip had worn her out.

"I'm sorry to end our picnic, but Sarah should rest for a while before the girls come over." Kate folded the blanket and Spencer packed the leftovers. Mrs. Pettigrew had packed enough for two armies.

"All good things must come to an end, they say." Spencer held Button and rubbed his back.

"You're always welcome, Spencer. You know that." Kate addressed him before turning the stroller toward the sidewalk. Sarah jabbered to the birds and squirrels in her sight.

Spencer shrugged and let Buttons down gently. He held his leash and followed the girls back to the apartment. Kate stopped to let another couple go past who were walking their cocker spaniel. Buttons went crazy for a minute, but Kate told him to hush. Kate was hoping that Sarah would fall asleep in the stroller during the short walk home. She was a heavy sleeper and Kate knew she could get her in her bed without waking her. Her jabbering seemed to slow down the longer they walked.

Kate took one hand off the stroller and put it on Spencer's arm but kept walking. "Listen, Spencer, I'm not mad at you. Please understand it's not that I don't want you around anymore. I do. I just can't love you right now. Alright?"

"Sure." Spencer looked away toward the street.

Kate put her hand back onto the stroller knowing that first she had to get used to John's death and parenting.

****

Spencer helped Kate unload the stroller and lifted Sarah to her bed. "Thank you, Spencer for the picnic. We enjoyed it."

"You're welcome." Spencer walked to the door. "See you later." *Maybe.*

He sprinted down the stairs feeling like a fool. To his credit though, he had been patient and honorable when John stole Kate's heart. Spencer wished he had been more vocal then. It wasn't as if he had any dibs on her.

He drove away upset with himself and not sure how to proceed anymore with Kate. He put the window down and drove around, not caring where he went. *Does she still think I feel obligated? Somehow I have to get her to understand that I love her and that's it not out of obligation to take care of her and Sarah. I'll send her some flowers from the base floral shop. That's a start anyway.*

While Spencer brooded and drove around town, Kate threw away the trash from their picnic and put their cups in the dishwasher. She made some lemonade and more tea. Then she stretched on the sofa with Buttons beside her. Her thoughts turned toward Spencer. *Am I free to love him? How do I know he's the one for me?*

After her brief nap, Kate answered the door to see Jen and Kelly in a cloud of pink. "Hi guys, come on in!"

Her two friends walked past her in a flurry of pink bags, pink balloons and bags of other stuff....also pink. "It's great to see you. But what's all this?"

Jen set her balloons on the dining room table, turned to Kate and answered, "It's what you call an adoption shower, on the fly."

"What? Are you kidding?"

Kelly set her own bulging bag down next to another gift bag. "Nope, and some of the gals from work are on their way in about half an hour." She gave Kate a sly grin.

"You shouldn't have—"

"Oh, but we did. Don't worry, we've got this." Jen slipped off her shoes, stepped on a chair and started taping pink and white streamers above the table.

Kelly started filling pink and white balloons with a small pump after she brought in a cake. Punch fixings were chilling in Kate's fridge.

Kate watched her friends in stunned silence. Kelly, who was wearing a leopard print top, paused in her work briefly and said to Kate, "We knew you wouldn't want us to go to the trouble, so we did it anyway. We figured this was the only way to get you to go along."

"You got that right. You know I'm not into frills and parties." She looked at her transformed dining and living rooms and couldn't believe how much pink frill she saw. But secretly she was pleased with the generosity and thoughtfulness from her friends.

Kelly rolled her eyes. "We know. Don't worry, it won't be fancy. Just a couple writing games and then opening gifts."

Relieved, Kate took a deep breath. "You guys are the best," she gave them each a hug. "This is really nice. I'll go get Sarah up and tell her about the party."

"Great; we're almost ready and the other guests should be here in a little bit."

Kate went down the hall to get Sarah up from her nap. She was glad her daughter could sleep through the party prep and get a decent nap. There were a couple of dresses in Sarah's clothing. Kate chose a purple dress and white socks with ruffles and got her dressed.

"We have company, Sarah, and we're going to have a little party."

"What party?" Sarah glanced at her with a questioning look.

"A party is when friends come over and share snacks and sometimes give gifts."

Sarah simply nodded at Kate like she knew exactly what she was saying. Kate couldn't believe she was the honored guest of a baby/adoption shower. It still seemed unreal to be caring for Sarah.

Since she didn't have time to take a shower, Kate changed into casual slacks and a matching top. She brushed her hair and put on a little blush to her cheeks. Then she ran a brush through Sarah's small curls and walked her out to meet her friends. Jen was opening packages of forks and plates.

"Oh, hi, Sweetie! You must be Sarah. I'm Jen." Jen bent down to the little girl's level and stared at her a little too long. She looked up at Kate as she stood back and mouthed to Kate, *she looks like John.*

Kate's look said, I know, I try not to think about it. Jen gave Kate a quick hug.

Kelly was scooping out sherbet into a punch bowl. "Hey there, Pumpkin, you must be the star of the show. I'm Kelly." She glanced at the full scoop in her hand before sliding the contents into the bowl. "Nice to meet you." Kelly gave Sarah a wink.

"These two nice friends are the ones giving us this party."

"I like party...pretty." Sarah was with all the decorations.

A few minutes later, Sarah sat on Kate's lap. Kate glanced around at the ladies assembled in her living room. She couldn't believe that her two friends put all this together for her so quickly. But their kindness sent a surge of pleasure and happiness through her heart.

Her friends were laughing and having a good time. Kate squeezed Sarah around the middle and asked her, "Isn't this fun?"

"Party fun," Sarah answered. Sarah eyed the gift bags in front of her and Kate. "These for me?"

"Yes, and me. We have to say thank you when we open gifts, okay?" Kate whispered in her ear.

Sarah nodded.

They had a lot of fun opening them. Sarah was Kate's little helper, bringing the bags or packages to her and yanking out the tissue paper. Sarah squealed when she saw new books, coloring supplies or wooden puzzles. She didn't get as excited when they pulled out a cute winter coat with matching mittens and hat. Everyone laughed when Sarah dropped it the floor quickly.

After the last one was opened, Kate said, "You guys are the best. I never would have expected this, thank you."

"Tank you," Sarah added.

Everyone smiled. "Glad to do it," Jen held up her punch. "To happy mothering," and all the guests toasted with her.

Chapter 27

The next morning Kate had to search for a day care for Sarah. Kate dreaded having to send her to one, but what was a single mom supposed to do? Kate pulled up Google on her computer and started looking.

She wouldn't need one until after the work exercise next week. *That Spencer.* He volunteered to work a lousy shift just for her sake. She shook her head. *What am I going to do with that man?*

Kate called a few places, but most of them didn't have any openings for two-year-olds. They had slots for infants or for three and up. She could try some home day cares, which were listed at the Family Readiness Center on base. She checked out their website.

With her constantly changing work shift, she couldn't narrow down her schedule enough for one of those, either. Frustrated, Kate closed out of the Internet. She watched Sarah as she worked one of her new puzzles, a picture of shapes and colors. Buttons sat beside her, and he seemed to enjoy having a little person around, which was a huge relief to Kate.

After lunch, Kate put Sarah down for a nap and worked on her thank you cards for the guests who came to the shower. She wrote a short note in each one, thanking them for coming and for their particular gift. She left the pile on the counter so Sarah could add her scribbled name. *Might as well start manners early.*

That task done, Kate pulled out the new clothes and cut off the tags, dropping them in the laundry basket. She folded all the empty gift bags and the best of the tissue paper and added them to her wrapping stash. The amount of pink wrapping items would last her for years.

Next, she called the base pediatrician and made an appointment for Sarah. She wanted her to have a well-baby check and meet the doctor. Kate pulled out the medical records she had and planned to make copies next time she was at the library so she could keep the originals for herself.

When Sarah woke up, Kate gave her a snack and showed her the thank you notes and a pen. "You can help me by adding your name right here," she pointed to the bottom of one. "Okay?"

Sarah was eager to 'write' her name. Kate helped her form the letters and then Kate slipped them inside the matching envelopes. She showed Sarah how to lick and close them.

"It taste funny," Sarah said after making a funny face.

"They do, don't they?"

On their way out of the complex to walk Buttons, they dropped them one by one into the mail box. "Now they'll go to the nice friends who came over with their gifts for us."

After a few minutes Sarah asked, "What's that 'mell?"

Kate sniffed harder to see if she could figure out what she referred to. "I think it's chicken. Somebody must be grilling. Do you like that smell?"

"It 'mells good."

"I think so too."

As they walked around the back bend of their walking path, Kate thought about how Sarah would adjust to daycare. And she worried about future orders to deploy. *What would I do then? Who can I trust to care for Sarah?* A headache started to form and Kate picked up her pace and headed home.

****

The next day during lunch Kate asked Sarah a bunch of questions so she could learn more about her. She felt like she was months behind on things a mom would know by now.

"What's your favorite animal?"

"Doggy."

"Favorite color?"

"Pink."

"Favorite things to do?"

"Color and books."

At least we have that in common already.

Kate felt that Sarah seemed more grown up in some ways and very much like a child in others. Maybe that was normal. How was Kate to know?

They were nearly finished with their tuna sandwiches when her phone rang. Kate got up to answer it in the kitchen.

"Hi, Kate, it's Spencer. What's up?" Kate spun around so she could keep an eye on Sarah at the table.

"Just finishing lunch."

"I won't keep you, but someone left a flier from the paper on the break room table for Babies-R-Us. They're having a big sale, furniture and stuff. Thought I'd let you know since you want a few things."

"Thanks. Could you go with us or could I borrow your car?" Her car was so small, big items wouldn't fit.

"Sure. When do you want to go?"

They made plans to go that evening after dinner, which Spencer would eat with them. Kate had some chicken in the freezer; she took it out to thaw for a casserole.

Kate said to Sarah, "Spencer's coming over for dinner tonight, and then we'll do some shopping."

"Okay." She pushed her plate away.

"All done?"

She nodded.

"Let's get you cleaned up and then it's nap time."

"No nap," Sarah said before frowning.

"Yes, nap. After we read a story." Kate cleaned her up and let her pick the story.

After putting down a sleepy toddler, Kate cleaned up the lunch dishes and made some of the preparations for their dinner.

An hour later, her doorbell rang and she went to answer it before Buttons went crazy and woke up Sarah.

Kate opened the door to see a large bouquet of flowers in front of her. "Miss Langston?" came a muffled voice behind it.

"Yes."

"Special delivery." He thrust the large vase toward her and pulled out a clipboard and pen from somewhere. "Sign here, please."

Kate set the flowers on the small table in the entry way and signed for them. She closed the door and pulled the little card out from amongst the pink carnations, fuchsia daisies, white baby's breath and fern-like greenery. They were beautiful and looked expensive. She read the card, *You're going to be a great mom. Enjoy the flowers. Spencer.*

Touched by his thoughtful gesture, Kate breathed in their scent before setting the fragile arrangement on the entertainment center so neither child nor pet could knock it over in their play. She planned to thank Spencer at dinner.

****

Later when Spencer arrived, he handed her the ad he mentioned on the phone. "Thanks, make yourself comfortable. Dinner will be ready in about twenty minutes."

Spencer took his shoes off by the door and spied Sarah peeking around the corner from the kitchen. He pretended not to notice and walked past her whistling, then turned around and winked at her.

She giggled and said, "Hi."

"Hi," he said continuing into the living room. "Wow! What went on here? Looks like a Pepto Bismol explosion."

Kate walked into the room and said, "I know, isn't it great? These are all the gifts from the shower." She left him with Sarah amidst all the pink and returned to the kitchen.

"Sure is a lot of pink." Spencer turned to Sarah. "Should we read a few books before we eat?"

Sarah ran to her basket which stored an assortment of board books, big and small. She snatched the two in front and brought them to Spencer.

Spencer read the first title, *Mr. Brown Can Moo, Can You?* He smiled down at Sarah who snuggled into his side. He mooed, which startled Buttons, making him bark. Spencer and Sarah laughed. She started to moo and Spencer said, "That's good. Mooooo." Then he read the story making all the appropriate sounds. The other book he read was *Clifford, the Big Red Dog.* Kate hollered that dinner was ready. "We're on the last page."

Spencer told Sarah, "Your new mom is a good cook. She makes lots of good dinners." Sarah gave him a smile and they walked to the dining room together.

****

After dinner, Spencer helped Kate clean up the kitchen while Sarah played with Buttons and looked at her books. "I know you're concerned about daycare for Sarah. How about you ask Mrs. P? I'm sure she'd love to do it."

"Spencer, Sarah is almost three. Would Mrs. P be able to keep up with her?"

"We're talking about the perfectly capable and trustworthy Mrs. P, aren't we?"

"I'll think about it. I'm not finding anything else right now." They left for the store after transferring Sarah's seat to Spencer's car.

On Kate's mental list was a bed and a small dresser or chest of drawers. When they arrived at the store, Kate strapped Sarah into the cart and they headed to the furniture area. Balloons were tied to several end displays and the lighting and décor were bright.

They picked out a cute white toddler bed with a small chest of drawers to match. Then Kate and Sarah picked out a bedding package with a coordinating area rug and lamp. When they got back to Kate's, Spencer offered to put the items together.

"That would be great. I'll give Sarah her bath." Before Kate ran the bathwater, she pulled out the bedspread, sheets and some outfits she couldn't resist buying and ran down to put them in the washer, taking advantage of Spencer's help.

Meanwhile, he got a few tools out of his trunk and began ripping open the cardboard boxes.

****

At Spencer's insistence, Kate finally decided to give Mrs. Pettigrew a chance with being Sarah's day care provider. It wasn't that Kate didn't like or trust her, she just wasn't sure she could keep up with her.

Sarah was a great little girl, but recently had begun to feel quite at home. Yesterday, little Sarah squeezed out all of Kate's toothpaste on the bathroom counter. Kate learned to keep it up in the cabinet, after she spent an hour cleaning it up and wiping down the bathroom.

Last week, Sarah overfilled Button's water bowl and Kate had to mop the entire kitchen floor. Yes, Sarah was cute and a good girl most of the time. But her curiosity and familiarity with things at home had caused a few mishaps.

Kate pulled up into the driveway Mrs. P and Spencer shared. She knew Spencer was at work until late afternoon.

She walked up to the door with Sarah in tow. Mrs. P opened the door with excitement. If Kate had any doubts about her wanting to watch Sarah, they flew out the window.

"Hello, Kate. Hi, Sarah, come on in." She shut the door behind them. Today Mrs. P wore denim jeans and a Rams sweatshirt over a collared blouse. Her smile and welcome were genuine. Kate felt somewhat better at the idea of this woman being able to care for Sarah.

"So good to meet you." She leaned over to Sarah's level and chucked her on the chin. Before they could get comfortable, Mrs. P asked Sarah, "Would you like a cookie?"

Sarah looked up at Kate. "You may have one; use your manners."

Sarah looked back at Mrs. P. "Yes, please," she said quietly.

Kate sat on the sofa where Mrs. P gestured she sit. Sarah followed Mrs. P to the kitchen. Kate could hear them talking and the rattle of a cookie jar lid.

A minute later, Mrs. P came back and asked Kate if she wanted anything. "I'm fine, thanks."

"She's a pretty little thing." Mrs. P settled into a wing chair next to an end table stacked with books, papers and magazines. She leaned forward as if to hear every word Kate would speak.

"Now, what can I do for you? I know Spencer hinted at some child care needed."

Kate nodded. "Yes, I need care for her. But, I have such a rotating schedule, I wasn't sure you'd be interested."

"Is at as crazy as Spencer's?" She gave her a knowing smile.

Kate smiled in return. "Sometimes, yes." She pulled a stray hair behind her ear. "Right now I'm on days, but with all the action in the Middle East and everywhere, I could go to second shift or mids anytime."

"I'm here, 24/7. The only thing I do regularly is go to the library and my monthly Friday night dinners with my class. I like to garden, can, and cook. I don't see a problem with a little helper in any of those activities."

Kate gave her a smile and then they began to discuss the details, like nap times, emergency contacts, pay rate, and Sarah's eating habits. "I go back to work next Monday."

"If you are comfortable, I'm comfortable. I'm healthy as a horse and finally got rid of that stupid walker that slowed me down. If I have any emergency, Spencer seems to be around. Or my neighbor on the other side."

Sarah came in and smiled at Kate, with crumbs stuck on her upper lip. "Cookies are good," she said, smiling at Mrs. P.

"I think we'll get along great," Mrs. P said, "but it's totally up to you."

Kate knew she could trust this woman. "You have a deal." She turned to Sarah, and said, "Mrs. P is going to watch you when I'm at work."

"I more cookies?"

The two ladies laughed. Mrs. P said, "I think there will be lots of cookies in your future." Kate whispered in Sarah's ear, "Say thank you."

Sarah said thank you to Mrs. P and they got ready to leave. Mrs. P walked them to the door and said, "I'll have some fun things for you to do next week."

Sarah gave her a smile, Kate thanked her and they left. Sarah babbled about the things she saw in Mrs. P's kitchen and Kate felt relieved at the knowledge Sarah would be well cared for.

Chapter 28

O range, maroon and gold leaves swirled from the oak and maple trees, and clusters of yellow and orange mums bloomed in many yards along Kate's route to work. She was a little nervous since it was her first day back to work after bringing Sarah home. But Mrs. P seemed to be ready for the energy of little Sarah. Kate sure hoped so.

When Kate walked into the hallway, Kelly and some of her other coworkers welcomed her back and she proudly showed them the few pictures of Sarah she had so far. Those who hadn't been to the shower and the guys who were interested (not many) said she was cute.

"Thanks," Kate said. She still had a hard time believing she was a mom and felt like it hadn't quite sunk in yet. Kate had a hard time concentrating on her work, wondering constantly how Sarah was doing. And Mrs. P for that matter. Mrs. P told Kate she could call at any time or stop by on her lunch break if she wanted.

At least with her and Spencer's different schedules, Mrs. P only watched Sarah a couple full days a week. Kate didn't think that was so bad. And Spencer filled in the roll of dad almost perfectly.

On days when Spencer kept Sarah they'd stay at Kate's. On warmer days they walked Buttons, or played at the park. They read books, played Candy Land and colored if it was chilly. Kate loved seeing them together. It made her really consider when she might be ready to get married.

November arrived and the leaves were falling from the oak and maple trees by the bagful, with the days gradually getting cooler. John's mom was coming Thursday to clean out his apartment. Kate had mixed feelings about the visit from Mrs. Kern, but she would have to overcome the ordeal as best she could.

Spencer offered to drive her and Sarah to the airport and she gratefully accepted. Because it was unseasonably warm, Spencer came over wearing khaki shorts and a red polo. Kate dressed Sarah in a cute Winnie-the-Pooh outfit. In the car, Kate explained to Sarah that her grandma was visiting for a few days. They rode in Spencer's car again since his had more room.

"My memaw? Who's her?"

Kate smiled at Sarah's grammar. "Your grandma is your daddy's mom."

"Mr. Daddy's mommy?"

Kate sighed. "No, John's mom. John was your daddy but he died, remember?"

"No...Mr. Daddy not my daddy?" Sarah's little nose was scrunched up and it was hard for Kate not to laugh at Sarah's funny face.

Kate gave up, turning back toward the front. "You'll like your grandma."

"Okay." Sarah's answer showed her complete trust, which helped Kate relax.

Spencer reached for Kate's hand and squeezed. "You tried."

"I know, but I don't know how to help her not to forget John. It wasn't like they lived together. Do you think I should worry about it that much?" Kate peeked back at Sarah, but she was already distracted, watching the traffic.

"She didn't see him more than once or twice. When she's older, it will be important for her to remember that he was a special man and that he died for his country. She's too young right now."

"I guess. Maybe I can get her a few photos or mementos from John's place to hold on to until she's older."

"Definitely. And in case you're wondering, I plan to adopt Sarah after we get married, if you want me to." He gave her hand another gentle squeeze.

"Spencer, that's great. Thanks for telling me. It will be nice to be a whole family, I admit. When I'm ready."

"I know." He squeezed her hand again before letting go so he could signal their turn onto the airport exit. He took a ticket from the machine in the parking garage and found a spot not far from one of the doors. "Shall we?"

"We shall. Ready or not." Kate and Sarah followed Spencer since he had the flight information.

After a minute of fighting crowds, Spencer asked Sarah, "Is it okay if I hold you?"

She nodded and leaned her head on his shoulder as soon as he picked her up. Kate smiled and took Spencer's remaining hand. Spencer squeezed it before giving her fingers a quick kiss. They walked through crowds of people coming and going and found an electronic arrival/departure board to see if Mrs. Kern would be on time.

"She should be here. Let's walk to the luggage pick up area." Spencer turned to the escalator and they rode down to the basement. They spotted Mrs. Kern with a navy medium-size suitcase on wheels and a matching carry on. She was standing next to her daughter-in-law who had two bags in a bright berry color.

"Hi, Mrs. Kern. How are you?" Spencer asked.

"I'm fine, thank you, Spencer. It's good to see you again." They hugged briefly before Mrs. Kern turned to Kate, "How are you doing, dear?"

Kate felt her shoulders relax at Mrs. Kern's friendly tone. "I'm okay, how are you?"

"Holding on, holding on. But you can both call me Lauren. This is my daughter-in-law, Judy."

"Nice to meet you," Kate held out her hand.

"Likewise," Judy replied. Judy was fairly tall with dishwater blond hair. She must be one of John's brother's wives, but Kate didn't know which one. Kate didn't remember meeting her at the funeral, but maybe she hadn't been able to attend.

"And this must be Sarah," Mrs. Kern said, smiling. She was quiet for a moment before saying, "I'm your grandma, sweetheart. How are you?"

Sarah gave her a wide grin. "I okay, too."

Lauren gave her a big grin. "I'm glad to hear it." She wiped away moisture in the corner of her eyes with a crumpled tissue.

Spencer offered to help with their bags. "I think we got it," Judy said. So they headed for the car.

Kate asked about the flight.

"A little turbulence, but otherwise it was good," Mrs. Kern answered. Judy seemed nice and Kate was glad Mrs. Kern didn't have to travel alone.

Kate let Sarah converse with her grandma while she chatted with Judy during the ride home. She learned that Judy was married to John's older brother who was also active duty military, and that he was currently TDY, so Judy had free time on her hands. They didn't have any children. Later after dropping off Lauren and Judy at John's and helping them with their bags, Spencer dropped off Kate and Sarah at her place. He walked them to her door.

"I'll see you later."

"Thanks for picking them up," she gave him a quick hug. "It helped a lot."

"You're welcome." He gave Sarah a quick peck on the cheek. He had to go home and get ready for work. Kate had taken a late lunch and planned to stay home with Sarah for the rest of the day.

"We'll see your grandma again later, for supper. She and your Aunt Judy are coming here to eat with us."

"For roni and cheese?"

"Maybe another day. I think we'll have chicken and rice. Do you like that?"

"I dunno. I like chicken." Sarah sat in the entryway and removed her shoes.

"Then you'll probably like this. It's time for your nap."

"I no take nap."

"Sorry, but you have to. Pick out a book to read first." Kate hung up Sarah's diaper bag in the coat closet and picked up Buttons who came running.

After putting Sarah down, Kate went to the kitchen and put on a chicken to boil so she could cut it up later for the casserole. As she worked around the kitchen she wondered what life might be like if she and Spencer were married. *What would be a good time for a wedding? It makes sense to wait until after my release from active duty, which should be late April. Perhaps a June wedding? Would Spencer propose since we've already discussed marriage several times? I like the idea of him getting down on one knee. The vision makes me smile.*

Later Kate and Sarah picked up Lauren and Judy around five. Kate hadn't been to John's apartment since his death. Her heart pounded and tears blurred her vision. She had a key, but didn't feel the need to use it. As a matter of fact, she'd have to give it to Lauren to turn in.

She took a deep breath when his mom opened the door. "Hi, Kate and Sarah, come on in. We're just about ready."

"Hi." Kate and Sarah stepped in. Kate looked around, half expecting to see John. She knew in her heart he was gone, but her mind still played tricks on her. She saw the sofa where they watched movies, the table where they shared meals. Most of the walls were now bare, and boxes were scattered around the rooms, ready to be taped shut. She swallowed the lump in her throat and silently handed her key to Lauren.

She was relieved when they left. John's mom sat in the back with Sarah, engaging her in conversation. Judy sat in the front and asked Kate questions about St Louis.

The casserole was a big hit and even Sarah seemed to enjoy it. Even with the "green" things in it.

Lauren said, "It must be difficult for you to be at John's place without him."

Kate nodded, not able to speak. Lauren seemed to understand.

Kate rested her fork on her plate before answering. "It is, but I'll help in any way I can. I'd like to have some photos of us, if that's okay."

"Of course, take anything you'd like for you or Sarah. I have our letters we've written back and forth and already packed a few special things, but most of the rest is going to charity." She was silent a minute before she added, "You don't mind Spencer helping, do you?"

"Oh, not at all. He's more than happy to. He said he'd be by in the morning after he picked up Sarah from here."

"Perfect. With the three of us, I think we can get the furniture loaded on the rental truck coming at nine. Do you know where we can drop off the larger items?" Lauren pushed her plate back.

"There's the thrift shop on base, or Goodwill a few miles away."

"Maybe we can take it to the base; that would be a great idea. Thank you."

"You're welcome. Spencer should know where the Airman's Attic is, where items are donated for younger airmen who can't always afford bigger items." Kate finished her dinner and asked, "Who's ready for ice cream?"

"Me!" Sarah shouted. They all laughed and spent the evening getting to know each other. Lauren read several books to Sarah which they both enjoyed. Judy and Kate cleaned up the kitchen and loaded the dishwasher. Kate took out her digital camera and snapped a couple photos of

Sarah sitting on the sofa while Lauren read to her. She took some of Sarah with Judy also, and then Judy offered to take some of Kate and Sarah together. "Thank, you I appreciate that." Kate put away the camera and said, "I'll send you copies when I get them back."

"That would be great, Kate. Thanks." Lauren smiled at Kate. "I have a few from when she was little; I'll make copies of those and send them to you as well."

Kate tried hiding her surprise, but said, "Thanks. I'd love to have them."

"Could I go ahead and take Buttons for his walk?" Kate asked Lauren.

"Of course," she answered. "I'll even get her into her pajamas if you show me where they are." Kate walked down to her bedroom with Lauren following her. "Her jammies are in the top drawer and diapers and wipes are right here," she pointed to the top of the dresser.

"Very well. Enjoy your walk."

Afterwards Kate and Sarah drove Lauren and Judy back to John's apartment.

"Good night, Kate, and thanks for the delicious dinner. We'll see you tomorrow."

"You're welcome. Have a good night." Kate watched Lauren unlock the door, not pulling away until she and Judy were inside.

Chapter 29

In the morning, Spencer came in with a long-stemmed pink rose for Kate. "It's beautiful, thank you." She gave him a quick peck on the cheek before putting the bud in a vase.

"Now, that's what I'm talking about," he said.

Kate set the vase on the counter. Her heartbeat quickened. "I suppose you'd like another?"

"May I?"

Kate put her arms around his neck and gingerly at first, then with more passion, kissed him on the lips. A tingly sensation spread throughout her body. She pulled away and asked, "How's that?"

"That was fabulous. I could do this all day." He leaned his forehead on hers, sighing.

"I'm sorry you haven't got all day. Let me see if Sarah's ready to go." Kate quickly left the kitchen to check on Sarah. She thought about their kiss just now. *Am I falling for him? I actually enjoyed that kiss. Maybe it was time to move their relationship forward. Slowly.*

After Spencer and Sarah left to help clear out John's apartment, Kate drove to work. She was relieved to cancel her appointment at the child care center on base, since Mrs. P was working out so well.

When she got to work, the office was abuzz. "What's going on?" she asked Sergeant James, another airman she sometimes worked with. His freckles stood out on a face that was paler than usual.

"They're asking for volunteers for early outs again for another round of cuts." He looked worried.

"How many?"

"I don't know, something around four to six percent across the board."

Kate went to her cube, her mind spinning. She'd been too busy to pay any attention to the news that much. The economy took a downturn recently and the government was trying to cut corners, which meant shrinking the country's protection—which never made any sense to her. That's the problem with a non-military president residing in the White House.

The cutbacks could be her opportunity to get out early, but she'd still have to support her and Sarah somehow. What would she do if she got out now? Ideas floated through her mind, making it hard to concentrate on typing up her reports. *Focus and I can think about it at lunch.* She had enough money built in savings to last several weeks, and didn't have any bills but rent and food. Then she remembered the monthly stipend for Sarah's care. That would relieve the pressure of finding something for a while and give her a little cushion.

She and Sarah had dinner again with Sarah's grandma and aunt. Kate was relieved neither of them tried telling Kate what to do or how to handle Sarah. She was grateful they could have a relaxed time together.

That night, Kate with her mind made up to take the early out, slept peacefully. In the morning, she requested the paperwork from Lieutenant Thompson.

"Are you sure? You have less than a year left."

"I know, but what's the point? I have Sarah to think about now and it guarantees I don't have to deploy."

He nodded. "I see. It doesn't make me happy, but I understand. I'll get the forms to you this afternoon. I'm on my way to a briefing."

"Thanks.

Glad that was over with, she went to her office and tackled the next pile of waiting reports. She felt like she was in charge again, and that made her feel a whole lot better. It wasn't just herself she had to think about anymore. Being a mom was the most important role she had and she would do whatever she could to protect her new daughter.

Kate had an email from her boss that included the forms she needed to get out early. A sticky note left on her monitor said, *We'll miss you.* She ate lunch at her desk and filled them out. After emailing them back she heaved a sigh of relief and felt a huge weight lift from her shoulders.

She hummed through the rest of her day, and then went home to Sarah. "Hi, I'm home," she called after shutting the door. Buttons came running, jumping on her uniform. "Down, boy," she said, laughing. Next, Sarah came running. "Hi, honey. How was your day?" she picked her up.

"Good. I make 'nakes and 'nowmen with play dough."

"Really? That sounds like fun." Kate turned as Spencer joined them in the entryway. "How did it go?"

"Fantastic. We helped at John's for several hours and Andrew was able to help for a while, so the furniture is gone."

"That's good. I guess we can go over after supper."

"That would be great. Mrs. Kern has some things for you to go through. They're cleaning now."

"Okay." Kate put Sarah down and she ran off to play. She went to the kitchen and Spencer followed. Kate leaned against the counter. "I put in my paperwork today."

"Are you sure about that?" He leaned on the opposite counter, a look of concern on his face.

"Absolutely. I feel much better already. I have to think about Sarah now." Spencer came close and rubbed her shoulders. "I understand. I'll help you anyway I can."

"Thanks. Are you leaving now?"

"I better. I brought my uniform, so I'll change before I go."

"All right, have a good night." Kate knew he'd be tired tonight, but he had called her earlier and said he was able to go home and nap while Sarah went to Mrs. P's.

He nodded and left to change in the bathroom.

Kate walked into the living room to see what Sarah was doing. She was having a little tea party with the dishes she had bought for her. Bo-bo was sitting on a blanket with some tea and some sort of imaginary snack on a plate. "Can I have some tea?"

"Sure. Sugar too?"

"Yes, please." Kate sat down beside the bear and stretched her legs out. She unlaced her boots and yanked them off and stretched out on the floor. "Thank you," she said to Sarah. "It's very good." She smiled at her and rubbed her soft head.

Spencer joined them, now in his uniform. "I'm off to save the world," he said.

Sarah looked up briefly and said, "Bye, Mr. Daddy."

Spencer grinned at her. "Bye, Sarah, you be good and I'll see you later, okay?"

She nodded as she gave her bear more tea.

Kate walked Spencer to the door. "Thank you for watching her," she gave him a hug.

"You're welcome. We had fun. I'll see you later."

****

Two weeks later, Kate was preparing Thanksgiving dinner. They were getting together on the Wednesday before, because some of her coworkers had to work the holiday shift or mids that weekend. Spencer and a few others from their squadron, who weren't traveling, were joining them. The sixteen-pound turkey was in the oven and she stirred a Jell-O salad before putting it in the fridge to set. Spencer kept Sarah busy, watching a parade on TV or coloring with her.

"Hey, how's it going in here? It smells good already." Spencer walked up behind Kate and wrapped her in his arms. "But not as good as you." He buried his nose in her neck. She giggled and turned around to face him. Their eyes met and he drew her closer for a tender kiss. She was more than willing.

Kate reluctantly pulled away and answered his earlier question. "Dinner prep is going well so far. Can you and Sarah set the table in a minute?"

"Sure. What else can I help with?"

Kate thought a minute. "How about putting the relish tray together?" She told him where to find the black olives, pickles, celery and cheese.

"Mmm. How I love this holiday."

Kate grinned. "Me too. Not to mention the pumpkin and apple pies."

"What's everyone else bringing again?" Spencer opened cans of black olives and drained them in the sink.

"Andrew said he'd bring some spirits and a green bean casserole; Jen is bringing a dessert; Matt's bringing a salad and stuffing; the new guy, Joel, is bringing biscuits and rolls and Kelly's bringing homemade cranberry sauce and a fruit plate."

"Wow, we're eating like royalty today." He continued working on his task.

"Mommy, Mommy, it's snowing." Sarah ran into the kitchen excited. Sarah had pronounced it 'knowing'.

Kate knelt down to her level. "It is?"

"On the TV. It's pretty. Come see." Sarah grabbed Kate's hand.

"I'm coming." She followed Sarah to watch the TV for a minute. "See? Pretty snow." Sarah's face showed her fascination.

"It is pretty. Every snowflake is different, can you believe that?"

She nodded, her curls bouncing on her shoulders. "I want one."

Kate smiled at her innocence. "It's fun to try, but they melt too fast."

Sarah sat down, watching a Santa and snowman floating by in the parade. Her attention diverted, Kate went back to the kitchen. Their company would arrive in about an hour and then they would set the food onto the table and share a toast.

Spencer had brought chairs from his place and Kate had taken a couple of odd wooden chairs from John's apartment when they cleared it out. The table would be crowded, but Kate looked forward to it. She loved having company and this was the perfect holiday for it. She and Sarah had made place cards decorated with stickers of cornucopias and pumpkins. Paper plates and napkins adorned with leaves and pumpkins sat at the end of the counter, waiting to be filled with all kinds of delicious food. The room definitely had a festive atmosphere.

Kate peeled potatoes and dropped them in the pot after cutting them into chunks. Spencer came in a minute later to finish the veggie tray. Kate watched him out of the corner of her eye to see if he'd sneak olives or pickles while he worked. He started to bring an olive to his lips and Kate said, "Uh, uh, uh."

Spencer offered it to her instead. "Now can I?"

She grinned and nodded. She was getting hungry, smelling the turkey. "The turkey should come out of the oven pretty soon." She peeked through the oven door window to check the pop-up timer but didn't see it yet.

There were five more potatoes to cut up and then except for carving the turkey, mashing the potatoes, and making gravy, her work was done. Spencer finished the relish tray and went to set the table with Sarah. Kate poured some lemonade and went to relax in the living room for a while.

Sarah and Spencer joined her a minute later. "Table's done," Sarah announced. "It's pretty."

"Good, thank you. Thanks for helping, that's a big girl." Sarah walked over to her and Kate hugged her. They sat together and watched more of the parade until Kate had to put the potatoes on.

"You seem distracted. Anything I can do?" Spencer whispered in her ear.

"Just wondering why my paperwork hasn't gone through yet."

"It's probably just the clogged bureaucratic channels." He squeezed her shoulder.

She leaned her head back. "I hope you're right."

A few minutes later, she got up to heat the potatoes. Guests would start arriving soon and she didn't want to be in the kitchen too long before they sat down. The timer on the turkey popped up, so she turned the oven off and left the bird in the oven until she could get to it. When the potatoes began rolling along she started the gravy.

"How's it going, need any help?"

"Can you get the turkey out for me and set it there?" She pointed to the counter. "It can rest for a few minutes before carving."

"Would you like me to do the honors?"

"Yes, please. I'll get you a platter and a knife."

They finished up their work right before the doorbell rang. Kate shushed Buttons and went to the door. "Hi, Andrew, Matt, come on in." They stepped in and commented that the aromas were tantalizing. "Thanks, I'll take your coats after you bring your goodies to the kitchen."

"Look who's here," she said to Spencer.

"Hi guys, come on in."

Andrew said, "She turning you into a pansie in here?"

"Hey, no grief to the chef's assistant. Or no turkey for you, Turkey."

Andrew grinned. "It looks good on you," he said, stepping through to the fridge. "I'll put these in here until we're ready."

"Thanks, Andrew."

"Where do you want this?" Matt asked, holding his salad. Matt was one of Spencer's friends who she didn't know very well.

"How about on the table," she answered, pointing.

"And the green bean casserole is in a slow cooker still in the car. I'll run and get it."

"It can sit behind the canisters where there's an outlet."

"I'll be right back."

Someone knocked on the door, and Andrew hollered, "I'll get it."

Kate stirred the gravy and took the potatoes off to mash. She snatched a piece of turkey from the platter. "Hey, no picking." Spencer pretended to poke her hand with the fork.

"The cook automatically gets special privileges."

"True. Here, have another," he held one out for her. She turned around as Jen and Kelly came in holding their offerings.

"We followed our noses," Kelly said. "Smells great. Where would you like this?" Kate told them where to put their dishes and stirred the gravy.

"As soon as the platter is full of turkey and the gravy's done, we can eat."

"Can I help?" Jen volunteered.

"You can stir the gravy while I finish mashing these, then we can pour drinks in a minute. Kelly, can you take your coats and throw them on my bed?"

"Sure. I'll take Matt's too when he gets back."

"Thanks."

Matt returned and had Joel with him. They made introductions again and then put the food on the table.

Spencer added the turkey platter to the table and brought out the relish tray and some butter for the bread. A few minutes later, they were ready to eat. Sarah was sticking close to Kate and Spencer. "It's okay, honey," she whispered. "Spencer and I work with these friends. They won't hurt you." She lifted her up and put her in her chair and pulled a bib over her head. To their guests, she said, "Spencer's here, and I'm here, the rest of you fill in where you find your name cards."

Everyone found their place and sat down.

"Hey, is that Cookie Monster?" Andrew asked Sarah. She shook her head, too afraid to speak. "Oh, I know who it is. It's Oscar the Grouch."

Again Sarah shook her head. "Elmo," she whispered.

"Oh, that's right. Elmo. I think he's pretty cool." He gave her a wink.

Sarah nodded, then looked at her mom and asked, "We eat now?"

"As soon as Spencer prays for our food, yes."

"Let's pray." He waited for everyone to bow their heads. "Dear God, We thank you for the many blessings you've given us, including this delicious food. We especially thank you for sending your Son to die on the cross for our sins and giving us your grace. We ask that you continue to protect our troops around the world and at home and thank you for our many freedoms we enjoy in this country. Bless our time together and continue to watch over us. In your name, Amen."

Several 'Amens' were heard around the table. "Everyone, start with whatever is close to you and we'll get the turkey passed around." Kate started to fill Sarah's plate so the hot food could cool a bit.

Andrew proposed a toast. Everyone but Sarah lifted their glass. "To the greatest country in the world, and to friends far and near and to good food."

"To John and our beloved heroes, and may God bless us," Jen offered.

"To the best da—" Matt caught himself, eyeing Sarah and finished, "dang air force in the world, and to our lost comrades, and to plenty of food and especially our freedom."

Kate lipped a thank you to him.

"To John and to family and friends, our country and great food," Spencer said.

Kate was touched with their toasts to John. They drank to the offered toasts and began eating. "This is fantastic," Matt said. "So much food in one place."

"Isn't this great? Better than the Chinese buffet," Spencer said.

"Yeah and it's going right here," Andrew poked his stomach.

"Not all of it," Jen said.

"Yeah, save some for us," Kelly added.

"Delicious, Kate," Andrew commented. "Thanks for including me."

The others around the table chimed in with their thanks also.

"You're welcome. I'm glad we could all get together. This is fun." The room grew quiet with just the forks scraping paper plates and their drinks moving up and down in almost a rhythmic pattern.

"How's it going with Sarah?" Kelly asked Kate.

Kate swallowed a bite of turkey. She saw the curious look on Joel's face. "She's adopted," she whispered. Then she continued in a normal voice. "Great so far. I'm just taking it one day at a time and try my best." She took a few seconds to cut more turkey. "There's a parenting class at the Family Readiness Center starting next week. I've read quite a few magazines, but that's not the same thing." She looked down at Sarah, gave her a side hug and a quick kiss on the top of the head.

Kate tried listening to Spencer's conversation with the guys. She heard words like torque, speed, awesome power, and other terms. Sounded like they were talking about cars. Or perhaps new airplanes.

Jen and Kelly and Kate started discussing their Christmas plans. "I'm not going anywhere this year, but I'm still taking the week off, of course. So, if you need any help with Sarah, call me," Jen said.

"Thanks, I'll let you know." Kate knew Jen's family was in Germany, as her father was still active duty as well. Jen was trying to make it over there for New Year's or early January before her family transferred back to the States.

The conversations around her made her feel happy and content. It helped having Spencer around and that he was so capable and helpful with Sarah. He had shared some stories about taking care of his nephew and nieces. Kate looked forward to being an aunt in the future. Spencer had an older brother and sister who were both married with kids.

Shortly after they finished eating from an assortment of pies, Kate's apartment phone rang. "I wonder who that could be." Kate picked up the extension in the kitchen.

"Hello?"

"Sergeant Langston, this is Lieutenant Thompson. I'm sorry to bother you, but we have a situation and we're putting everyone on alert. Do you by chance have any guests from the squadron over?"

"Several...Spencer, Kelly, Matt, Andrew and Joel." She didn't mention Jen, since she was from the Supply Squadron. Kate walked back around the corner to face them and found them all staring at her. She listened a minute longer and said, "Okay, Sir." She hung up, her face white.

"What's happening?"

"What's going on?"

"Who was that?"

Spencer held his hand up for silence. "I think Kate will tell us if we give her a chance."

Kate gave him a grateful smile though it was short lived. She swallowed hard before adding, "We're at war. Everybody's been put on alert. I can't get out yet. Excuse me," she said and rushed out of the room.

Spencer went after her. "Hey," he said, his voice just above a whisper. He sat beside her on the bed and began rubbing her back.

"This isn't going to work," she groaned. Her shoulders shook with her outburst.

"We'll work this out together, okay? I know you're worried about Sarah, but she'll be fine. She'll adjust."

"I'm scared for her, what if something happens to me?"

Spencer held her in his arms for a few minutes until Kate regained her composure.

A minute later they rejoined the others in the kitchen. "I'm sorry guys," Kate said. "I just needed a moment."

Kelly was washing the serving bowls and pots and pans while the guys finished clearing the table, tossing plates into the trash can. "We're here to help you in any way you need," Kelly offered. She rinsed another pot and placed it in the drainer.

"I'm not worried about me, but for you know who," Kate gestured with her head toward the living room where Jen was reading books to Sarah.

"Understandable. I don't know how families do it," Matt shared. Heads nodded in agreement.

"Do we need to report or anything?" Andrew asked.

"Not yet. We're just on alert for now, they're doing roll call. Just stay in the area and keep your cells on." Kate leaned on a counter watching everyone gather their dishes. Spencer brought in the turkey platter and set it down. "What a way to end the day." He picked at the turkey.

"Thanks, Kelly, for washing up," Kate said.

"Of course." Kelly dried her hands and gave Kate a hug.

"Thanks." Kate tried not to worry.

Spencer rubbed the back of his neck.

"Thanks guys for coming and bringing your dishes." Kate walked their guests to the door.

"Oh, Kate," Jen said, joining them. "I'll be praying for you. Let me know if you guys need anything, okay?"

"Sure thing, Jen. Thanks." Jen gave Kate a hug and there was a flurry of goodbyes. Spencer shut the door slowly and returned to the living room to pick up where Jen left off reading to Sarah. Kate said she'd join them in a minute. Spencer read aloud to Sarah, but his mind was elsewhere. *If Kate had to deploy, it would break her heart. How would Sarah handle it, really? The poor thing had been through enough trauma for such a short life.*

Kate came out in her pajamas and robe. She saw Sarah yawn, so Kate said, "I'll put her down. Be right back."

Spencer poured two glasses of wine and took them to the living room. It had been a busy and fun day until the phone call that ruined the party atmosphere in a hurry. He put his feet up on the coffee table. Christmas was coming up and he hoped that neither of them would have to deploy.

She came back a few minutes later and sat down next to him. They watched a Christmas movie mostly in silence. Spencer held Kate close and rubbed her shoulders, trying to ease her worries.

During a commercial, Kate asked, "What if I have to leave her?" She swallowed a lump in her throat.

"I don't know, Kate. Hopefully it won't get that bad. But with the cuts already made, and now this, we're stretched pretty thin."

"That's what I'm afraid of. I can't be a good mom if I'm half a world away."

"One day at a time for now. You know Mrs. P and all of us will help you. We're like family." *I hope we can become our own family.* Spencer pulled Kate closer and held her. "Try not to worry," he said.

Kate nodded, "I'll try not to. Thanks."

Chapter 30

A few days later, the air was tense in the security forces offices and the squadron as a whole. More troops were being deployed overseas and the ramifications were felt base wide.

Whether of republican or democratic background, most troops agreed that the White House wasn't serving its military personnel well. The country's service members were doing more work with less manpower and money, causing a spike in grumbling.

One of those complaining was Kate, after she learned she was deploying again, right before Christmas. She worried about leaving Sarah, and wrestled with the idea of sending her to her grandparents. She knew Kelly and Jen would help, but with a long deployment, she didn't feel comfortable with all the back and forth for little Sarah. It would be too much. Mrs. P said she could care for Sarah while Kate was gone, but Kate thought it was too much to ask of her.

Not at all hungry at lunch time, Kate drove to the gym to exercise some frustration out of her system. She changed in the ladies' locker room and walked into the room with the weight machines. She pumped her arms up and down, moved to the machine for legs and shoved them back and forth against the pulleys until her muscles ached. She sat up and wiped sweat off her face with her towel. Out of time, she took a quick shower and returned to work. Unfortunately, the workout didn't help her anxiety nearly as much as she'd hoped.

When she returned to the SF building, she ran into Spencer in the hallway.

"What's the matter?" he asked. He had to hold her a step back so he could see her face.

"I have orders to deploy. Now what am I going to do?" With that, she stalked off.

****

Spencer's heart sank when he heard Kate's announcement. He continued on to his station, where he dropped into a chair and blew out his breath. Kate always put her heart into things full force, but when steered where she didn't want to go, she's like a raging bull.

Patience, patience. She would need some time to deflate and figure things out. The best thing he could do was give her space and continue praying for her. *I'll have to give her a few days before talking to her unless she approaches me first, which seemed unlikely.*

At the moment, he had to put her problems aside and get back to answering the phone at the help desk. Pulling up a sagging sock in his boot, he took a deep breath and answered the phone, his mind on the woman he not only loved, but who also sometimes confused him.

When his shift was over, Spencer drove to the BX and took care of his Christmas shopping and let the charity of the evening wrap everything. Many nights during December, organizations offered to wrap gifts for customers in exchange for donations. To him it was always worth the few bucks to get his packages wrapped and not worry about buying paper and bows that matched. He didn't care much about that stuff. He was happy to get a gift wrapped in grocery sack paper for all he cared.

****

Kate drove her assigned work car, the Chevy Impala, around the base, her thoughts swirling in all directions, but mostly worrying about how she would care for Sarah. Kate slowed down for the stoplight at the corner that would lead her to the back of the base where the flight line stretched between empty fields at one end and railroad tracks at the other. The day was blustery and cold, but little snow had fallen, except for the freak storm back in October.

At the end of her workday, Kate drove to the shooting range in Belleville and shot some rounds through paper targets. When she was done, she felt a little better. The man behind the checkout counter noticed her shredded paper targets and seemed impressed. She didn't bother to explain she was supposed to be a good shot in her line of work.

That evening after a quiet dinner and putting Sarah to bed, Kate decided to pull out her Christmas decorations. Her only carton of Christmas items was in the storage area of the basement. Some years she put out her things and some years not. She didn't have much, but had a few snowmen and a wreath.

She brought the box up and Kate unwrapped her wreath, straightening its red velvet bow. She hung it on her apartment door and felt a little better, thinking about happier times and getting into a more festive mood. Next she unwrapped ceramic and glass snowmen and snowflake candle holders. She did not have any stockings or a tree.

While she decided where each item should go, she thought about when she and Sarah could celebrate. She moved the carton aside and pulled out her day planner and sat on the couch.

Perhaps on the 18th. She wouldn't prepare a huge meal, but a ham at least and invite Mrs. P, Jen, Kelly and Spencer, of course. This plan gave her twenty days to prepare, which was adequate.

Her phone rang and she put the planner down to answer it. "Hello?"

"Hi Kate, it's Lauren."

"Hi."

"How are you and Sarah doing? Did you have a good Thanksgiving?"

"We're fine. Yes, we had a nice Thanksgiving, thanks for asking."

"Good. Dale and I are inviting you and Sarah up for Christmas if you don't already have plans. Timothy will be back and we're having a small reunion."

Kate knew that Timothy was John's older brother and that Lauren's use of reunion probably meant 'memorial' of some kind. Kate was silent a minute but finally said, "I would love to, but I'm actually deploying on the 20th and we were going to celebrate early."

Lauren sucked in her breath but didn't interrupt. "I'm sorry to hear that. Well, we'll be here, Timothy and Judy will be here on the 7th, so if you can make it, you're most welcome. We have plenty of rooms."

Kate asked if she could think about it. She didn't think they'd go, but she didn't see a problem with at least thinking about it first.

"Of course. I didn't expect an answer right away. But call us in a few days and let us know, okay?"

"I will."

"Tell Sarah we love her and we'll talk soon."

"Okay." Kate hung up, considering a trip with a two-year old, luggage, presents, coats, diaper bag—

The phone rang again. *Did Lauren forget to mention something?* "Hello?"

"Kate, it's Spencer." *Definitely not Lauren.*

"Hi," she sighed. "Sorry about my—"

"Forget it. When do you have to leave?"

"The 20th." Kate plopped into a chair at the dining room table, fidgeting with the phone cord.

"I called to offer assistance with Sarah if you need to do some Christmas shopping."

"I do. And I need a few more decorations." They made plans for her to shop later in the week. He again reassured her they would all help to keep Sarah safe and happy while Kate was gone. She hung up, hoping so.

****

Three days after their phone conversation, Spencer came over to watch Sarah. He handed Kate a small Christmas bouquet of red and white carnations, baby's breath and greenery.

"They're lovely, thank you." She gave him a lingering kiss before finding a vase. She set it up high on the entertainment center where it added fresh fragrance and beauty.

"Pretty," Sarah commented.

"They are, aren't they? Spencer was nice to give them to us."

Sarah smiled at him. Then she pulled on his arm, ready to play. Buttons was ready too, jumping up on Spencer's legs.

"Well, I'm off. You two have fun."

"Will do."

Kate drove to the mall, glad for a few hours to herself. Decorations hung from street lights throughout the area, different themes in each of the small towns she drove through on her route. She played her favorite Andy Williams Christmas CD in the car, which helped to put her in a festive mood.

In the middle area of the mall, a huge display was set up for Santa to sit in his chair and listen to wishes from children. Kate watched for a few minutes while a photographer snapped shots of each child on Santa's lap.

In the children's store, she found two outfits and new winter pajamas for Sarah. In the electronics store she bought a gift card so Spencer could pick out a video game. She also found a soft scarf and gloves to match in a pretty shade of blue he would look good in.

For Mrs. P, she found a new cardigan for her to wear to church. Kate noticed the one she often wore had a missing button and a hole in one elbow. She also picked out a blanket for the living room sofa. In the toy store she bought some tray puzzles and some new Clifford and Little Critter books for Sarah. She also bought two mugs and added some chocolates to fill them for Jen and Kelly. Satisfied, she drove home, singing her favorite Christmas carols.

She left everything in the car to wrap later. "Thanks Spencer, I got a lot done." She was happy but tired. The crowds hadn't been too bad, but she was relieved all her shopping was done except for decorations and food.

"You're welcome. We had fun, didn't we?" He looked at Sarah.

She sat on the sofa, bathed and ready for bed. "We played lots."

"Sounds like a good time was had by all."

They said their goodnights and Kate put Sarah to bed after reading her a book. Kate brought in her packages and wrapped the ones for Sarah and then put them up in the coat closet out of sight. She had bought paper and bows at the BX earlier in the week. She would wrap the rest at another time.

On Saturday morning, Spencer came over so the three of them could pick out a small tree at a nearby tree farm. As they drove, Kate told him about Lauren's invitation.

"That makes a tight schedule," Spencer said.

"I know. I'm not sure I'm up to it. That's a lot of extra stress."

Sarah sat in her seat, lost in her own world. After Kate told her they would be getting a tree, she asked, "We have tree...in house?" Kate laughed at the amazement on her face.

Before they trudged through the fields, Kate made sure Sarah's coat was zipped up and she had on her hat and mittens. Spencer looked rugged and handsome in his own coat, boots and knit cap. "Here we go, let's see what we can find, okay?"

Sarah ran ahead of them and looked at all the trees. She would look up, up, up and almost fall over. She found almost every tree a perfect candidate, but Kate found flaws in most of them, mainly because they were too tall for her apartment.

Kate guided her to the shorter ones. "Sarah, see if you like one of these." Kate had been snapping photos with her camera and laughing at some of Sarah's faces. They enjoyed their stroll through the fields of Scotch Pines and Blue Spruces.

They finally found one and Spencer cut it down with the saw. They tagged it and then waited for it to be shaken and wrapped in red netting for the journey home on top of Spencer's car. He paid for the tree, after Kate's mild protest. Then he pulled out a tarp and wrapped the tree in it and roped it to the car's roof.

On the way home, Spencer asked, "What it would take for you to make the trip north?" "An extra set of hands and a barrel full of patience, I think."

"My hands are available. And I believe I have some use-it-lose-it time to take anyway." He had taken his hands off the steering wheel for a second and wiggled his fingers.

"Hey, mister, keep them on the wheel." She sighed. "I'll think about it. So much to consider."

"It's beautiful up there. Their property is near a wooded area and it's quite peaceful. Just let me know."

They drove the rest of the way home in silence. Before long the tree was in the stand and the adults were stringing on the lights. Buttons came to investigate soon after the tree was brought in. Kate admonished him, "Don't you dare!" Spencer tried not to smile, but Kate saw it. "Not funny."

"I'll leave you to it."

"Thanks, Spencer."

After Sarah's nap, the two of them added all the tree ornaments Kate had. The tree was quite festive and she was pleased with how it looked. The mild pine scent added to the ambience. Kate took pictures of Sarah putting ornaments on the lower branches. Most of them had fallen off, but Kate helped her put them back on. She showed her how to bend the hooks a little over the branch to help them stay put.

Later that evening Kate considered Lauren's invitation and Spencer's offer of help. *On the one hand, Sarah should spend some time with her grandparents. But she just saw her grandma a couple weeks ago. It would be so awkward to be at John's childhood home for the first time, and John not being there. But like Spencer, she also had some leave time to use. Is this how she wanted to use it?*

I'll think more about it tomorrow.

Chapter 31

Kate found herself once again as a passenger in Spencer's car. This time the three of them headed to the Kern house. Kate was nervous but excited too. She loved Christmas time and she thought being in wintry Minnesota this time of year might make it more special. And both adults checked and rechecked the weather this time.

The drive went well. Kate was glad Sarah was an easy traveler. She seemed happy to look out the window or read books.

"When we get out of the suburbs, I'll have you call Lauren for the rest of the directions. I remember how to get to their town, but not to their acreage."

"Okay. Thanks for coming with us." Kate had thanked him at least three times already.

"You're welcome...again." He smiled at her, knowing how grateful she was. He reached for her hand and gently squeezed. Half an hour later Spencer drove down a rocky driveway where he pulled in front of a sprawling ranch home surrounded by pine trees on three sides and smoke rising from the chimney.

Kate didn't think it would take her long to settle in. Just the property was peaceful to look at. A long porch ran along the front of the house where a porch swing and several chairs with flowered cushions made it look inviting.

"I can see why you liked coming home with John," she said while taking in the crisp white and woodsy scene through the windshield.

"Yep, and Mrs. Kern is a great cook, too."

"Yes, you've mentioned that. Is that why you offered to come with us?" Kate slid out of the car and stretched. She breathed in fresh cold air, with a scent of pine. She unbuckled Sarah and let her down in the gravel driveway. Sarah stared at all the trees surrounding the house.

"Get more tree?"

Kate and Spencer both chuckled. Kate scooped her up and said, "No, Honey, these trees belong to your grandparents. This isn't a tree farm." Kate tightened down Sarah's knitted hat.

"Oh..." She still looked around and then said, "It pretty here!"

"I agree, Sarah. I agree."

Spencer said, "In answer to your earlier question, yes, that's partly why I offered to come. And because as you can see, the setting is a perfect backdrop for this time of year."

"You can say that again." Kate put Sarah back down and grabbed her wallet and the diaper bag.

"Come on in," Lauren already had the door open wide. "It's so good to see you all." Her smile was genuine and she hugged each one of them. Her Christmas cardigan and slacks made her look a little like Martha Stewart.

The visitors stepped in and stomped snow from their shoes. "Don't worry about a little snow, now," Dale said. "We're used to it, aren't we Honey?"

Lauren gave him a brilliant smile and a gesture that said, "yes indeed."

"Dale can take your coats and I'll show you to your rooms where Spencer can put your bags. Spencer," she turned to him, "you can have the blue room, and you, Sarah, can have the pink room. Kate, you can pick from the lavender or the green room." Dale hung their coats in the large closet and then the guests followed their hostess down the hall.

Kate chose the lavender room, liking it right away. The walls were a soft purple and there were darker purple flower accents on the bedding, rug and curtains. A club chair in pastels sat in the corner near the window. Kate felt at home right away. Spencer left her bag on the bed before going to his own room.

Kate unpacked her things and put Sarah's in the room she would occupy. Sarah's room was similar, but had two twin beds with white headboards, a chest of drawers and a matching nightstand. The curtains, rugs and lamp were in a pastel pink with white flowers.

The house John grew up in was beautiful and Lauren knew how to decorate on the level of a professional. Kate glanced around at the greenery woven around candlesticks on the mantel, an adorable collection of snowmen spread across the top of the piano, and plants and figurines tastefully placed around the house.

Apples in various forms, some in prints, some as ornaments and some as figurines were throughout the house, no doubt gifts from students during her teaching career.

Dale and Lauren were warm hosts with lots of smiles and a positive outlook. Kate felt awkward though being in John's home for the first time and being with Spencer instead. She thought it would be awkward for the Kerns as well, but they seemed to have no qualms. Kate couldn't tell if they were at peace or merely putting on a brave front.

After their guided tour of the house, Lauren offered them refreshments. "Dinner will be ready around six." They sat in the living room with cheese, crackers and hot cider.

They could already smell something with garlic and tomatoes from the kitchen. "Sarah, I found some books you might like," Lauren picked up a basket of board books from the hearth where a fire blazed. She patted a place next to her on the sofa and Sarah readily climbed up ready to "read."

"Spencer, why don't you and Kate take a walk along the property? I don't think it's too cold yet and the snow is slowing."

"Sure thing, Mrs. K." He pulled their coats from the closet and they were soon walking along the edge of the woods. The temperature was near 40, and Kate could hear the crunching of their boots on older snow. They spied Dale gathering another pile of wood for the stove. The whole house was heated from one of those stoves that pumped heat through pipes in the house.

They gave him a wave and he said, "Have a good time."

The scent of pine was heavy from the trees all around the property. "I have a feeling that she wanted Sarah to herself," Kate said, once they were out of listening distance from the house. Not that she worried about being heard.

"Perhaps. Or maybe she wanted you with me." Spencer eyed her with a grin. He took Kate's hand and pulled her closer.

"Oh? And why would they want that?" Kate played along.

"Maybe so we could—" he let go of her hand, bent over, scooped up some snow, formed it into a ball and lightly tossed it at her, "have some snow fun."

"Hmm. I don't think so." She quickly made a ball of her own and tossed it at him, not so gently.

They continued to play in the snow; Kate determined she would hit Spencer more than she would miss. The chance to exert some built up energy along with the brisk and fresh air proved invigorating. *Perhaps Mrs. Kern knew what she was doing after all.* They had gotten up early and got on the road by six to be here before dark and— important to Spencer—before dinner.

Their snowball fight took them near a small clearing. "What's this?" Kate asked spying a log cabin that looked every bit as cozy as the Kern's house.

"The cabin."

"'The cabin?'" Kate echoed.

"Yep, its' their guest house/cabin for extra guests."

"Looks nice." She stepped up to the porch and peeked through a living room window.

"I'll give you a tour." To her surprise, Spencer opened the door.

"We can just walk in?" Kate slowly followed him inside after brushing off most of the snow from her clothes and stomping her boots a few times on the outdoor rug. Spencer followed suit and then shut the door. She shivered since there was no one staying in it and the cold seeped in.

"It's usually left unlocked unless they're out of town. I've been in it myself a time or two."

Kate loved the beamed ceilings and log walls. The floors were covered in beige carpet and scatter rugs sat near the doors for wet boots. The many blankets and natural décor around the place made it homey. Kate wondered if Mr. Kern built it himself.

Kate thought about how nice it would be if she and Spencer could stay in it. She imagined them watching a movie by firelight—another stove, though smaller, stood at the front of the living room. A large basket of kindling and newspaper knots stood at the ready.

Spencer watched her wander from room to room while he waited in the living area, perched on the edge of a leather ottoman. He wondered what she was thinking. And if she was thinking the same thing he was.

****

When they walked back, Dale was playing in the snow with Sarah. They were filling up a yellow beach bucket with small shovels and then making walls of a fort. "Looks like fun, Sarah!" Kate called to her.

"I having fun, Mommy!" She laughed as they dumped another brick for the fort.

Spencer stayed with them, but Kate went inside to warm up after giving Sarah a quick hug. Lauren offered Kate hot tea and she accepted. They visited in the formal living room, just the two of them. Kate had a hard time, seeing all the family photos of John. It was disconcerting to be in his home, knowing he would never be there again.

Kate gave Lauren a half smile. She took a deep breath and said, "I feel bad—"

Lauren interrupted her, somehow knowing what she was going to say. "Don't, Kate. We know why John never told you about Sarah. But we didn't know that until just a few months ago. We couldn't figure out why he hadn't said anything about you two getting serious. He kept saying, in due time, Mom. We had to trust that he knew what he was doing. I only wished he had told us why and we could have prayed more specifically about it." She paused to sip her tea after blowing across the top of the cup.

Kate liked the room they were in which was well appointed with cherry wood tables and an antique motif fabric covering the sofas and chairs. Kate sat on a love seat with comfortable cushions while Lauren sat opposite on a matching sofa. The coffee table between them gleamed from a recent polish. A red candle sat amidst fresh pine cones and glittery snowflakes.

"I realize I don't know you well, Kate. John always said nice things and that you were serious about not having any children. I don't know your reasons, but I can tell from the short times I've seen you with Sarah, that you're already a good mom." She smiled at her.

Kate swallowed down surprise. And wiped her eyes. *How could she know that already?*

Lauren must have read her mind, for she said, "A person can tell a lot about the interaction someone has with other people. I see only love in your eyes when you interact with Sarah. It's not an act." She smiled again and added, "And listening to Sarah chatter about you proves it."

This was an emotional revelation. She didn't have any idea Sarah would talk about her to anyone. It was reassuring and a relief to hear Lauren share this. Kate toyed with the idea of telling her the reasons she never wanted to be a mother. She sipped her tea and thought it wouldn't hurt. Lauren and Dale seemed to see through her anyway. She took a deep breath. "My mother left when I was eight…"

When she finished, Lauren remained quiet for a few minutes, absorbing Kate's story. She said, "I'm sorry. That has to be awful, to be abandoned like that. I can't imagine your pain. I will pray for you and your family."

Kate blurted out, "How do you do it? How do you not get mad or scream that your son is gone?" She gripped the cup so tightly; she had to set it down before she accidently broke it.

Lauren gently set her own cup down and looked at Kate for a full minute. Kate thought she might get angry at her outburst. Lauren answered, "Oh, Honey. Don't think we haven't had words with God. We have, believe me. But it isn't worth fighting against him. We don't always understand his ways, but we know he loves us. These kinds of things happen, mainly because we live in a sinful world."

She sighed and looked toward the tree in the corner, the lights sparkling. "I still wonder why John is gone, don't get me wrong. But I trust God knows what he's doing and I can have peace in that. And we take it one day at a time."

Kate listened to Lauren, finishing her tea in silence. She didn't know God very well, though she had been reading her Bible more. Maybe someday she would understand John's death. And then maybe not. For now, she had Sarah to think about.

If John's own parents don't understand, why would I? Maybe it's time to realize I won't get any answers and that God knows what he's doing. Isn't that what faith is about? At least I can rest knowing I loved John and don't have any regrets.

****

That evening Timothy and Judy joined them for dinner. They had been out shopping earlier and were staying in a bedroom at the other end of the house. It was good to see Judy again, and Sarah remembered her.

Kate thought Timothy was more like Spencer than John. Timothy was more outgoing and playful, where John had been serious and reserved. Timothy was taller than John by about three inches and looked more muscular than most who were active duty. Perhaps he worked out more for himself than the air force.

The lasagna they ate was amazing and Spencer wasn't kidding when he said Mrs. Kern was a good cook. Kate had seconds which she hardly ever did, anywhere. She took comfort in the cheesy pasta, with sausage, tomatoes, garlic, basil and onion. The fresh bread was soft on the inside with a slightly crunchy crust, just the way she liked it.

Shortly after dinner, Kate put a sleepy little girl to bed. The fresh air, fun in the snow and the long drive wore her out. Kate read her a book they brought from home and said their nightly prayers.

"If you need me, I'll be right next door, okay?" Kate sat on the bed, rubbing Sarah's forehead. She left the lamp on in case Sarah woke up and didn't remember where she was.

The little girl nodded, already half asleep. Kate rejoined the others in the living room. "Will she be comfortable enough?" Lauren asked.

"She'll be fine. She's already asleep. She doesn't move around much, but I put the extra pillows on the side so she doesn't roll off."

"Good. If you need anything, let us know."

Kate nodded. She was pretty tired herself and stared at the flames through the glass in the wood stove door. Earlier when the guys came in with Sarah, Spencer had brought in a load of wood to keep the fire going.

She listened as the Kern's talked about past Christmases. Timothy said he and John used to unwrap their presents and tried to hide it. But when their mom caught on, she would wrap old socks or towels and rocks and put those under the tree.

"We were quite nervous that Christmas," Timothy said. "We didn't know if we were getting rocks or presents."

"I put a stop to that, didn't I?" Lauren asked, with a twinkle in her eye. She didn't seem to be the type to get bested by her sons.

"That's for sure. I told John, if we get rocks and no presents, I'd pummel him." They had a good laugh and then one by one, turned in for the night.

Kate checked on Sarah first, and found her sound asleep. She went next door to read for a while, but was too drowsy. She clicked the lamp off and snuggled under the comforter and fell asleep in minutes.

Chapter 32

After another Martha Stewart worthy dinner on their second night, Lauren approached Kate in the kitchen. "Kate, I was wondering if you and Spencer would want to be alone for an evening to spend some time together. We can play with Sarah and put her to bed."

Kate was grateful for the offer, but didn't know if she wanted to leave Sarah. Though grateful, Kate was also curious. *Why is she willing for them to be alone?*

Lauren took her hesitation as consideration. "You don't have to decide right now, but talk it over with Spencer."

Kate sipped her coffee wondering what was going on. *Are they trying to pair her up with Spencer? Are they worried that Sarah wouldn't have a dad?* She obviously couldn't ask Lauren these questions. She took her coffee into the living room, lost in thought.

Sarah was tucked into bed and the adults were talking in the warm living room, the fire crackling along, and Christmas carols playing through the speakers. Kate asked Spencer if they could talk in another room. "Of course." He got up and led her into the small family room.

This room was as nicely done as all the others. The walls were covered in a cream and blue wallpaper on the top, with white wainscoting on the bottom. Dark blue curtains were drawn against the December weather. The two sat on the same small sofa, the fabric covered in blue and cream stripes. "What's on your mind?" Spencer asked quietly.

"I don't know what to think." She set her empty coffee cup on the table in front of them and turned toward Spencer, leaning her shoulder on the sofa. "Lauren offered to keep Sarah if we wanted an evening to ourselves."

"And?" Spencer didn't seem surprised by this at all.

"Why would she ask that?"

"I think so we could have some time alone?" he asked, as if he didn't understand why she didn't know.

"But why? Why does she think you and I need time alone?"

Spencer looked at Kate waiting for her to answer her own questions. He looked at her with tenderness and waited in silence. Slowly, as if the sun was coming up across her face, Kate seemed to come up with the answers. "What do they—, what did you—why do they—," and then finally she spluttered, "Spencer!"

"Yes?"

"They know you're in love with me, don't they? And they want to encourage us to get together, don't they? Why?"

"Really?"

"Spencer!"

"Kate, don't overcomplicate things. It's not that difficult."

"Yes it is. This doesn't make any sense whatsoever."

"Kate," Spencer slid across the sofa and took her hand, "life is not lived in neat little boxes we check off as we go. It's always changing, never the same. Nobody thought

John would die when he left for his last deployment. We all miss him. You, me, his parents, his siblings." He cleared his throat. "But now, you're here. Sarah's here. I'm here. His parents and siblings are here. There isn't any reason for us not to fall in love. We both know how short life can be." He swallowed hard. "And his parents knew about you and they know me. And they want what's best for Sarah as much as you do.

"Life goes on for the living and we have to take what comes. I love you and have for a long time. But I can't go on waiting. Not for much longer." He let go of her hand after squeezing it gently. He got up and walked around the room giving her time and space. He slipped his hands in his pockets, clenching and unclenching them while his heart pounded in his chest and his breathing rate sped up. There was little sound in the room, except for the north wind blowing against the windows and the sound of their breathing.

Kate didn't know what to say. She had had similar thoughts just last night. John was gone. Spencer and everyone else he mentioned were here. *I do like Spencer. A lot. But do I love him? If I try not to analyze things too much, I'd say yes. Even though I don't understand how to love two people at once, one man who is gone and one man who is here. This is the part that trips me up.*

Her thoughts went back and forth for several minutes. Finally her brain told her what her heart knew all along— that it was big enough to love them both.

She got up and walked over to Spencer who stared at the floor while leaning on a writing desk. He stood up and waited.

Looking him in the eye, she whispered, "Yes. I do love you." Saying these words out loud warmed her from head to toe and she tingled all over. Just as she reached for him, he held out his arms and held her in a tight embrace. She recalled hugs they shared before and knew that she truly did love him.

Spencer mumbled, "Oh, Kate." He pressed his lips to her head and held her close. His heart nearly burst when he heard Kate's answer.

She tilted her face up toward him and their lips met for a lingering kiss.

After a few minutes she sniffed and leaned away from him. "Are you going to be okay?" He wiped her cheeks with the back of his finger.

"I think so. It just almost feels wrong to love someone else. But I know in my heart that John's gone and you're here. It's just taking time for it to sink in and not feel like I'm betraying him."

"I totally understand, Kate. I'm here for you."

"I know and I'm so glad you're here. I love you."

"I love you too." He leaned in and kissed her, his heart soaring.

****

Kate wanted to remember their trip forever. She had loved the slower pace, the quiet and peace of the woods, meals with friends and family, evenings by the fire. And of course, admitting that she loved Spencer.

During the drive back to Illinois, Kate was quiet. She fretted about her upcoming deployment and leaving Sarah behind. She made a mental list of things to do as Spencer drove. She recently updated her will to name Spencer as legal guardian of Sarah if anything should happen, which Kate sincerely hoped not, for Sarah's sake more than her own. Spencer would keep Buttons for her and would check on Sarah when he could.

After Spencer dropped them off, Kate unpacked their luggage and made a large laundry pile to tackle. They got a later start back home than they intended, so it was dark and near Sarah's bed time. "Let's get you in your pajamas and I'll read you a story."

"Okay." Sarah picked through her books and brought one to Kate.

Just then her phone rang, so she told Sarah to hold on a minute. As a member of the air force, she had to always answer the phone in case of an emergency.

"Hello?"

"Kate, Lieutenant Thompson. How are you doing?"

Kate's stomach dropped at the sound of his voice. "Fine, Sir."

"I'm sorry to bother you so late, but I didn't think you'd mind after hearing why I called."

"Oh?"

"Good news for a change. You're not deploying after all."

"I'm not?" The volume of her voice rose two octaves. She was afraid to ask why she wasn't leaving, so didn't.

"No. It seems that Sergeant Alexander and his wife are having some difficulties and he asked for an assignment to give them some time and space, so we quickly made the switch." He paused briefly before adding, "Merry Christmas, Kate."

"Merry Christmas to you, too, Sir. And thank you!" She hung up the receiver in a daze. *I don't have to go!* She was so stunned, she couldn't think straight.

Her whole body felt electrified. The overwhelming relief of not having to leave Sarah was so huge, Kate could hardly breathe. She leaned on the kitchen wall after hanging up the phone, trying to regain her composure after hearing such great news. She took deep breaths and waited for her heartbeat to return to its normal pace.

Kate put the news at the back of her mind and read Sarah the book she chose. After teeth brushing and face washing, Kate kissed Sarah good night.

She called Spencer.

He answered on the third ring. "Miss me already?" He teased.

"Not exactly. But would you mind coming back to my place for a bit? I want to talk about something. In person."

"Be there in a few."

****

Spencer had been home long enough to throw a load of clothes in the machine and glance through the mail pile Mrs. P left on the table. He was about ready to plug his cell in to charge, when it rang.

He was a bit surprised that it was Kate and hoped there wasn't an emergency. But she sounded fine, almost giddy. He wondered what was up as he retied his shoes and left.

****

Kate jumped up and down after she put Sarah to bed, but Buttons started barking, so she stopped. She scooped him up and danced around the room. "Buttons, how did I get so lucky?" She set him back down. Not able to sit still, she dusted the living room and vacuumed. After that, she turned on some Christmas carols in the CD player and sang along while waiting for Spencer.

Manheim Steamroller and Andy Williams filled the living room with holiday cheer. Kate wondered if she had anything in her refrigerator to celebrate with. She highly doubted it. She found some carrots and celery that were still decent and some veggie dip. She started crunching on a stick of celery.

She took her plate to the living room and had just set it down when there was a knock on the door.

"Everything okay?" Spencer asked after she let him in.

"Wonderful. Come on in."

He followed her to the living room.

"Sit down and make yourself comfortable."

"I need some water first." He headed to her kitchen.

Kate followed him. "There's some wine left from Thanksgiving."

"That works." *Must be good news.*

They settled in the living room a few minutes later, each with a glass of wine and the veggies.

"Okay, you got me. What gives?"

"I don't have to go."

"Go? Go where— oh!" He set his glass down. "Fantastic! But how come?"

"I got a call from Thompson and he said somebody else volunteered, they made the switch and presto."

"Well, well, well. I'm happy for you. Have you told Sarah?"

"No. I thought I'd wait until morning so she could sleep."

"Good idea." He sipped his wine.

"I'm so excited and relieved. Now Sarah doesn't have to be shuffled back and forth between caregivers and we can celebrate Christmas here."

"I'm thrilled for you."

"I know you're leaving for Christmas with your family in a few days, but do you want to celebrate with Sarah and me?"

"Of course. Let me know what you have in mind and what I can bring."

"I'll let you know as soon as I figure it out." Spencer was leaving in four days to spend Christmas with his family in Tennessee.

They finished their wine and Spencer said he better get home and finish his laundry.

"Thanks for coming back. I know you're tired."

"Never too tired to see you. And you're welcome." They shared a passionate kiss and reluctantly Spencer pulled away. "I'm happy for you, Kate. I know this is a big relief to you."

She nodded and gave him a tight hug. "Good night."

"Good night."

Chapter 33

Kate and Sarah celebrated Christmas a few days later. She helped Sarah open her presents to squeals of delight. Buttons was happy with his new bone too. They ate a simple breakfast of fruit, pastries and milk. Then Kate showered and put on the new outfit she had bought.

Kate put the ham in the oven on low and she and Sarah set the table. She played with Sarah and her new kitchen toys.

Spencer arrived at noon. "Merry Christmas!" He announced as he came in. His arms were loaded with bags and packages. "Let me help you with those." Kate took the brown grocery bags to the kitchen and unloaded them.

Spencer put his gifts around the tree, hung up his coat in the closet and watched Sarah happily putting new puzzles together. He sat on the sofa jiggling his leg like it was full of Jell-O. He smiled at Sarah's excitement when she added the last piece to her glitzy flower puzzle. Buttons chewed so contentedly on a new bone; he hadn't even bothered to greet Spencer.

In the kitchen, he asked, "Can I help with anything?" Kate was peeling potatoes.

"Nope. Not much left to do, I'll join you in a minute."

"Okay." He swiped a piece of fudge from a dessert tray. "Help yourself, we have plenty."

He grabbed a couple of cookies and took them back to the living room. Sarah was cooking with pink pots and pans. *I'm happy with what I bought Sarah and think my gifts will expand her horizons perfectly.*

Kate soon joined them and they exchanged the gifts they had for each other. He opened his gift card, and his cologne, which he immediately sprayed on, and his outer wear. Kate opened a new leather journal, the robe he bought on their trip, and several books on parenting he ordered from Focus on the Family. She promptly started flipping through one.

Sarah was busy coloring in a Superwoman and Superman activity book from Spencer. He had also given her a box of Lincoln Logs and a set of cars and trucks, which made Kate smile when Sarah unwrapped them. "Trying to share the male perspective, are we?"

"Can't have too many superheroes or building toys, you know."

"I see." Kate gave him a gentle bump on the shoulder. "Thanks. She's already enjoying them." Kate picked up her new book again.

"Kate, I'm glad you like your presents. But I have one more."

"Oh?" She set the book down and waited for him to give it to her since there weren't any more packages under the tree.

"I'll get it." Spencer left the room for a minute which puzzled Kate. She waited for a minute before he returned with a small square box.

Spencer knelt on one knee in front of Kate, opened the box and asked her, "Kate, will you be my wife?"

Kate looked at the beautiful marquis diamond ring, then at Spencer and back at the ring. It took her all of two seconds to answer, "Yes. I would love to be your wife."

Spencer smiled a million-dollar smile and slid the ring onto her finger. "I love you, Kate Langston, and I will love you forever." Their lips met for a tender kiss.

"Mommy, Mommy, let me see." Sarah climbed onto the sofa next to her and oohed and aahed over her mom's jewelry. "It pretty."

"Thank you, Sweetie. Now, Spencer and I are engaged."

Sarah asked, "What 'gaged mean?"

"It means that I promise to marry Spencer. And that I love him."

She nodded as if she understood. "I love him too." And with that matter-of-fact announcement, she climbed back down and returned to her toys.

"Well, it sounds like you got a two-for-one deal," Kate teased Spencer.

"I couldn't be happier." He kissed her again, long and slow.

Spencer helped Sarah build a cabin with her new Lincoln Logs. They chose the doors and windows and then he showed her how to lay the foundation and build upwards. Buttons napped in his bed, tired from all his chewing.

Spencer got a kick whenever he noticed Kate staring at her sparkling finger. "Kate, are you there?"

"Hmm?" Kate looked up at Spencer. Then she smiled and said, "I'm here. Just admiring my best gift this year." She returned her gaze back to her finger. Amidst the opened boxes, torn wrapping paper, new toys for both Sarah and Buttons, music in the background, and the scents of baking ham and a hot pumpkin pie, Kate zoned out admiring her ring.

Spencer smiled. "That's great. But it's time to eat. The timer went off five minutes ago.

"Oh! Let's eat!" She jumped up as if a firecracker went off and jogged to the kitchen.

Spencer was amused by her enthusiasm. He was thrilled he could finally propose to the woman he loved. They enjoyed their meal and were satisfied both in stomach and spirit as they listened to holiday favorites and played with Sarah and Buttons.

It was a Merry Christmas indeed.

****

One evening shortly after Christmas break, Kate fixed dinner for the three of them. The scent of spaghetti sauce with garlic, onions and tomatoes permeated the air. Spencer had fed Sarah earlier and given her a bath. After Sarah was in bed, the two adults enjoyed their pasta and salad. Kate had also baked a loaf of wheat bread.

After discussing their week at work, the weather and other light topics, Kate asked, "Spencer, can I ask you something?"

He looked at her, gauging her mood. "Of course. Ask me anything." He reached for her hand, showing his concern. "What is it?"

"Do you have your heart set on an actual wedding?"

Spencer let go of her hand and leaned back in his chair. "To be honest, I don't know. I always wanted to get married, but now that you ask, I haven't really considered the actual 'how'. I guess I always thought it was the bride's domain to figure out."

"It usually is. But this bride doesn't have anyone to walk her down the aisle and doesn't particularly like lace and flowers that much."

Kate rested her head on her hand and stared at the table. She looked at him and asked, "What do you want?"

Spencer didn't hesitate. "I just want you to be happy." He took her hand again, and got up from his seat, coming around to her side of the table. He knelt down to her level and kissed her on the forehead. "Whatever you decide is fine with me. If you want nine bridesmaids, three cakes, a full band and a limo, you got it. If you want just you and me and the JP and witnesses and a ring, we'll do that. If you want somewhere in between, just name it. That's the long way of saying, I want what you want."

"I'll have to think about it. Your family will—"

"Hey, now." Spencer knelt all the way on the floor and held her shoulders. "If I'm not worried about my family, you don't need to worry about them either. Now, I'll admit my mother mentioned a wedding of some sort with the flowers, music and all, when I was home for Christmas, but this isn't her gig. And I love you; that's what matters most."

"Oh, Spencer, I just don't know." Kate had met Spencer's parents at one of their gatherings back when she was dating John. From what she recalled, they seemed nice. Kate and Spencer stood up, and she leaned against his strong frame, thinking. Spencer wrapped his arms around Kate, gently brushing his hand up and down her back.

"You don't have to decide tonight, you know. Think about it for a few days. The world isn't going to end no matter what you decide."

"Are you sure?" Kate pulled away to look Spencer in the eye. "You really don't care if we have a wedding or a reception?"

"I would like a reception at least, yes, but we don't have to have a full wedding, no. With my family all over the place, it's going to be hard enough to get them all in one place for whatever we decide. They are not the issue. *You* are all that matters."

"Thank you. And thanks for being honest." Kate started to move away from Spencer, but he pulled her back. "I love you, Kate Langston. *That's* what matters." Then he kissed her again, long and slow.

****

In mid-January, Spencer left for a short TDY for some training. Mrs. P kept an eye on his place, as was customary, and still watched Sarah. While Spencer was gone, Kate slowly started moving some of her household goods over to his place.

As the day got closer for them to get married, Kate grew more excited. She was actually looking forward to being a complete family. Mrs. P helped Kate give Spencer's place a good cleaning before Kate started moving in her belongings. She hung pictures, (Spencer gave her full reign of the decorating, which he had little of), and added small appliances to his kitchen. Kate left very little in her apartment, but only what was essential for her and Sarah for a few more weeks.

And after the wedding shower that Jen and Kelly gave her, Kate took over new linens, some board games, and other gifts. She had fun putting away their household goods and looked forward to using them.

****

Kate and Sarah waited in the cell phone lot at Lambert Airport on the day of Spencer's return. When her phone rang, she answered it quickly. "Hello?"

"Hi, Kate. I'm back."

"Oh, good. We'll be right there."

"Can't wait to see you."

"Me either." She drove around to the passenger pick up lane and pulled into the line of cars waiting for loved ones. Kate was relieved to hear his voice.

On the drive to the airport, she and Sarah had been listening to a Paddington Bear story on CD while Sarah followed along in the matching book. Kate was glad Sarah enjoyed books as much as she did. Kate hoped Spencer would someday enjoy reading as much as she and Sarah did.

Spencer jogged out to the car and Kate pushed the button that popped open the trunk. He threw in his suitcase and slid into the front passenger seat. "Missed you." He gave Kate a hug and kissed her.

"Me too." She kissed him back and then had to drive away.

"How are you, Sarah?"

"I fine. See book?" She held it up so he could see it.

"Paddington Bear is a good one."

"We've listened to it three times now." Kate glanced at Spencer with a 'please rescue me' look.

"Ah, maybe we can listen to some music now. Is that okay, Sarah?" He turned to ask her.

"Mhhm. I tired."

Spencer grinned and tuned the radio to Joy FM, a newer station that played popular Christian music the three of them enjoyed.

"How was your trip?"

"Okay. Missed my girls though. I did manage to improve my marksmanship skills, which was nice."

"Well, we're glad you're back. We missed you too."

****

April brought more sunshine and milder temperatures. Kate took Sarah and Buttons to the park on warmer days. Kate was excited about the big day coming up.

Kate and Jen went shopping to look for a dress Kate approved of.

"How about this one?" Jen asked. She held up a simple navy sheath dress with a lace overlay. So far Kate had turned down all of Jen's other suggestions. Jen knew Kate was picky and not frilly, but they were running out of options.

"I like that one! Let me see it." Kate took the dress from Jen and held it up against herself while looking in a nearby mirror. "It's a good color. Not too fancy." She smiled at Jen. "I'll go try it on."

Jen held her breath while she waited for Kate to come out of the dressing room. "It's perfect!" Jen said. "Do you like it?"

Kate turned around in front of the three-sided mirror. "I love it. And I already have pumps to wear with it."

"Good. Let's go look for one for Sarah. My treat."

"Jen! You don't have to do that."

"I know; but I am. Come on. After we find one for her we can get lunch."

"After?" Kate's stomach already growled.

"Yes. Let's go."

As much as Kate disliked dress shopping, she saw several for Sarah that she thought were adorable. Jen held up a frilly dress in navy and white. "What do you think?"

"It's really cute. And we can get little white gloves and a purse to match. Look," Kate saw a display of accessories that would go with it.

"It's a done deal. She'll look so pretty all dressed up."

Kate agreed. She was relieved she found a dress for both Sarah and herself. And she was hungry.

****

Kate and Spencer held a barbeque at his place on the evening of Kate's last duty day. She was thrilled that her paperwork was finally signed and she could stay home with Sarah.

Mrs. P came and many of Kate and Spencer's coworkers. There was much laughter and delicious food. Burgers, brats and chicken along with many side dishes were spread across Spencer's outdoor tables.

Kelly proposed a toast. "To Kate and her new career as mother. And of course the tough job of being Spencer's wife soon."

"Hey," Spencer mildly protested. He winked at Kate and she smiled back. They held up their plastic cups and everybody cheered.

"I'll miss my little charge," Mrs. P told Kate. She had brought her delicious baked beans and a platter of cookies.

"Don't worry, we'll be close by." Kate smiled at their friend and soon-to-be neighbor. "It won't be long before we're right next door. Maybe when Sarah is in one of her chatty moods, I'll send her over," Kate joked.

"That would be just fine," Mrs. P answered.

"I was just kidding." Kate promptly clarified her statement.

"I wasn't." Mrs. P gave Kate a big smile.

****

Two weeks after the barbeque, Kate and Spencer stood in front of the justice of the peace and exchanged marriage vows. Kate wore her navy dress with matching pumps, and a sprig of baby's breath in her hair. Spencer wore a dark suit adorned with a white rose pinned to the lapel.

Sarah loved the new dress Jen bought for the occasion. Sarah seemed more comfortable in dressy clothes than Kate did. Sarah also wore cute lacy socks and white patent-leather shoes. She was probably the dressiest of the bunch. Jen stood with Kate and Andrew with Spencer. Kelly was in charge of photos.

After exchanging their vows, the justice said to Spencer, "You may kiss the bride."

Spencer drew Kate closer to him, wrapped his arms around her and kissed her fully on the lips, happy this day finally arrived.

He pulled away, looked right in her eyes and said, "I love you, Kate Coleman."

"I love you too, Spencer." She kissed him back.

Their friends congratulated the new couple. Kate and Spencer each hugged Sarah. "You married now?"

"Yes, we are," Spencer answered. He scooped up his new daughter and then grinned at Kate.

"Yay! We married." The three of them shared a family hug, all of them smiling.

Kate and Spencer had a great time at the reception with friends and family. The day before, Kate, Kelly and Jen decorated the church fellowship hall with streamers in blue and white and put up balloons. They covered tables with navy blue tablecloths and then shook out wedding themed confetti in the middle of each one. In the very center of each table, a candle was enclosed in a small glass hurricane cover.

"Time for cake, everyone," Kelly announced. "I want this to be good." She arranged the new couple behind the cake table and gave them each their slice of cake. Earlier Kate and Spencer promised each other they would be nice. Kate was afraid Kelly would be disappointed, but that was too bad.

"To my beautiful bride," Spencer said as he offered her a bite of cake. Kate swallowed it and then offered one to Spencer. "To my wonderful and handsome husband," she said before Spencer took his bite. They were completely dignified and filled with love as they gazed into each other's eyes. The crowd aahed.

"You two are too nice," Kelly grumbled. But she grinned as she took photos.

Shortly after, the newlyweds left for a short honeymoon in Florida. Mrs. P kept Sarah for them.

****

When Memorial Day came, Kate, Sarah and Spencer drove to Minnesota for the weekend. They again stayed with the Kerns, but now the newlyweds were both occupying the purple room which Kate loved so much.

The Kerns drove Kate and Spencer to the cemetery where John was buried. At the grave site, Spencer squeezed Kate's hand. "He would want you to be happy, you know," he whispered.

"I know."

"I miss him too." They stood in silence, lost in their own thoughts. Sarah stood by the car with John's parents. When Spencer and Kate finished their time at the grave, they stayed with Sarah to give John's parents some time. They had all attended a local Memorial Day service earlier in the morning.

If anyone had asked Kate if she thought she would become a wife and a mom in the same year and live to tell about it, she would have tested their sanity. However, she had grown and stretched over the last several months and loved all the new people in her life.

Granted it took some getting used to being a mom overnight and then shortly after, becoming a wife. But Kate vowed to do her best for each member of her new family.

Epilogue

A re you ready?" Spencer asked Kate.
"Just about. I need to fill Sarah's cup first."

It was Saturday morning and they were headed for the park with Sarah and Buttons in tow. It was a warm summer day, in the mid-eighties. The sky was a pretty blue with scattered fluffy clouds.

Sarah loved the park near their new home and they went there often. In late June, the new family had received orders to move to Nebraska where Spencer was stationed at Offutt Air Force Base. In August they moved to a suburb of Omaha, called Papillion, which means butterfly in French.

From the bucket swing, Sarah giggled. Kate sat on a nearby bench, holding Buttons' leash while he enjoyed the smells of a whole new environment. Spencer pushed Sarah and she said, "More, Daddy!"

Kate smiled at them but gave Spencer a warning look that said not too high or too fast. It had taken Sarah several weeks to drop the 'Mr.' from her name for Spencer. Now, it was just Daddy and both he and Kate loved to hear it.

They now lived in Big Red country, so they all had bright red Nebraska Cornhusker T-shirts in their wardrobe. They had already made a trip to Lincoln, to see the state capitol, the only unicameral in the country. Kate thought the city was well laid out and planned well, with their street system easy to navigate.

They were still looking for a church home and had visited several over the last few weeks. They were taking their time and sometimes attended the chapel on base. Kate was sure they would find one soon.

Kate enjoyed being a mom and a wife. She took her roles seriously and kept their new home clean and cooked healthy meals for her new family.

On Tuesday mornings, Kate took Sarah to the base library's story time. Both mom and daughter were slowly making friends with others who attended each week. Sarah was always excited to check out new books.

Spencer was still getting used to a new group of coworkers, but most of them seemed like a good bunch. He and Kate had already hosted two couples for a barbecue last week.

Kate stayed in touch with Jen and Kelly often, either by email or texting. And Dale and Lauren Kern planned to visit soon. Kate saw them as allies now and enjoyed their time together. Sarah loved them as real grandparents. Before their move, the new family drove to Tennessee and spent a week with Spencer's family. With all the new family members in her life, Kate felt especially blessed. Spencer's parents were thrilled to have Sarah and Kate join the family as well.

Kate's body was changing and a roundness barely showed in her midsection. Only Spencer knew that they were expecting a baby. Kate was in shock at first when she saw the pink plus sign on the pregnancy test, and it took her several weeks to adjust to the idea. The more she thought about it, the more she thought about her own mother. *Is she alive? What happened to her? Is she being cared for?*

Kate and Spencer held hands on the walk back home. Kate held Buttons' leash in her other hand and Spencer held Sarah in his free arm. Kate's heart swelled at all the love and support she'd gotten over the last few months. She stopped walking, looked at Spencer and said, "I love you so much.

"I love you, too." He leaned over and kissed Kate on the forehead before they resumed their walk. Sarah chatted the whole way to the birds, squirrels and to Buttons.

When they got home from the park Spencer went outside to do some yard work. Kate put Sarah down for her afternoon quiet time, when she either looked at books or colored until she fell asleep. Kate sat down at the computer desk and glanced at the framed photo of her and Sarah as her fingertips hovered above the keyboard. Then she placed her fingers on the keys and typed 'Sylvia Langston' in the search engine. Maybe she could find her. Maybe she couldn't. But she would at least try.

Acknowledgements

This book could not be made possible without help from many people. I wish to thank United States Air Force Chaplain Erik Tisher, for his help with the military funeral process. I also talked with Grant Meyers, former United States Air Force Airman, regarding the daily duties and operations of those who work in Security Forces. I also thank the Scott Air Force Base Security Forces Squadron for the tour of their newer facility and their K-9 demonstrations our homeschool group watched in the last couple years. May God continue to bless your service to our country. It is much appreciated.

Any mistakes in the story are mine alone.

I can't forget my writing friends, members of Paddle Creek Writers, who have been there since the beginning when Heir Force was just a dream. Bev Lindbo, Pat Meyers, and Susan Korich, you guys are the best. I couldn't do this without you. I love you guys!

My first readers are the tops! A huge thanks to Vickie Styles, librarian at Scott Air Force Base Library; Ruby Walker, former nurse; and Pat Meyers, author of Caitlin's Summer Adventure.

To my great editor, Amy Middleton, for making this book the best it can be through your terrific editing suggestions.

And to my cover designer, Lucy Burton, for another stunning cover.

During the many hours it takes writing, editing, doubting, writing some more, editing constantly, and wondering if I know what I'm doing, I continually thank my family for putting up with an author in the house. I zone out often, jump up at odd times to jot a note and sometimes I don't listen to the person talking to me. Our dinners aren't stellar, and the house is often cluttered with books, magazines, rough drafts, office supplies, research notes, etc. Thank you Mike, Madelyn, Molly, Michael and Mariah for putting up with me.

And to my parents, Aaron and Sharon Reed, for spreading the word about my books to anyone they meet. And for sharing the love of reading with me as I grew up, taking me regularly to Gere Library in Lincoln, Nebraska to get my own stack of books.

To my Savior, for giving me a love of words early on and allowing me to use them to encourage others through letters, cards, emails, and now novels.

From the bottom of my heart, I thank you all. Forgive me if I've inadvertently left anyone out.

Author's Note

The idea for Heir Force came to me in a dream several years ago when I attended a writer's conference. I woke up on the day I was headed home and had to unpack a notebook and pen to write it down. The opening scene between Kate and John was as close to the dream as I could remember.

When I began working on their story, I did not know in the beginning that Kate didn't want to be a mother. I am a write-by-the-seat-of-your-pants-writer (a pantster) so this was an interesting development. So, then I came up with the title Heir Force, which was the title of the newspaper column in the base paper announcing new births when my youngest two children were born at Offutt AFB, NE. I thought the title fit Kate's situation very well. Thus Heir Force was born!

I know that many things changed in the military after 9/11 and since Mike was already retired, I chose the year 2000 to begin Kate and John's story. I also didn't want them to have access to Smartphones to check the weather when they were on their adventurous trip.:) But it's also a work of fiction, so some things I made up like how paperwork is done, and other work related tasks.

Did you enjoy Heir Force? Share the love by adding a short review to Amazon, GoodReads, or B&N. Every review helps get the word out and is much appreciated.

Please visit https://www.michelleconnellwrites.net and sign up for Michelle's newsletter for giveaways, contests and updates about her other books.

Have a question or comment? Write the author at mc.romwriter at gmail.com; she will do her best to respond.

About the Author

Michelle Connell is an AF veteran spouse, homeschool mom, and former reviewer for CBA, Christian Home & School, and other markets. She is a member of RWA, CSPA, and She Writes. She is the author of Cookie Encounter, coauthor of Prompted to Write, and contributor to Tyndale's Life Verse Devotional. A native of Nebraska, she now lives in southern IL with her family. Visit michelleconnellwrites.net or paddlecreekwriters.com for more information.

To arrange an interview or to request a review copy, please contact Sharon Reed at Paddle Creek Publishing: pcpubsvs@gmail.com or 618.491.4042.

www.ingramcontent.com/pod-product-compliance
Lightning Source LLC
Chambersburg PA
CBHW031213120726
47905CB00002B/324